ABSTRACTION

Sam Weis

Kasva Press

Make its
bowls,
ladles,
jars and
pitchers
with
which to
offer
libations;
make them
of pure
gold.

וְעָשִׂ֣יתָ
קְּעָרֹתָ֧יו
וְכַפֹּתָ֛יו
וּקְשׂוֹתָ֖יו
וּמְנַקִּיֹּתָ֑יו
אֲשֶׁ֥ר יֻסַּ֖ךְ
בָּהֵ֑ן זָהָ֥ב
טָה֖וֹר תַּעֲשֶׂ֥ה
אֹתָֽם

St. Paul / Alfei Menashe

Cover design & layout: Yael Shahar

First edition published 2023
Kasva Press LLC
www.kasvapress.com
Alfei Menashe, Israel / St. Paul, Minnesota
info@kasvapress.com

Abstraction

ISBN
Trade Paperback: 978-1-948403-31-3
Ebook: 978-1-948403-32-0

9 8 7 6 5 4 3 2 1

To my brother, who taught me to read

ABSTRACTION

Sam Weis

Chapter 1

The explosion was a thundering wave pushing at the wall of plate-glass windows. The banquet room's tables shook, and wine glasses skittered like nervous ballerinas before spilling like delicate waterfalls of merlot and chardonnay to pool on the carpet.

Moments before, Wren Willow Hendrix had watched the Mayor standing at the microphone, pushing his dark brown hair out of his eyes with his right hand, then with his left. Wren had watched as he jammed his hands into his pants pockets and bumbled through his speech, pausing every twenty seconds to flash his election-winning smile. It looked like an affectation, but he might simply have been trying to gather enough of his scattered thoughts so that he could proceed with the speech. Distraction was everywhere. The Mayor wiped at his lips with his sleeve as he glanced out the rain-streaked windows, down to the marina just below the restaurant. Boats bobbed and tugged at the lines that held them to the dock.

"I know you are eager to get to dessert, and I think you've pretty much heard enough of me."

"Hell, we've got three more years of listening to you, Jack," boomed a voice from the back of the room. "Can you blame us?"

"Thanks, Mike," said the Mayor, "it's always nice to have your support."

Laughter skittered through the restaurant's low-ceilinged banquet room. Mike Johnson, the Mayor's brother and the town's biggest realtor, raised his coffee cup with a smile and a nod, gesturing a toast. The Mayor buttoned his suit jacket and sipped from his water glass as the room quieted.

"Our little town is lucky to have two of our nation's most admired living painters as residents. On behalf of the City and the Chamber of Commerce, I am honored today to be presenting a plaque to each of these women. The Outstanding Citizen Award is given to those residents who have brought exceptional honor to our little community."

Applause echoed sharply off the large window panes. As if taking a cue, a gust of wind shook the windows as rain threw itself at the glass like tiny pebbles. The sky was dark and heavy, and seemed as though it were sagging to the ground from the sheer weight of the rain it held.

The Mayor gestured toward the guests of honor to come up to the podium. Wren winked at her friend Julia Burlow, set her glass of Riesling on the table, brushed crumbs of bruschetta from her skirt, and rose, her movements as precise and tidy as her paintings. Julia looked up at her co-honoree and raised an eyebrow as she tossed the cigar she had been alternately fingering and chewing onto her salad plate. Julia's hair was wildly bushy and she wore paint-stained jeans under her black pinstripe designer jacket. Yet somehow, she looked stately, in possession of a powerful secret.

They were greeted with continued applause and smiles as they walked to join the Mayor. A few people reached to quickly shake their hands.

Another gust of wind hit the windows, and the lights flickered. The room gasped.

"OK, I guess Mother Nature's telling me to move this along," the Mayor said through a toothy smile.

Turning toward Julia, the Mayor got to work. "Julia Burlow," he said, "I admit that I don't really understand your pictures, but I do appreciate the things you have achieved. You are highly regarded as an abstract painter, and I'm just a guy with a high school diploma who thinks the picture of the dogs playing poker is pretty good."

The room laughed again. Julia Burlow smiled, and Wren hoped that her co-honoree had not had enough wine to let unfiltered truth escape her lips.

"Truly," the Mayor continued, "it humbles me, and gives me great pleasure to give you this Outstanding Citizen Award plaque."

Julia took the plaque in her right hand, then fumbled it to her left so she could shake the Mayor's hand. She turned to the applauding assembly, raising the plaque above her head, like a winner at Wimbledon.

"And now," the Mayor went on as he stepped in front of Julia, "I am honored to present this plaque for 'Outstanding Citizen' to Wren Willow Hendrix."

He never got to describe his understanding of Wren's work, because that's when the explosion shook the building.

As nearly everyone ran to the windows to see what had happened, the Mayor dove to the floor beneath a table by the podium.

"It's a boat," shouted Mike Johnson. "Good God, a boat blew up. Damn, there's a man in the water." Mike pulled out his cell phone and hit 9-1-1, gave a quick report, then went over to his brother. "You OK, Jack?"

The Mayor looked up at his brother from beneath the table, eyes wide.

"Yeah. I, uh, I think I tripped on the carpet," the Mayor stammered.

"I called for help. I think we ought to go down there and see what we can do."

The Mayor blinked rapidly, discretely checked to make certain he had not pissed himself, and nodded agreement. He looked up at his brother, at his perfect composure, almost as though seeing him for the first time. At sixty Mike looked like forty-five, lean, with a neat white mustache and hair so perfect that it resembled a helmet the color of dry pavement.

Mike pulled the Mayor to his feet, as he had done frequently since Jack started his political career.

"Let's go have a look," said the Mayor.

The two men hurried away, down to the docks.

Julia approached the podium and picked up Wren's "Outstanding Citizen" plaque from the floor. "Don't forget your award, Ms. Hendrix," she said, handing Wren the plaque with a deep bow.

"I almost forgot," Wren said, returning the bow. "I suppose dessert isn't going to happen after all, much less our acceptance speeches. I guess that's a fair trade-off."

As Wren and Julia were about to sneak out of the room, a petite elderly woman approached Wren and said, "My name is Hilda Enquist. I'm your neighbor. I just wanted to say that I'm so glad you received this award. Your paintings are just so pretty. They are just lovely in the Lord's eyes, dear."

As she stepped away, Mrs. Enquist looked at Julia with a frown and narrowed eyes. She made a little grunting sound, then left the room.

The two artists looked at each other and giggled like seventh-grade girls.

"Was it something I said?" Julia offered.

"It would seem," said Wren, "that the Lord's eyes don't like seeing your pictures."

Wren and Julia stepped, otherwise unnoticed, from the room. When they got out to Julia's car they stood and watched the boat burn. Bystanders had fished the man from the icy bay, and an ambulance was just arriving to take him away.

Light-hearted a moment ago, Wren now found herself feeling strangely taken by the scene. The burning boat was captivating, and she couldn't look away. She stared, as though in a trance.

"Hendrix," Julia said.

Wren was barely breathing.

"Wren, are you in there?" Julia said, a little louder.

Wren blinked and trembled slightly. "...Yes. I don't know what it is. I feel something. I feel something odd. About the fire. Like a déja-vu, but not exactly. More like an..." Her voice trailed off.

Julia watched her for a moment, then looked at the burning boat. "Let's get the hell out of here. It's cold and you look like you just stepped off an alien spaceship."

Wren got into the passenger seat and Julia closed the door for her. Pausing for one last look at the boat before getting behind the wheel, Julia shivered.

"Just a boat accident," Julia whispered as she dropped into the driver's seat. Withdrawing a skinny cigar from her raincoat, she bit down on it, started the car and drove out into the rain-puddled street.

Chapter 2

*C*offee cup in hand, Wren pushed the door open and a shower of birdsong floated into her studio. It was May in the Pacific Northwest, and although the rain had paused, the air was chilled and sodden. Only the blossoms made spring discernible from winter. She gently shut the door behind her.

Her nostrils flared slightly, an involuntary response to the mild tang of drying acrylic paint. Sipping occasionally from her coffee, she moved around her newly-finished painting. The four-foot by six-foot canvas stood on a large wheeled easel at one end of the big room — a room that was surprisingly spotless for a painting studio. Wren was obsessively tidy, believing that extreme order in her physical world allowed her to roam the realms of imagination unhindered.

She studied the painting with a hypercritical eye from arm's length. Then she stepped back twenty feet. She waited. She drank her coffee and again stepped closer to the painting. Silence filled the open spaces. Can a room hold its breath?

The painting was a realistic landscape of perfectly balanced composition. The tone and colors were muted and hypnotic. The viewer was immediately drawn into the world of mountains and streams and roads the artist had made on the stretched fabric, as the painting appeared to radiate its own interior light rather than merely reflecting the light of the mortal world.

Wren walked to the sliding glass door that looked out upon the trees — alder, fir, and cedar. Beyond the trees lay the salt water. Bringing the coffee cup to her lips, she sipped, swallowed and whirled toward the painting as if to surprise it. Coffee splashed on the floor, unnoticed. She walked the length of the painting with her nose just inches from its surface. Then, setting the cup on a table at the far side of the room, she returned to the painting, selecting a small brush from one of the ceramic vases on her workbench, which also held about sixty bottles, jars, and tubes of paint. Grabbing a large bottle of black paint, she squirted out a silver dollar's worth of the gleaming liquid onto a 6-inch Melmac plate. Dipping the brush, she carefully signed the painting in straight and legible strokes.

"Wren Willow Hendrix," she said aloud — a strong signature, and a singularly curious name.

Wren's mother was a hippie, a true character, with flowing tie-dyed dresses, Isadora Duncan scarves, and wild long hair leaping out toward space as she danced with spaghetti arms to the Grateful Dead by moonlight. Back when her daughter was born, she was living in The Peace, Love and Understanding Commune in northern California — although it would have been more honest to call it The Crazy Sex and Lots of Drugs Commune.

Anyway, it was August of 1969, so where else would she be? Woodstock, of course. She'd avoided the infamous bad brown acid, but that was about the only thing she missed. The atmosphere was electric. She met a dark-eyed, reed-thin young man and they dropped acid (the good stuff, not the dreaded bad brown stuff), tripped, and danced together in the pouring rain.

By the time Jimi Hendrix took the stage on Monday morning after the rain had given up, the stars had aligned. It was a pure and perfect moment, and the dark-eyed boy and the spaghetti-armed girl made love right there beneath a rain-soaked blue blanket on the muddy ground in the middle of the crowd of half a million people. No one really noticed; everyone was tripping, and love is a beautiful thing after all. Wren was conceived right there in the sacred mud of Yasgur's Farm while Jimi's guitar screamed "Purple Haze" to the sky.

The girl never saw the magical dark-eyed boy again, but she didn't mind. Back home at the commune, everyone looked after her, and when it was time for the birth she waddled into the redwoods with a midwife, squatted, and dropped Wren out onto the duff of the forest floor. The cooing midwife wrapped the baby in a blanket and handed her to the new mother, who was humming a peculiar little lullaby. The infant made hardly a whimper, but her dark eyes were wide open, curious orbs taking in every possible shape in her new world.

The infant's mother closed her eyes and decided she would name the child for the first thing she saw when she opened them again. She sat and rocked and hummed and rocked and meditated with the child suckling at her breast. After an ocean of time had passed, she opened her eyes and saw a tiny brown wren sitting in a willow tree at the edge of the creek. The Woodstock baby became Wren Willow, and, of course, Hendrix would be her last name. Naturally.

The painting was done and signed. Wren Willow Hendrix regarded her work for a few more long minutes. Finally, sighing, she dropped into her squeaky office chair, quite satisfied.

"Well," she proclaimed, "that doesn't suck."

Wren was an artist who was comfortable and confident in her work. She had achieved the recognition she had hoped for — recognition that at times had seemed out of reach. Looking again at the new painting, she thought about what she was feeling. She decided that she felt safe, and safety felt good.

Wren stood, cleaned her brush, and left the studio by the side door, walking down the narrow path fifty feet to her house. The air was heavy with the dense molecular exhalations of vegetation. On either side of the path, rhododendrons, overgrown from benign neglect and burdened with fat buds, brushed her shoulders and face as she passed. Soon burgeoning blood-red blooms would brighten the path, each blossom as wide as Wren's hand could span.

A cedar tree towered sixty feet above the yard, its boughs reaching down like fingers, tickling the tops of the rhododendrons. At one time, paving stones had marked the path; but Wren had no talent for landscape maintenance, and now a thick soft carpet of cedar duff, moss, and twigs had buried the stones.

She paused midway to look out at the waters of Puget Sound, an inlet of the Salish Sea. The smell of the salt water made her smile. She could live anywhere, but this was the place that chose her. The shapes of the water, the imposing height of the distant mountains to the east and to the west, and the lowering clouds captured her imagination, informing her work. Wren had come to view the rain, nearly omnipresent in the winter months, as conversational. A light shower had things to whisper, but a ten-hour downpour had larger and louder messages.

The sound of a hissing rattlesnake in her pocket brought her back to the moment. It was her cell phone.

"Hey, Wren, you got a minute?"

"Hi, Julia. Good timing, I just finished a painting," Wren said, scraping a spot of chromium green paint from the toe of her boot. "What's up?"

"I need you to come over and look at what I'm working on," Julia said. The poor phone connection made Julia's booming voice sound like someone dropping a box of nails down a flight of stairs.

Wren grinned, looking out toward the Sound, hoping to see a whale or a seal, and said, "I'll be right there."

She pushed off on her bicycle, her tall, muscular frame easily pedaling the half-mile to Julia Burlow's place. What passed for landscaping around Julia's studio was an extraordinary array of bare dirt, wilted flowers, and thick weeds. Wren dropped her bike into a clump of last summer's dead daisies and walked toward Julia's studio door.

Wren loved Julia like a sister, although she did not love Julia's ever-present little cigars that gave off the aroma of a burning moldy carpet. It seemed to Wren that fate had dropped them both in this quiet little off-the-map place. Unlikely denizens... Wren loved the solitude. She had preferred playing alone even as a child. For Julia, however, this locale was a self-imposed exile from urban excitement. The city for her was one big 24/7 party zone, and she loved the party life. She had to choose between working and having too much fun. Wren often told Julia that by choosing to work she had given the world one of the greatest abstract painters it would ever see. Julia always responded by lighting a cigar and puffing a fat smoke ring.

Julia opened the door a second before Wren knocked.

"What do you have?" Wren asked.

Julia stood there in paint-smeared jeans and a navy-blue sweatshirt. Slightly taller than Wren at five foot nine, Julia had an aura about her that always made her the dominating force in any room.

"I've got a line I'm uncertain about," said Julia, stepping into the center of her cavernous studio. Light poured in from clerestory windows twenty-five feet above the floor. Julia's words bounced around the room, echoing like a cavern or a cathedral.

Wren looked at the huge canvas: eight feet by twelve feet of crashing six-inch-wide black lines forming alarming geometric shapes filled with primary colors, so bold it made her ears ring.

She was always astounded that someone who made art this impressive would bother to ask her opinion of it — her opinion of anything, for that matter, even the weather.

"Julia, you are the best living American abstract painter."

Julia looked up from lighting a skinny cigar and grinned at Wren. "Yes, I am aware of that." She stepped up to the painting, squinting at something apparently only she could see.

"The thing I am bothered by," she tapped the canvas while puffing out an accidental smoke ring, "is this line. What do you see?"

Wren studied the massive painting, waving away the cloud of cigar smoke. *Are you kidding? This picture is complete perfection,* she thought.

Wren said, "Are you sure it isn't upside down? Like that Mondrian...?"

Julia scowled, then laughed. Then they were both laughing, releasing some of the pressure of their expectations about acceptance or rejection, avoiding the shadow of insecurity that trails alongside most artists, even the best ones. *Especially* the best ones.

Wren froze and pointed to a place on the painting near the bottom. "What's this streak? It's like a bolt of lightning. I can feel it in my chest." Wren walked toward the painting, then backed away, transfixed. "It's fantastic," she said in a whisper.

Julia observed her friend with mild consternation.

Wren could not even blink. In that moment, she threw away her art-school training about how paint could create images that evoked feelings. Now she fully grasped it — how the paint itself was something alive and breathing. Inhale blue, exhale green, inhale yellow, exhale red.

"You should do more of that," she said absently.

"What? Do I look like Jackson Pollock? It's just a paint drip. I'll clean it up," said Julia, as she carefully wiped at it with a rag.

But Wren was spellbound by that little drip, that thin streak of paint, and couldn't let it go. Her body was vibrating, nearly shaking. "Julia, that was hypnotic. Really, you should do more with this," she ventured quietly.

"Yeah? Why the hell don't you?" Julia said definitively, putting an end to that line of conversation. She took several shallow drags on her skinny cigar.

Wren watched wispy smoke dragons fly around Julia Burlow's curly black-and-white hair, and felt something slip sideways in the universe. She felt like her cranium was an empty chamber in a very large and very deep cavern.

She looked absently at the huge canvas and said, "It's good." She nodded. "Don't change a thing."

The two women stood silently together, regarding the huge painting for several minutes. Wren felt a bit dizzy. She thought she probably had inhaled too much of Julia's smoky Cuban security blanket. It was a spectacular painting, but Wren could not stop obsessing about that streak, that one unwanted drip of paint.

"Hey, really, thanks for lending an eye," Julia said finally, wiping cerulean blue from her hands with a paper towel, "Sometimes I just get too involved, too close to the bone. You know what I mean? Can I get you a glass of wine or something?"

"No. No thanks. I've got two more paintings to crank out for Huxley-Lavelle by the end of the month. Big show."

"Big show, big gallery. Ahh, the price of fame. I'll come by tomorrow and check out what you've got done," Julia said, smiling as she puffed out another Havana Honey cirrus cloud.

Back home, Wren skidded to a stop in front of the door, let her bike slide to the ground, and burst into her studio. She stood in silence for five full minutes looking at her perfect new landscape painting. It was beautiful. Wren knew that she was nearing a vital career plateau, that she was about to catapult into a new sphere of the art world. Her work was already part of some important private collections, and she had been shown in many prestigious galleries. This was truly not the moment to take a risk, to make a drastic change. Yet as she stood there studying it, she felt suffocated by the new painting, as good as it was.

"OK. OK. I'm just going to do it. It's just an experiment, just letting off some steam. This is not an irreversible condition," Wren said aloud.

She walked to her ancient CD player and the room came alive with pulsing electronic music. The day crackled with possibility.

Wren pulled the new landscape from the easel and kicked the easel away, its wheeled frame squealing across the room. She threw the canvas to the floor. Looking at it, she thought of one of her favorite Richard Diebenkorn statements about beginning a painting. He had said, "Attempt what is not certain. Certainty may or may not come later. It may then be a valuable delusion."

She picked up a squirt bottle of burnt orange paint and shot an arcing volley of color across the canvas. The paint seemed to suspend in air, then fall both as a languid stream and as separate droplets in slow motion. She mixed ultramarine blue and teal blue in her mostly empty coffee cup and scooped it out with a thick brush, releasing bombs of color around and over the burnt orange as she weaved a rhythmic dance around the canvas. Sweat slid off the end of her nose and dropped into the paint.

Wren wiped her brow on the arm of her crisp white shirt and then rolled up both sleeves while plotting her next color. She decided upon the exact four colors she would use, as well as black and white. Then she stopped thinking. She quickly pulled back her long, straight, coppery hair and confined it with a rubber band.

Wren's eyes, the color of the darkest-roast coffee on the barista's menu, flashed her intensity as she studied the canvas.

She mixed colors, poured, splashed, and moved color through the air above the canvas, throwing, shaking and dripping paint. Did she notice that she was painting air, never once touching the canvas with a brush or a knife or her hands?

Too present in the moment to be fully conscious, Wren was reaching for a towel when she realized it was nearly dark in the studio. Frowning, she flipped on the lights. She was surprised that many hours had passed, and was further surprised to realize that the painting was done.

Wren stood, panting like a long-distance runner, watching the painting suspiciously, feeling as though she was awakening from a trance. She walked around it, looking at how it changed completely when viewed from different angles, although it had a definite orientation in which it demanded to be set.

Wren turned away from the painting. She had been looking at it and circling it, as though in a labyrinth, for half an hour. She was tired, but began to notice that she also felt happy — had never felt so happy in her life. Euphoric! Maybe two fat doobies' or three martinis' worth of euphoria. She closed up her studio and walked to the house, hoping for sleep. From the narrow path she could hear the waves whispering on the beach, and she thought she heard the long, sighing water-spray exhalation of an Orca.

Chapter 3

"*Really*, Hendrix, what the hell did you do?" Julia exclaimed. "I mean, shit, have you just gone off the cliff?! Have you given up on your career and just decided to wreck things in some existentialist tantrum? Is that what you're doing here? You're a solid realist. So what the fuck is this thing?"

Wren did not feel chastised. Placing her hands firmly on Julia's shoulders, she pushed her friend around to face the painting and held her there, and calmly said, "Julia, keep looking at it. Just keep looking. I don't know what it is, but something weird happens."

Julia looked long at the painting, opened her mouth for a snarky comment... Instead of speaking, however, she sighed loudly and eased into a chair by the wall. She had a smile on her face like the kind you see in movies about people who have had a transcendent spiritual experience.

Wren watched as Julia sat grinning, held by the painting for fifteen minutes. Could someone overdose on a painting?

"Julia? Julia, let's go outside and you can have a smoke."

Wren took Julia's arm and guided her out the door. The wind was cold and blustery off the water, but they sat outside anyway, in the glider on the small flagstone patio in front of the house. Julia giggled occasionally, looked at the choppy gray water, then at Wren, and giggled some more.

"Wren, what is it? Is there something wrong with the air in your studio? Should you open a window or something?" Julia finally asked.

"I don't know what it is, but it's intoxicating, or even hypnotic, isn't it? I'm a little scared."

"Yes, it's weird. It's..." Julia trailed off. She tucked away from the wind and lit one of her favored Havana Honeys. The smoke didn't have time to become a ring or a dragon before the breeze whipped it away. She shook her head and watched the whitecaps on the bay. "I feel like I could never be angry about anything, ever again. That's weird," Julia said. A long moment passed, then she added, "Is this what art is supposed to do?"

"I don't know," Wren whispered, looking at the sky, the cold wind causing her eyes to water. Wren pulled her jacket tightly around her as a light mist began to fall. Julia's Havana Honey had gone out from neglect.

"Maybe we should invite a couple people over and see if maybe it's just us having a shared hallucination," Julia suggested.

Wren looked slightly alarmed and said, "Oh, I don't know about that. Let's go inside and have some hot coffee and Bailey's and think it over."

As the two painters went into the house, their backs to the water, they failed to notice two things. First, seven otters squabbled and frolicked their way from the water up the gentle slope of the lawn, taking shelter under the hydrangeas beside Wren's studio. Second, nine J-Pod orcas chose that moment to take a food-finding jaunt in the waters between the studio and the island a mile to the north. This in itself was not unusual... but if anyone had looked, they would have seen all nine whales pointing their noses toward Wren's home, not a salmon dinner in sight.

Chapter 4

Reality can be a tyrant and a taskmaster. Wren turned the new painting to face the wall in the storage room. She still felt a bit wobbly, but needed to work now. Twelve paintings were required for her Huxley-Lavelle show, and now she had ten.

Swinging a five-foot by six-foot canvas onto the easel, she began to rough in a mesa, a river, a road. She selected the colors of her palette: orange, umber, red, ochre, and blue. When she turned back to the canvas, she stood looking past it at the paint streaking up the walls, rivulets and blobs across the windows, and ruinous layers of color on the perfect wood floor — all reminders of the wild giddy painting she had done. *What a grand mess*, she thought. She smiled.

Not wanting to accept that she'd already permanently damaged the wood floor, in a fit of neatness she climbed the ladder to the storage loft and pulled out a long roll of canvas and spread it on the floor. With no thought or pause, she tossed the rough-sketched picture on top of it, and in seconds she was in it again, painting the air above the stretched canvas, rocking and dancing around and around it. Hours passed, paint flew, dropped, spattered, dripped and threaded across the surface.

Wren paced. She danced. She scowled and she laughed as the paint set itself free through the air and onto the canvas. Music radiated and roared and floated from the stereo. Time also flew, and the painting was done.

Wren lay the newly finished painting to dry on the floor in the storage room and thoughtfully seized one of the finished landscapes intended for the show. It was beautiful, a desert scene burning with a compelling light. She threw it on the studio's newly paint-strewn canvas floor and poured ultramarine blue in foot-long loops across the picture. Blue was the moment, and Wren was fully in this moment. Now came layers of phthalo blue, teal blue, cobalt, and cerulean. She stopped for less than ten seconds to regard her work, and then began to build layers of vermillion threads, layers of brown ropes, streaks of white and, finally, delicate threads of black. Her new painting completely covered the desert scene.

Oddly, Wren could faintly smell the presence of the desert. Was it simply because she knew it was there under the shocks and loops of color? So much mystery... *Maybe,* she thought, *in religious myth there never was a single lone tree of knowledge, only forests of mystery.* It was like that with this.

By the time Wren stopped painting, it was five o'clock the next morning. She shut off the lights and closed the door behind her. She was exhausted, but still paused to gaze at the water for a moment. Dawn was a little way off, but the water of Puget Sound glowed like liquid silver as it lapped at the rocks on the beach. She thought she heard laughter in the hydrangeas.

"Ms. Hendrix," she whispered, "you are completely baked."

Her fatigue also skewed her perception of the J-Pod orca family circling a hundred yards offshore, resting. She thought it was just a rippling wind-current, and shuffled off to bed.

After five hours of deep sleep, Wren awoke from a dream about the Puget Sound Naval Shipyard being turned into an amusement park. In the realm of the wakeful world, the shipyard was in the business of repairing, rebuilding, or dismantling floating and submersible instruments of war. However, in Wren's dream anyone could buy a ticket and take a two-hour submarine tour around Sinclair Inlet through Rich Passage and under the Agate Pass Bridge. Solar-powered subs had been fitted with windows, and for twenty dollars people could sit and have a view out to see all the sea creatures that swam up to look in at them.

Wren pondered the dream as she ate a bowl of cereal.

Reading her favorite comic strips online, she drank a cup of coffee laced with cocoa and cinnamon. In her thoughts, an idea for a painting was forming. Outside her window the sky and water merged in the same shade of silver-gray. Gradually, the clouds lowered and darkened, and when they could hold back no longer, fell open and released a torrent of rain.

Wren set down her coffee cup and hurried to the studio, dodging cold fat raindrops. Quickly, she painted a black-and-white sketch of her dream. Then she began to use color. She loved sea pens, and painted them in electric orange against a teal blue sea. Then it began again — the dance of painting air.

Her phone hissed.

"Hi Wren. Julia here. How's it going?"

Wren had grabbed her cell phone with cobalt blue fingers, smearing the phone. "I'm in the pink," she answered, and then immediately considered that she might in fact need some pink accents in this picture.

She searched her workbench for just the right pink while she talked. "I've been busy. I've only got three more new paintings to finish, and then I'm ready to take them to Lavelle."

Silence.

"You're making the whole show these mysterious new paintings, aren't you?"

"Yes, I am."

Julia paused for half a minute. "All right. I'm on board. Want me to go with you? You might need backup when Bertram Lavelle sees the new work. I'm guessing that he'll be pretty … excited."

"Oh, I think he'll be excited, for sure, but it probably won't be pretty. I'll call you when I'm ready to load the van. Thanks."

Dropping her phone on the bench-top, Wren found a jar of Iridescent Hibiscus, a delightful name for a radiant pink, and threw four thick globs in carefully chosen places on the painting. She then proceeded to bury most of it under about twenty layers of lush green paint.

Wren was careful not to look too long at her new paintings, as she was not immune to their peculiar effect. She walked cautiously around the last one, looking down at it where it lay on top of the thickening paint on the surrounding canvas and floor. She was checking for balance and composition and tone, things she was certain most viewers would feel at first glance. Things that, by the time they were looking deeper and the painting had its way with them, she suspected would not matter anymore.

"Julia," Wren spoke into her cell phone, "it's time to load the van. Bring sunglasses, but definitely *not* the polarized kind."

Wren was amazed at how tiring constant euphoria could be, like too much chocolate or too much champagne or too much sex. It all ends with some kind of hangover. After a bit of experimentation with various methods to protect herself, she had found that ordinary sunglasses did the trick. Polarized lenses, however, magnified the effects of the paintings to a dizzying extent. She'd had to lie down for a while after that experience.

Wren had tried looking at the paintings from a greater distance.

She tried looking at them through the studio window from the outside, but found herself backing knee-deep into the salt water at the edge of her lawn. It had been at that moment that her peculiar neighbor, who always dressed to some degree in seventeenth-century pirate garb, showed up. Wren avidly detested the man, but now found herself smiling at him and inviting him into her house for coffee. She even laughed as he punctuated every other sentence with "yaaahrr". He declined the coffee invitation, saying he had seas to sail and islands to pillage. Usually, she had the urge to unwrap the ridiculously long bandana from his bulbous balding head and strangle him with it. Now, she just wondered how long the peaceful effect of her new painting style would last.

Julia arrived, looking like an incognito Hollywood celebrity, wearing wraparound sunglasses and jeans crusty from the paint she habitually wiped on them. She had an intense natural beauty. Wren wondered why Julia and her husband had divorced. It might have had something to do with his inability to stay out of the gay bars. Or maybe he'd finally figured out that in Julia, he had a Bengal tiger on a short leash.

"I look like I'm in a TV commercial for freaking Ray-Bans," Julia said, entering the studio.

The paintings leaned against the wall, facing in on each other. Feeling a margin of safety, Julia took off her shades.

Wren's studio was a square building with twelve-foot ceilings. The north side was glass and the east was a solid wall with two small openable windows. The west side had a four-foot-wide mandoor that opened onto the path to the house. The south side of the studio had a fourteen-foot-wide garage door that could be raised with a touch of a button.

Julia hit the button, the door slid up, and Wren backed her old white Ford Econoline van into the studio. The two women looked at each other and donned their sunglasses in one synchronized motion.

When the van was loaded and secured, Wren realized that you could look in the side windows and see more than half of four different paintings. "Well," she offered, "I guess it's OK... You can't see a whole painting, and I think the auto glass may offer some protection. Maybe. Anyway, I have to scoot if I'm going to make the ferry."

The two women hugged quickly and Julia said, "You sure you want to do this alone?"

"No big thing," answered Wren. "I'm just a delivery girl."

The ferry was only five minutes from Wren's studio. Wren paid the fare and drove on board just as the gate closed behind her. As Wren switched off the van's engine, the vessel's diesel engines increased in pitch and the huge boat pulled from the dock.

Though small compared to other Washington State ferries, this one could hold eighty-seven cars and 1,092 passengers; it had a comfortable lounge area with video games, newspapers, Wi-Fi, restrooms, and a full galley — a floating rest stop on a watery highway.

It was a perfect spring day. Some early tourists were standing at the rail, taking in the bracing sea breeze. The rain had moved on and the sun was shining, elevating Wren's mood considerably. Her van was near the bow of the ferry, where the sun made it shine like a beacon. Wren hopped out of the van and ran up the stairs to the galley for some coffee. Water from the holding tanks imparted a special flavor. She had tasted worse... besides, it wasn't the quality of the coffee; it was the ritual of sitting on a ferry sipping coffee, watching the water and the mountains while floating above the deep canyons of Puget Sound.

In her haste to acquire a caffeinated beverage, she failed to notice that her van was garnering attention. Six passengers and one crewmember were standing beside Wren's van looking in through its big side windows. Their mouths hung open. The crewmember had tears in her eyes.

Wren was drinking coffee and speaking on her phone with Bertram Lavelle, the tightly-wound owner of the gallery representing her work. Bertram was carrying on in his remarkably shrill voice about his stable of unstable artists and the high price of cocaine, so Wren did not hear the captain's announcement.

"Folks, if you look out over the stern about a hundred yards away, you may catch a glimpse of some killer whales," the captain's voice crackled over the ferry's loudspeaker.

While many passengers hurried to the boat's stern, six dazed passengers and an emotionally overwrought crewmember still circled Wren's van. One of the six was a portly gentleman with thin hair so slathered in gel it stood six inches straight out from his head. He was attempting to climb the short hood of the van, but he slipped off the bumper, lost his balance, fell on his butt and slid toward the bow of the ferry. The crewmember leapt for him and grabbed his jacket collar with one hand while her other hand snatched the safety netting strung across the vessel's open bow.

The passenger's feet kicked in the air over the end of the car deck, salt spray soaking his pants. He was laughing. The other painting-dazed passengers were laughing. The crewmember was panting and tugging the laughing, wild-haired, crazy-eyed man back onboard, but she was joining in the laugh fest, too. The seven people joined together in a group hug.

The ferry bumped to a stop at the dock as Wren got into her van. She closed the door and snapped on her seatbelt. Glancing in her rearview mirror, she did a double take when she saw two crew members herding six passengers to their cars. One crew woman was being assisted to the crew quarters. Wren wondered what she had missed, but then recognized an unmistakable look in the eyes of one of the passengers.

Apparently, auto glass enhanced the effect of the paintings, and even partially obstructed views did the trick.

The Captain of the ferry, disturbed by any interference with the work of his crew, filed a Mysterious Incident report with Homeland Security. These were treacherous times.

The dock's ramp was lowered to the ferry deck and Wren sped off the boat, up the ramp, and out onto the street. With haste, she edged over the speed limit and got onto the West Seattle Bridge without obvious incident; but on the bridge, traffic slowed to the pace of a brisk walk. She was pinned in the middle lane and noticed faces of curious people in cars on either side of her. Wren held her breath. Then, without apparent reason, the pace of the traffic picked up.

She was certain she could make the short distance to the gallery's neighborhood without incident; but when she looked in her side mirrors, her heart nearly stopped. Two cars remained at a complete stop. The driver of the car in the right lane was now sitting on the hood of his Toyota Prius, meditating in lotus position. A white-haired passenger in a Buick sitting stationary in the fast lane was merely waving her underpants out the window.

Wren moved to the now-open fast lane and accelerated without giving any thought to a speeding fine.

Her rusty white Econoline pulled into the loading zone directly in front of the Huxley-Lavelle Gallery. Traffic here was light, and few pedestrians would be in the area this time of day.

Bertram Lavelle's assistant, Jeanette Perdot, spotted the van as Wren jumped from the driver's seat. Jeanette opened the glass double doors, securing them to hooks embedded in the sidewalk.

Jeanette Perdot was a serious Goth in her dress and manner. Tattoos crawled around her neck; piercings sparkled from ears, nose, lip and eyebrow. She sported the requisite black lipstick and thick eyeliner, and her form-fitting black dress was accessorized by a spiked dog collar and black five-inch stiletto heels. Jeanette's dark exterior persona was betrayed, however, by her beaming, welcoming smile. Wren was sure Jeanette had more than the normal human allotment of shining white teeth. All of this made the opening of the gallery doors quite a spectacle.

"Oh, fly to me, my little Wren!"

Jeanette always greeted Wren this way, even though Wren was

nearly six inches taller, broader, and nine years older. Of course, Wren flew to her.

"Listen, Jeanette, I've got a bit of a surprise with the paintings. I can't imagine what Bertram's going to say, but I want you to take a look before he gets here."

"OK, little bird, let's see."

"Put these sunglasses on first."

Wren slid a painting out the back door of the van and leaned it against the plate-glass front window of the gallery. Jeanette drew in a breath so sharply that Wren thought she might choke. Then Jeanette removed the sunglasses from the bridge of her pierced nose.

"Oh," said Jeanette softly. "Oh my."

A delivery truck was cruising past the gallery when the driver slammed on his brakes. The driver of a Land Rover following close behind could not react in time, and crunched half his car's hood under the back of the delivery truck. Both drivers were out on the street, the truck driver smiling beatifically, the Land Rover driver irate. The truck driver put his arm around the man who had run into the back of his truck and gestured with a nod of his polarized sunglasses toward the large painting on the sidewalk.

It took only a minute. Then the Land Rover's driver was smiling and hugging the truck driver like a brother who had just returned from six months at sea.

Meanwhile, two more cars had piled up on the street near Wren's van. An ample middle-aged woman in an oddly outdated beehive hairdo glided out from a beige Cadillac that had just bashed into a dark blue low-rider. The low-rider bounced up and dropped down, left front fender up, right rear down, entire front down and entire rear up, maneuvering like a cat in heat in an attempt to free itself from the Cadillac. The driver got out, an Asian man in his mid-twenties, *so* hip in his wrap-around polarized sunglasses, fired up and ready to unleash a few words on Miss Beehive. It only took a brief glance at the painting to get him weeping with joy. Miss

Beehive, already soothed by the painting, brought him a tissue and they held hands in the street.

This was the scene Bertram Lavelle saw when he rounded the corner a block away. His first thought was that his gallery had been the victim of art theft, which made him feel important and cheerful. Insurance money! Notoriety!

He straightened his little red bow tie and smoothed the front of his tight silver-gray suit jacket. His resemblance to the entertainment icon Pee Wee Herman was uncanny. As he put on his tinted glasses he saw no police cars and the crowd was calm and quiet. There was no broken glass, save for the automotive damage in the street. Still, it was a scene of promising disarray.

"Jeanette," Lavelle said, hoping concern showed as much as happy anticipation, "is this a robbery?"

"No. It's magic," Jeanette beamed.

"Bertram," said Wren cautiously, "I've brought the paintings for the show. I'll finish bringing them in."

She pulled a canvas out of the van and took it inside the gallery. She got another, and another.

Watching her, Bertram Lavelle stood with his hands pressed to a face the color of fresh beets. He began to scurry around the paintings, pulling at his hair until it formed a brown and white widow's peak that looked more like a pot handle than a hairstyle.

"Wha', wha', uh?" babbled Bertram. "Wren Willow Hendrix, what the hell is this supposed to be?" He was screaming now.

"Bertram," Wren said calmly, "look at them. Take a minute and just look."

Lavelle did not look at them. He whirled around to face her. "Are you crazy? Are you just fucking b-batshit crazy? I'm supposed to present a show of the best realist landscapes by the best realist landscape painter in the region. That's what I'm supposed to do. That's what you are supposed to do. I. Want. Realism!"

He enunciated the last three words so separately that they each stood like a pillar. Lavelle was literally foaming at the mouth, saliva droplets flying as he spat his words. He flailed his arms and pounded his fists against invisible air-walls. His eyes were bulging so much that Wren thought he'd either have a stroke or simply explode. Bertram Lavelle spun on his heels and ran inside the gallery.

Lavelle stormed around the back of his desk, jerked open the top drawer, and pulled out a small plastic baggie containing his favored medicinal white powder. He reached into the bag with his long manicured right pinky fingernail and scooped up a bit of joy and shoved it up his nostril with a sharp inhalation. Thus fortified, he rifled through a file cabinet, throwing aside papers until he seized upon the file he was seeking. Clutching a handful of pages, Lavelle shoved the baggie back into the drawer and ran out onto the sidewalk to stand toe to toe with Wren.

Wren could hardly believe this crazy scene. By now, the police had gotten word of the unusual activity, and two officers were trying to sort out the traffic.

"Hendrix, this is your contract." Then Bertram Lavelle grinned a demonic little smile and tore the contract into little strips of twenty-four pound clean white non-recycled paper. "I swear to God, all of you artists are unreliable, egocentric narcissists. Can you not follow the simple road map of your own making? You are a *realist*. I don't know what you are trying to do to me with these insane paint-vomit canvases. Jesus, I should have become a lawyer like my mother wanted."

He paused for a ragged breath and began again, "Now, get the hell out of my gallery, take these stupid globs of indecipherable paint with you, and do not — do not ever — *ever* come back."

With that, Bertram Lavelle's eyes rolled skyward and he passed out, pointy nose down, on the sidewalk in front of the elegant Huxley-Lavelle Gallery.

The police officer standing nearby quickly radioed for an ambulance and hurried to Lavelle to administer any required first aid. Jeanette held Wren by the arm.

Wren nervously watched the surreal scene and asked Jeanette, "What will Huxley think about this?"

Jeanette looked at her, a little surprised, and said, "You never knew? 'Huxley' was Lavelle's invention. He thought the name 'Huxley-Lavelle' sounded classy, and whenever things hit the fan he just blames Mr. Huxley, who is always conveniently in Paris or Milan."

Jeanette and Wren started to laugh, and then everyone within sight of the paintings that were now leaning on every available gallery wall joined in. Bertram Lavelle, beginning to regain consciousness, did not even chortle.

He would recover, but it would take many months of intense rehabilitation.

Wren and Jeanette put the paintings back in the van, except for one.

"Look at this painting carefully when no one will interrupt," said Wren, handing the big blue and orange looped canvas to Jeanette. "And I mean *be careful* when you look at it. You'll see what I mean. It's yours now."

Wren looked down at the moaning Bertram Lavelle, her shock dissipating and her confidence returning. She leaned down close to his face and hissed, "If you want realism, take a damn photograph," and strode triumphantly to her van.

Jeanette smiled broadly, her spiked collar glinting in the late-morning sunlight. She would hang the canvas where she could always see it.

Eliot J. Stern was engaged in a staring contest with his computer screen. His left hand held a cell phone and his right hand was wrapped around a paper coffee cup. One thick, light-brown curl escaped his perfectly greased pompadour and clung to his dark-framed glasses. Eliot's face was cherubic, a bit doughy from too many hours at the keyboard and too few at the gym. At thirty-eight, his boyish face astonished people when they learned that he was the tenacious, super-aggressive reporter whose byline was seldom absent from their daily paper. He was smugly satisfied that he, unlike most of his former colleagues, had not been relegated to the wasteland of the blogosphere. Eliot had credentials, respect, and an ego to match.

The police scanner on the edge of his densely cluttered desk sizzled, popped, and screeched a message. Stern lifted a pile of papers and squinted at the scanner. *It's the damn twenty-first century, and these things still sound like a pair of tin cans with a string,* he thought.

A bit easier to hear without five inches of paper on it, the scanner squawked its message: "10-51, 10-52 at our 20. Possible 10-96."

Stern knew all the police 10-codes, and this didn't sound like anything new or particularly interesting...until he heard the dispatcher ask the reporting officer why he was laughing. Eliot caught the location — an art gallery — and bolted for his car. This might be a rare opportunity to combine a heartless-cop story with the public's disdain for art.

Eliot Stern unfolded from his Smart car beside the Huxley-Lavelle Gallery, grabbing his cheap "conflict zone" sunglasses on the way out. He snapped a few photos of a car jammed partially under the back of a delivery truck, and several other cars with flat tires, broken side mirrors, and accordion-folded hoods scattered in the street.

Eliot watched as a man with a nose so sharply pointed it could spear fish was strapped to a gurney and loaded into an ambulance. The man was screaming "realism, *realism!*" over and over. Two women were filling a van with paintings. Was this a robbery?

The oddest thing was that all the onlookers, except for the screamer on the gurney, were calm, laughing…occasionally hugging. Even the police officers seemed to be in a transcendent, euphoric state. Eliot sniffed the air in an attempt to detect the aroma of marijuana.

He walked through the scene, taking notes and snapping photos of the pile-up, the tripped-out drivers, and the paintings leaning against the disreputable-looking van. He learned that the beak-nosed screamer was the gallery owner, the gorgeous copper-haired woman was the painter of the canvases being loaded into the van, the Goth was the assistant director of the gallery, and everyone else was a group of incompetent-but-happy drivers.

"Officer," Eliot said to the nearest police officer, "Eliot Stern, Seattle News. What happened here?"

"The truck driver saw a painting," the officer answered. He paused and then doubled over with laughter, hardly able to catch his breath.

Eliot tilted his head and watched. Laughter was contagious, and even he could not restrain a broad grin. He wrote "saw a painting" on his notepad. "Yeah, I'm sure that happens all the time. What about the other cars?"

The cop took out a white cotton handkerchief and wiped tears from his eyes and cheeks.

"Ah, that's better," he said. "I just feel so darned good today. Well, the other drivers, *they* saw a painting, too." Then he started laughing again. "Sounds crazy," he managed to say between spasms of laughter.

Eliot shook his head, wrote something more in his notepad, and hurried over to interview the Goth girl just as the painter drove away in the old white van.

"I really wanted to interview her. Who is she?" he asked while he watched the van speed away.

Jeanette regarded Eliot carefully. "Why?"

"I suspect she's newsworthy."

"Would you like to see one of her new paintings?"

"Oh, of course."

Stern looked at the canvas, unimpressed. "Well, that's a traffic stopper, isn't it? Where can I find her?"

Jeanette, baffled that the reporter did not react to the painting, said, "Her name's Wren Willow Hendrix, and…"

Eliot's piercing cell phone ringer interrupted her.

"Yes," he shouted into the phone. "What? Why? Well, damn, where is this? …OK, I'm on it."

Turning back to Jeanette he said, "Sorry, dear, I've got a funeral to attend. I'll call you later."

Chapter 5

*L*akeview Cemetery was silent and pastoral, even though it was in the middle of the city. Eliot Stern drove past tall grave monuments rising out of perfectly trimmed grass punctuated by elegantly pruned Japanese maples and towering cedars. History buffs strolling through the cemetery sought out the graves of some of the many Seattle founding families in eternal residence here. Every year hundreds of tourists from all over the world prowled these grounds in search of Bruce and Brandon Lee's graves. Walkers and bicyclists, enjoying their cardio workouts on roads that rolled up and down the hills through the cemetery, overcame any superstitions about conducting such life-affirming activities in the presence of the dead.

About a hundred yards ahead, Eliot spotted the tent that shielded a few mourners from sun, rain and the Angel of Death. He parked and approached, remaining at a respectful distance. The deceased was Army Corporal Gil Walston, blown into the next world by an improvised explosive device on a dusty road in Afghanistan. This had become so commonplace that the military spokesmen pared the information down to mere initials: simply another IED. The funeral was over now, and a terribly young soldier was presenting the carefully-folded flag that had recently covered the coffin to Corporal Walston's softly sobbing mother. Nearby, another soldier gave commands, rifles were shouldered, and a twenty-one-gun salute rang in the air. Birds exploded from the surrounding trees as if they had been shot from those guns. A bagpiper played "Amazing Grace" as the mourners began to walk away, leaving Walston's parents alone. As the corporal's mother sobbed, her husband engulfed her small body in his huge arms. The couple wobbled as she wept. Eliot saw them as corks bobbing on a bottomless lake of grief.

He swallowed the lump in his own throat as he noticed Walston's father looking off into the distance. Eliot thought perhaps the man was going into shock, but as he followed Mr. Walston's gaze and saw what Mr. Walston was seeing, he realized this was what he had been dispatched to report on.

There were three — no, four — men and three women. Good God, thought Eliot, there were also four children, and the youngest could only be about eight years old. Each person was carrying a placard stapled to a long wooden stake. Eliot supposed those stakes might have some valid use if driven through their hearts, if they had hearts, because the placards read, "God Hates Fags", "God Hates America", and "Thank God for IEDs". Stern thought the last one was especially cruel here, today.

So this was The Repentance Undeviant Tabernacle, led by the Reverend Billy Joe Bobb. Eliot had seen photos of Reverend Bobb, but he didn't see him here with his flock.

Mourners were pleading with the protesters to go away. The Repentance Undeviant Tabernacle members retorted to these heartfelt pleas with sneers and snarls of "Spawn of Satan", "You will drown in fag semen", and, of course, "Repent!".

Eliot, who thought he'd seen just about everything, was horrified that these supposed good Christians were shouting such ugly things at elderly people and a grief-stricken family — and, even more bizarre, that their small children were shouting the same slogans and insults, smiling while they did so.

The young soldier who had presented the flag now politely asked the group of picketers to leave. A tall, thin, stringy-haired woman spat on the front of his uniform jacket. The soldier calmly removed a tissue from his pants pocket and wiped away the spittle.

Eliot walked closer to the scene and spotted the Reverend Billy Joe Bobb moving around behind a minibus. He recognized the man's long, wispy, sandy hair. Billy Joe Bobb, wearing a blue work shirt and khaki Carhartt pants with a hammer loop, looked older than his sixty-two years, his skin papery and wrinkled. His haunting eyes, an icy sky blue, were bloodshot — perhaps from too much talk of hellfire. He moved his bony six-foot frame quickly from behind the minibus, bullhorn in hand.

"Jesus wants fags to die," Reverend Bobb's high-pitched, tinny voice screeched from the bullhorn. "God is punishing America for letting homosexuals live. Jesus doesn't like you!"

Then, pointing a finger at the late Corporal Walston's parents, he shouted, "God is dancing in Heaven today because he's glad your faggot son is dead."

Mr. Walston sat his wife down firmly on a chair next to their son's coffin, stood erect and straightened his tie. His face reddening as he moved, Mr. Walston blasted toward the Reverend Billy Joe Bobb like a cannonball.

"I'm gonna break your lousy skinny neck, you son of a bitch."

Reverend Bobb smiled, lowered his bullhorn, and began to back away, wiping his sweaty palms on his blue shirt. Walston was almost within reach of that skinny neck when two Seattle Police officers arrived. A soldier and a cop stepped in and halted Mr. Walston's advance while a policewoman began to herd The Repentance Undeviant Tabernacle members back to their bus.

Billy Joe Bobb lifted the bullhorn for one last verbal swing. "God will smite thee, fag lover. Fag father."

Eliot Stern was shaking his head, wondering if Billy Joe Bobb stayed awake at night thinking up this weird crap, when Mr. Walston responded, his voice constricted with emotion.

"You're too low to garner even one tiny second of God's fleeting attention. That's the only reason you still exist: you're just not worth the trouble of killing. My son was a kind and honorable man who just happened to love another man instead of a woman. What in the name of heaven does that have to do with you? With anything?" Walston paused, drew a ragged breath and continued in a tightly restrained voice, "A piece of dog shit is more worthy of God's attention than you are."

The Reverend Billy Joe Bobb dropped his bullhorn on the ground, raising his arms to protect himself from Mr. Walston, who looked ready to resume his charge, cops or no.

Then Walston's broad shoulders sagged as the cop and the soldier led him back toward his wife, who came gently to him. They walked away arm in arm, looking like a couple just going for a romantic walk in the park instead of parents who had just buried their only child. Eliot sighed and watched as they joined the other mourners heading for their cars.

The Reverend Bobb bent to retrieve his bullhorn. When he stood up he found himself nose to nose with Eliot Stern.

"Get away from me," Billy Joe Bobb squeaked, skittering backward two steps.

"I'm not going to hurt you. My name is Eliot Stern and I'm from the Seattle News. Would you answer a few questions for our readers?"

"No."

"Why is The Repentance Undeviant Tabernacle picketing this funeral?"

"It's not a funeral, it is evidence. It proves that God detests homosexual abominations."

"Hmm. But that young man died defending your country."

"Not my country! God has cursed America for denying Jesus Christ and for spitting in God's face with the sin of homosexuality."

"You really don't have a live-and-let-live attitude, do you?"

Reverend Bobb made a chuffing sound and started toward the Repentance Undeviant Tabernacle minibus. Something about the man brought the image of an iguana to Eliot's mind. It might have had to do with the way his tongue occasionally flicked out between his thin, bloodless lips when he spoke.

At the door of the minibus, Billy Joe Bobb raised his hands, rolled his eyes skyward until only the whites showed and proclaimed, "Listen ye blasphemers! God will kill the fags and bring this country to its knees. It is foretold in the scriptures." Then, turning directly to Eliot, he growled, "Tell your hell-bound readers we will be bringing God's message to that sinful Fremont Solstice Parade next month. That's Sodom and Gomorrah rolled into one, and God hates it! God hates sun worshippers."

Stern sighed and put away his notepad and pen. He unbuttoned his suit jacket and jammed his hands into his pants pockets, rocking back and forth on his heels a little.

"Reverend Bobb, what are you so afraid of?"

The Reverend Billy Joe Bobb did not answer; he got in the bus and slammed the door. Glaring at Stern, he started the engine, put the bus in gear, and drove away, much too fast to be considered respectful of the departed.

Chapter 6

Blood-red paint drooled from the end of a bent dinner fork as Wren walked it around a small canvas — twenty by twenty-four inches of cobalt blue, cadmium yellow, and black. Now she punctuated the painting with red: a red that, no matter what she did, refused to budge from a somewhat gruesome arterial glow.

She didn't fight it. Wren had figured out, after thirty-two of these paintings, not to fight the will of the paint, to simply flow with the dance that each painting demanded.

Finishing off the red, she stopped, unsure of her next move. Something wasn't right. She wasn't feeling the dance of this painting. Wren put on Bach's Third Brandenburg Concerto and watched the painting. Nothing. She walked around the canvas. Nothing. She had hit the painter's equivalent of writer's block, and she knew the cure. She needed to look at a face instead of a canvas, to hear another human voice, not just the scuff of her boots on the canvas-covered floor.

She pressed a speed-dial button on her phone. "Julia, let's go have a drink."

Twenty minutes later Julia and Wren sat in the local martini bar. It was cozy and dimly lit, the perfect atmosphere for properly reacquainting oneself with vodka and gin.

Julia sipped at her martini and ate the olive, a faraway look in her eye. Wren ordered a second blueberry martini while she finished her first. She wondered at Julia's uncharacteristic silence, thinking maybe it had to do with the drink ratio — this was Julia's third.

"Are you thinking about your ex-husband again?" Wren ventured.

Julia laughed out loud, "No...the poor dumb bastard." She sipped a bit of her drink, then gulped down the whole thing. "You know, I did love him. Still do, on some level. We might have been able to come to some arrangement if he'd been honest."

Wren asked, "Do you think you'll marry again? Or even date someone?"

"Only if whoever he is has the courtesy to tell me up front that he's mostly gay."

Julia tipped back her martini glass, working to extract one more drop. They sat in silence for a few minutes, watching the people at the other tables, listening to the musical clinking of glassware and the hive-drone of conversation.

"What about you?" Julia asked, an olive skewer clamped between her teeth.

Wren frowned, "You know, I'm getting pretty comfortable in my life. I don't think I want to throw the monkey wrench of love into the works anymore."

Julia choked on the first sip of her fresh martini. "*Monkey wrench of love?* Really, Wren, is that your view of an intimate romantic relationship?" Julia laughed. She kept repeating "monkey wrench of love..." and laughing, until she needed to stop for a deep breath.

"Are you finished?" Wren asked, frowning. "I have a deep and intimate relationship with my work. You know that. You have that, too."

"Wren, work is work. You need someone to talk to, someone to hold you. You certainly need to get laid. You have to take a chance sometime."

Wren smiled and shook her head, "Sometimes my art holds me just tight enough."

They fell into their own private thoughts for a few minutes, studying their drinks.

Running an index finger around the rim of her empty glass, Julia said, "What is an artist? What is it that we do?"

Wren searched the ceiling. "I suppose we're interpreters," she replied after a moment. "Interpreters of nature, of society, interpreters of myth."

"OK. Maybe. Maybe we use symbols and metaphor to help explain the universe. Hmm... OK, interpreters of our world," Julia agreed flatly. She leaned back in her chair and looked intently at Wren. Then, lurching forward in her chair and leaning across the table, she said, "I think we also interpret the supernatural world, the hidden universe. At least, I think *you* do. I think you are making visible the invisible."

The waitress arrived and set a new electric-blue martini in front of Wren. The artists were silent while their empty glasses were cleared away.

Julia continued excitedly, "I think you have tapped into some deep well of information previously unavailable to artists. Hell, to anyone, for that matter."

"You're scaring me a little." Indeed, Wren felt gooseflesh tingling her skin. She had been so intent on making more paintings that she had not taken time to think about what this phenomenon was, or how it could even be possible.

"Really, Wren? This is just so exciting. It's a place where art has never been. It's not a trick of the light or a manipulation of color. And even if it was, so what? Holy shit, Wren, I think this is huge. We can do something big here. We can change things. You've seen how people react to your new paintings. I've experienced it. You've experienced it yourself."

Wren sipped the blue liquid, regarding Julia through squinting, suspicious eyes. "So... what are you proposing?"

"Well, I was thinking maybe I would take a couple of your smaller paintings, easy to handle and travel with. I'll take them someplace where there is conflict. I'll start small. There's a county council meeting next week, and those're always a hotbed of short tempers and disagreements. Then, if that goes well, I'll move up the conflict food chain."

Wren was now frowning deeply. She had spent so much of her life being careful and methodical, probably as a kind of antidote to her free-form hippie upbringing. Julia's idea wore a veil of trouble, and shook her solidity with a thunderclap of spontaneity. But Wren had to admit that things had changed. She was no longer painting delicate clouds and babbling brooks; she was throwing paint around like confetti and being delighted with how it came to rest on a canvas.

"I don't know...Julia, you don't have time for that," Wren rationalized.

Julia cut her short. "Look, you just keep painting and I'll handle my time management."

Perhaps it was the ambiance of the martini lounge, the dim lighting with streaks of neon color. Maybe it was simply the drinks. Whatever the reason, Wren was certain she now saw the painting that had stymied her, finished and reflected in her friend's eyes, like a promise.

Like an omen.

Chapter 7

*A*rlen Divine had just consumed his third boilermaker and was slumped like an old overcoat on the bar at Chuck's Tavern. A Seattle Mariners baseball game roared from the TV mounted high in the far corner of the bar.

Chuck, the bartender, owner, and bouncer, was chewing on a toothpick while polishing a glass. Not quite six feet tall, at forty-six years he was experiencing male pattern baldness and sporting a slight paunch. Okay, a major beer gut if he was being honest about it. A guy has to do a quality check on the products, doesn't he? Still, Chuck had biceps that rippled under his shirtsleeves and a look that let potential troublemakers know he would tolerate no monkey business. None. The toothpick was the result of compromise with his wife. "Dump the cigarettes, sweetie. I want you to live to see sixty," she had said. *Toothpicks will never replace cigarettes*, he thought, tossing the pulped little stick into the trash.

The home team scored a home run, and the crowd on TV and the one in the bar produced a cheer that, to Arlen's ear, sounded like screams of terror.

Arlen had left Afghanistan years ago, but Afghanistan had forgotten to leave him.

He raised his head and squinted at the TV in time to see the replay. The batter crossed home plate, pointed an index finger toward the dark sky and knelt briefly on one knee. "Huh, look at that," Arlen slurred, "it appears that the God who doesn't give a rip about geno-cide, hunger, and disease has an interest in baseball."

"Well, he is batting .375," said Chuck.

Arlen jerked his head around, frowned at Chuck, and said, "God's having that good a season?"

Chuck set the glass down and leaned close across the bar. "Arlen, I think it's time for you to head home. I don't want you passing out in my bar again."

"Just a quick pint, OK? I'm a thirsty guy."

Chuck turned his back to Arlen and poured nonalcoholic beer into a mug. *No point pouring gasoline on a raging fire,* he thought as he set the mug on the bar. Privately, Chuck thought Arlen momentarily resembled the fellow on the old Jethro Tull album cover...a real life Aqualung.

Arlen looked at Chuck with rheumy eyes as he drank half the mug in one draught. He expelled a long, resonant Clydesdale-sized beer belch. Then he passed out, face down on the bar.

Chuck looked at Arlen like a disappointed parent. "Shit."

Chapter 8

The new painting was four feet square. Wren had propped it on an easel and faced it toward the studio's north window.

She went outside to the yard facing the water and sat in the glider. She rocked back and forth in the bright morning sunshine, looked at the ebbing tide, and wept. She had been alone for five years and was comfortable with it, but sometimes she opened the wrong door a little too far, and she could not bear what she saw there. Wren put her whole being into her work; not much was left to give to someone else. Relationships came and went.

Wren also knew that these paintings were taking something extra from her heart, even as they gave her energy. She pulled a ragged tissue from her pocket and wiped her eyes and blew her nose. Putting on polarized sunglasses, she stood and turned to face the studio's large window. The new painting instantly took charge of her emotions, and her sorrow vanished like a dream.

After a minute, she began to observe that other creatures were also looking at the painting. Eight otters lounged between her and the studio, hypnotized by the sight. Wren quickly removed the polarized lenses, replacing them with regular dark glasses. She stepped toward the animals. Their little heads were weaving to the left and to the right as though they were keeping time with a slow waltz that only they could hear.

"Hey," she called to them softly.

The otters did not startle and run, but rolled onto their backs, wriggling their long bodies and kicking their webbed paws in the air. The sound they made was musical, like the sound of children laughing, high pitched and carefree.

Wren took a step closer and waited. All at once, the romp seemed to remember their instincts. They turned and loped to the water's edge. One, whiskers bristling, turned briefly to look back at Wren; and then they all slipped into the water and swam away.

Wren wrapped her arms around herself, feeling truly amazed. Had she just seen an otter wink at her?

She walked back to the studio. She felt like working again. In less than an hour she finished the painting she had struggled with and put aside, the one she had seen complete in Julia's eyes.

Then she took two already-dry paintings out to the street side of the studio and hung them on the walls to either side of the roll-up door so she could spray them with varnish. She went inside to get the varnish, and as she stepped back outside, was surprised to see her neighbor Hilda Enquist standing there. Wren was somewhat relieved to see that the old woman was wearing dark glasses, protecting her from the euphoric effect of the paintings. Mrs. Enquist was about seventy-five years old and looked thin and fragile. Her neck sagged in a turkey wattle, and her dull gray hair was tightly curled from a recent beauty salon visit.

"Hello, Mrs. Enquist. It sure is a beautiful day," Wren said cheerfully.

"I want to tell you about your paintings," the old woman said. "I think you should know that your soul is in peril."

Good grief, thought Wren, *who talks this way?*

"Oh, thank you, Mrs. Enquist." she said. "I'll be careful."

"No, girl, it's too late. I am certain you are possessed by a demon…maybe more than one," the woman said, shaking a finger at Wren. "These paintings, they are of the devil. These are evil images straight from Hell, and there will be retribution."

Wren stood as still as she could, trembling a little from the shock of being accosted in such a strange manner. "Why would you even think such a thing? We're neighbors. You know me." *But apparently I don't know you.*

"The Reverend told me. The Reverend Billy Joe Bobb from The Repentance Undeviant Tabernacle. He says things like this are visions of Hell, and people who make images of these visions are speaking for the Devil. You'll see, girl, you'll see. Now, take those away so nobody else has to see this blasphemy."

Mrs. Enquist stomped away and fled down the street to her house, where her husband was quietly sneaking rum into his coffee — the elixir that sustained him through the interminable bondage of his marriage.

Wren shook her head and pondered what retribution might be coming her way...from Satan? From God? Or just from Mrs. Enquist? She began spraying varnish on the paintings. Her sunglasses were tucked into her pocket, and she was smiling.

On a drizzly Wednesday morning, Wren confronted the reality of her empty refrigerator, tossed her shopping bags into her old van and drove the nine miles to the grocery store. When she phoned Julia to ask if she needed anything from the store, her friend asked for French roast coffee beans.

Julia ended the call, debated with herself for three minutes, and drove to Wren's studio. Then Julia Burlow added a new career to her resume: art thief.

She walked boldly through the studio side door and started to look for two small paintings. Julia realized that she was laughing and feeling deeply contented. She put on her lightly tinted non-polarized sunglasses, and thus protected, she easily found two twenty-by-twenty-inch paintings and placed them carefully in her black Audi hatchback.

"Let the fun begin," she said to herself, smiling at her reflection in the rearview mirror.

As she had proposed over martinis, Julia intended to start small with a county council meeting; what they lacked in significance, they always made up for in animosity. She headed toward town, scanning the radio for the appropriate soundtrack to her life.

"...And the Mariners lose, 6 to..." "...save and shop at Wal-Mart..." "...I'm on the highway to Hell..."

She kept AC/DC on for a verse and a chorus, banging on the steering wheel, keeping time, then went searching again. "...Traffic backup on Highway 3 at the exit to Bangor Sub Base due to an anti-nuclear-weapons protest..."

Julia stayed on that channel and kept listening as she changed course, wheeling her car toward the freeway. The little county council meeting couldn't compete with nukes.

She learned that Ground Zero, the spiritual anti-nuclear weapons group, was holding a peaceful demonstration at the main gate for Naval Base Kitsap, Naval Submarine Base Bangor. Perfect! Julia had always wanted to stand alongside these peacemakers, but she was too short-tempered to be of much value to their cause. She always imagined herself carrying a "No Nukes" sign, being approached by some angry nuclear weapons supporter, then altering his dental work with her placard. Today would be different. Today she had Wren's paintings to do the real work for her; all she had to do was be a human easel.

She threaded her car through the traffic waiting to be cleared at the gate and rammed the Audi halfway up over the curb, leaving two fat tire marks in the grass. Parking propriety was not at the top of Julia's agenda.

She had a sketchpad on the back seat, and she found a black marker in the glove box. She was so pumped with adrenaline that her "NO NUKES" sign came out as "NO NUKS". As she approached the crowd, a slender man with a thick shock of white hair was directing demonstrators to their specified positions and helping to unfurl a twenty-foot-long banner that read, "GIVE PEACE A CHANCE". Julia especially liked that because she had recently seen a car with a bumper sticker reading, "GIVE WAR A CHANCE" that caused her to wonder what the hell was wrong with people these days.

The old gentleman came over to Julia, reached over to take her hand, and said, "I'm Steve. You must be new to our little group."

Little group? There must have been sixty people there — old, young, younger, and very old — roughly an equal number of men and women. Many appeared to be almost itching to be arrested, hopeful that perhaps this one simple act would save the whole world from the horrors of nuclear destruction.

Julia was moved by their courage. She took Steve's hand in hers. "I'm Julia. May I join you?"

"Of course. Have you been to our nonviolence training?"

"Well, no, but I can behave."

"Good, Julia. Stand here and smile that lovely smile and hold your…uh…interesting sign."

Not wanting to reveal the power of the paintings until the time was right, Julia clutched one of them close to her chest, covered by her sign. She thought it odd that people were looking at her sign quizzically. She looked down at the lettering: "NO NUKS" blazed out at the world. An elderly man with a walrus mustache carrying a placard reading "6,000 HIROSHMAS" looked at the words, then directly into her eyes. "Spelling isn't my strong suit, either."

He smiled, and Julia grinned in return.

"What's your sign mean?" Julia asked.

The older fellow's walrus mustache danced as he answered, "Well, each Trident W88 warhead is 475 kilotons. The Hiroshima bomb was 14 kilotons. You get the picture? That's the human cost, the planet's cost. One Trident II D-5 missile sets our wallets back a tidy little sixty million dollars, and each submarine is armed with enough of those warheads to destroy eighteen cities. I'm glad you're here today to help."

He strolled off to join the group a few yards away. Julia felt like her shoes were filled with lead, and as she absorbed the man's grim statistics she worried that maybe her heart was leaden, too.

All at once, the group tensed and looked toward the gate. Three armed Navy guards approached and took positions near the demonstrators. It was shift change at the base. Cars and trucks began streaming out of one side of the gate, even as two lines of vehicles were attempting to enter the other side. Most of the people in the exiting cars did not even look at the Ground Zero group. But a few waved, while others frowned and shook their heads. And a few presented their middle fingers for inspection.

It seemed almost dull, until one young man got out of his big knobby-tire pickup and stomped toward the clump of demonstrators nearest Julia. He wore chinos with a knife-sharp crease, a white dress shirt, a tan zip-front windbreaker, and a dark blue tie that hung loosely from under his shirt collar. His crew cut bristled nearly as much as his attitude. He began to speak, but one of the guards asked him politely to please get back in his truck.

Julia panicked. Was this the moment to show the painting? The young man shrugged and retreated to his truck. Not yet.

More cars, more trucks, and the signs waved and bobbed.

Two older women from Ground Zero sat down in front of cars waiting to enter the base. The guards waited a minute, and then asked them to get up. The women remained seated on the asphalt. A man sat down between them, holding hands with the women. A woman of about forty got out of her car, slamming the door, and lunged at the three protesters, attempting to kick them. The guards moved to restrain her...and it was time. Julia stepped forward, flipping the "No Nuks" sign out of the way, and revealed the painting to all.

It took only seconds for the effect to set in. The guards stepped back, wearing the deer-in-the-headlights look that was now so familiar to Julia.

The angry woman looked at the painting for a long moment. Then she reached down and tenderly touched the cheek of the man who was sitting on the road. He stood and embraced her. She quietly got back in her car, pulled over to the side of the road, and sat watching the low gray clouds run across the sky.

The guards were issuing citations for trespassing, handing them out to the demonstrators with peculiar comments like, "Thanks for coming. Have a nice day."

"There's something odd about this citation," one woman said. "It's a cookie recipe."

Several people looked at their tickets. Yes, chocolate chip. Two other citations were thank-you notes, signed with a little heart drawn around the guard's name.

A small elderly woman wearing a red scarf examined the cookie recipe at length. "Ooh!" she said, eyebrows arched in surprise. "It's got cinnamon!"

Julia thought this would be a good time to leave. As she walked to her car, she saw a man wearing a dark suit step out of the guardhouse. Their eyes locked for a moment, then he examined her license plate number, scribbled in his notebook, and reached for his cell phone.

Julia quickened her pace, her heart thumping faster than her footfalls. She fumbled for the key fob, dropped it, and it skittered under the car. Leaning the painting against the bumper, she lay flat on the ground, reaching, reaching for the key. Finally, key in hand, she rose and saw that the suited man had stopped.

She stood, clutching the painting in front of her like a shield. The man in the suit was looking at her, smiling like a kid who had just caught the biggest frog in the pond. The painting…he had been captivated by it and had forgotten that he was coming to restrain her.

Julia hurriedly tossed the canvas into the back seat, started her car, and bounced out of her impromptu parking space. She spun the car around, skinny cigar clamped in her teeth, and waved to her new admirer as she crossed under the overpass and embraced the anonymity of the freeway.

Homeland Security Agent Levi Bitters was standing in the roadway, hands hanging limply at his sides, looking up at the towering fir trees and smiling innocently, when his buzzing cell phone brought him back to full awareness. He blinked rapidly, emerging from his reverie.

"Yes. Bitters here. What? Please detain him. I'll be right there."

Agent Bitters ran past the guardhouse and into the inner sanctum of the nuclear submarine base. A worker was attempting an act of sabotage, shouting something about how the painting had shown him the error of his life's work and how he needed to close this place forever.

The possibility of some serious action heightened Agent Bitters' situational awareness. Yet something deep in his being was moving — something more than an emotion. He wanted to see that painting again.

Julia pulled her car into Wren's driveway as the rain began to fall. Wren was in front of her studio scrubbing furiously at the overhead door with a long-handled brush.

"Hey, painter," Julia shouted, "have I got a story for you!" Julia got out of her car and stood gaping at Wren. "What's this, spring cleaning in the rain?"

"Some moron pelted the side of the studio with eggs while I was at the store — ironically, buying eggs."

"Who would do that? Neighbor kids?"

"I don't think so." Wren told Julia about her odd encounter with Hilda Enquist.

Julia was quiet for a moment. "I can't really see an old woman flinging a carton of Grade-A Large at your door. Here, give me that brush. I'll scrub while you listen to what I did today."

Julia gave her full report, even confessing to having borrowed the two paintings without asking. She left out the part at the end about the man in the dark suit. It was *her* car's plates that he'd recorded, after all, so it didn't seem important to share. She wondered, though, why the omission weighed on her...

The two artists finished the cleanup as the rain poured down. They flung the brushes and hose aside and ran through the cold rain to find shelter.

Wrapped in bathrobes, they sat in Wren's living room sipping cups of strong hot coffee. Silently they watched the rain bounce on the salt water a few yards away. This view was always soothing.

"OK, Wren. Out with it! The rest of the story."

"You really should consider giving up painting and join a traveling carnival as a mind reader," Wren said with a laugh. "Madame Julia will read your future!"

"So?"

"Nothing much, really. A couple of anonymous phone calls. One yesterday, one at about three o'clock this morning. They never say anything, just breathing and a sound like papers being shuffled."

"That cult preacher your neighbor mentioned...I've heard of him, and I don't like this." Julia ran her hands through her hair, stood up, and paced in a tight circle. "I think we should move your new paintings to my studio to store them for a while, until you get a new gallery on board…" She paused, looking bemused.

"What?" Wren asked.

"Just trying to imagine what the opening night party for these paintings might look like!" She shook her head. "But anyway, I just think you might need more room to work. I've got loads of space — I just shipped three big canvases and the place looks too empty. Let's move them now. You could even work there if you wanted… Plus, I think you should report the vandalism and the weird phone calls to the Sheriff."

Wren was unnerved by Julia's thinly veiled urgency. "Look," she said, "It's just a couple of crank calls and some teenage vandals. You're getting wound up for nothing." Wren ruffled her damp copper hair with a thick towel.

They watched the rain some more. Julia stirred her coffee.

"I saw some things today," Julia said quietly, "things that made me worry about the power of these paintings. They do things to people, these paintings. They change them. *I* think change is good, but I suspect that not everyone wants to be changed. To believe a new paradigm, or even take on a different personality, they'd have to give up their old one. That makes them afraid, and scared people sometimes lash out and do stupid things. So humor me, OK?"

Wren looked down at her hands and sighed in resignation. Finally, she nodded and looked at Julia. "Let's go get something to eat," she said, "I'll put on some dry clothes, then we can drive to your place and you can change too." She stood and turned to Julia, "And I'll bring a few paintings to your place… but for the record, I think you're being paranoid."

Julia smiled with relief.

As they walked out of the studio, Wren said, "You drive, and I'll call the Sheriff about the crank calls and the scrambled eggs."

Paradigm shifts, choices, and changes… Julia and Wren drove twenty miles to dine at their favorite restaurant, where they always ordered the same things: always Lemon Chicken, always Pinot Grigio, and always coffee.

Tonight, in the spirit of change, they ordered steak and Cabernet Sauvignon. In the end they stuck with black coffee, unable to completely ditch that particular part of their ritual. The artists laughed and forgot about the crank calls. They joked with their waiter and forgot about the vandalism. Wren's neighbor and her threat of retribution was forgotten, like a badly acted scene from a low-budget movie.

But Wren had not been forgotten.

The Reverend Billy Joe Bobb, leader of The Repentance Undeviant Tabernacle, lived in a world of his own construction. His nephew, Delbert Florian Bobb, followed his uncle's blueprint religiously, and that was why he now stood inside Wren Willow Hendrix's studio.

Delbert Florian *believed* what his Uncle preached — believed with all his heart. He *knew* that homosexuals and free thinkers were at the root of the world's trouble. He *knew* that a trusted follower of The Repentance Undeviant Tabernacle, Mrs. Enquist, had phoned his uncle, practically hyperventilating with righteous hysteria, shocked to see that her formerly decent neighbor was now doing the work of Satan.

Mrs. Enquist had always been a little wary of her neighbor, Wren Willow Hendrix, because she never worked; she just stayed inside that big garage, painting pictures of places that Mrs. Enquist had never seen and doubted really existed. At least the pictures were pretty, and seemed harmless enough. But now Mrs. Enquist had seen evidence that something much more sinister was going on in there. She had phoned Reverend Bobb to describe the images of Hell she'd seen on that painter's wall.

Her husband, meanwhile, was unsympathetic to her plight. He drank his coffee quickly and stretched out on the couch, falling immediately into a peaceful dream about being alone on a distant tropical island. He dreamed he heard monkeys shrieking in the distance.

Mrs. Enquist shrieked into the phone that something had to be done. Reverend Bobb told her to sit down with a cup of herbal tea and stay home with her husband tonight. Everything would be alright. God — as championed by The Repentance Undeviant Tabernacle — would prevail, protect, and persevere.

Delbert Florian Bobb always trusted and obeyed his uncle, so when Billy Joe Bobb called him into his office, he perched his bony behind on the cold metal seat of a folding chair, unzipped his jacket, and listened attentively. Billy Joe Bobb's office was a visual cacophony of crosses, stacks of bibles and bumper stickers, hate-signs stapled to stakes leaning against the walls, and gold-framed photographs of The Repentance Undeviant Tabernacle's many demonstrations. All this was stuffed into a dusty room lit only with one bare bulb in a brass floor lamp.

The Reverend Bobb conducted services in a storefront (formerly an adult bookstore) in a nearly vacant low-traffic strip mall. These worship meetings occurred sporadically, depending upon the Reverend's need to be elsewhere to spread his message — the word of The Almighty as interpreted by Billy Joe Bobb. He truly was divinely inspired, according to his small group of devoted followers.

Uncle Reverend Bobb had been clear about his vision as he sat behind his big white desk instructing his nephew. He folded his hands prayerfully, leaned forward on the desk, and said quietly, "You are doing God's work here, Delbert Florian, and you are fighting the Devil. Be fast, be careful, and be clean."

Billy Joe Bobb then stood and came around the desk to his nephew. He seized the young man by the front of his jacket, his face so close to his nephew's that his bad breath made the boy's eyes water. The Reverend added, "And don't get caught."

Reverend Billy Joe Bobb took a step back, smiled, and smoothed the front of his nephew's jacket.

Delbert blinked and wiped his sleeve across his nose. "God's work, Uncle Reverend," Delbert said, barely above a whisper. He zipped his jacket, turned and went out to perform his sacred duty.

Now, standing in Wren Hendrix's studio, Delbert Florian's biggest dilemma was where to pour the gasoline, and how much. He was not a man given to excess. One gallon of low-octane Chevron gasoline was all he had needed to invest. He splashed the fuel carefully, not allowing even a drop on his clothing. He had seen photos of burn victims, and thought he'd prefer not to be one of them.

He set the plastic gas can on the floor, walked to the side door, and looked around. *This will be the last anyone sees of this place*, he thought. He switched off the light, struck the match, tossed it on the floor, and walked away.

A loud low reverberating *whoosh* shook the building, startling the ten otters napping in the hydrangeas. They grumbled and squealed, loping for cover in a neighbor's blackberry thicket.

The orcas offshore spied the flames and decided maybe it was time to head north for the summer. The surface of the bay rippled and swirled, then rolled and flattened like a sheet of dark glass.

Chapter 9

*J*eanette Perdot sat behind her desk in the dark at the Huxley-Lavelle Gallery. She switched on the desk lamp, got up, and checked that the front door was unlocked. She poured three glasses of Chardonnay in the kitchenette that was hidden from public view at the rear of the gallery.

On the way back to her desk, Jeanette turned on a spotlight illuminating the painting that Wren had given her. It hung alone on a large black wall, but the wall was at an angle that kept the painting from being seen by anyone passing by or entering the gallery. Being careful not to look directly at it for the moment, she draped a piece of black velvet over the painting and hurriedly set up three straight-backed chairs in front of her desk facing it. It was nearly nine PM and she was ready.

Precisely on the hour, Jeanette opened the front door. The air pressure in the gallery changed slightly. The Mayor and a City Councilman walked through the door and into the softly-lit gallery. Jeanette felt the air pressure change again as she closed and locked the door.

"Good evening, Madame Mayor, Councilman Yates," she said, handing each of them a glass of wine. Mr. Yates nodded hello and draped his jacket over Jeanette's desk while the Mayor declared she was chilled and wrapped her coat tightly around herself.

"Well," Jeanette forged ahead, "thank you for coming. As you know from my email, I am the new director of this gallery. Mr. Huxley is in Paris…No," she glanced at the laptop on the desk, "Milan. And Mr. Lavelle, the previous director, is recovering in a rehabilitation center in California. What I am about to show you is the reason for Mr. Lavelle's unfortunate breakdown, but it is also a reason for hope and for awe. I'll be showing you a painting by Wren Willow Hendrix."

"Oh, I know her work," said the Mayor. "We've got one of her large landscapes depicting Mount Rainier in our offices."

"Yes, and no," said Jeanette. "Ms. Hendrix recently made an abrupt and inexplicable change in her painting style. But even more shocking is the thing you are about to experience. Do you recall an incident at the gallery two weeks ago involving a six-car pile-up, compounded by Mr. Lavelle's health issue, that required an ambulance and several police officers?"

The politicians nodded and gulped their wine in unison, their attention riveted on the Goth gallery manager.

"The painting I'm about to show you is the cause of all that. I've asked you to see this because I've been looking at this painting for two weeks, and I've concluded that Ms. Hendrix's work could be used for truly incredible change in our world. I know this sounds ridiculously optimistic, but I think this painting and the others Wren has produced could be a catalyst to facilitate the end of conflict as we know it on our poor, beleaguered planet."

Her guests merely stared at her and drained their wine glasses.

"Really," Jeanette said, "I can understand your skepticism. But please, sit in these chairs and look at Wren Willow Hendrix's new work while I refill your glasses."

The Mayor and the Councilman moved to the chairs Jeanette had indicated, and Jeanette got up, plucked the black velvet away from the painting with her free hand, and stepped away toward the kitchenette. She had barely finished pouring the wine when she heard laughter. She returned to find two completely different personalities than the ones she had left seconds ago.

"Madame Mayor," Mr. Yates began.

"Oh, please, just call me Caroline."

"Well, Caroline, I am so sorry about the fight we had yesterday about the homeless shelters. I don't know how I could have missed your point."

"Yates, I regret that I may not have listened closely enough to your observations. I really appreciate your work on the issue. Your insight will help those in need, save the city hundreds of thousands of dollars, and create meaningful work for many, many people."

Jeanette knew this mutual adoration fest could go on and on and probably devolve into endless giggles, so she moved things along for them. She handed the city leaders their wine, replaced the scrap of velvet over the painting, and waited for the painting's effect to subside enough for them to have a coherent conversation.

Two glasses of wine, a bowl of cherry tomatoes with baby carrots, and a family-size bag of tortilla chips later, the Mayor and the Councilman settled down.

The discussion went on for an hour. Councilman Yates tried hard to tweeze out some sliver of trouble, but finally he could see only good coming of using the painting to bring people to agreement. The Mayor concurred.

"We should put reproductions on buses," said Yates.

"We should put them on billboards," the Mayor added.

Jeanette, who had been sitting behind her desk observing the pair, said, "I don't know that reproductions work the same. I tried photographing the painting and looking at it on the computer, and I didn't experience anything unusual."

They sat in silence, mulling over what that might mean. Councilman Yates twisted around in his chair and lifted Wren's canvas off the wall to look at the back.

Holding out his empty wine glass to Jeanette for a refill, he asked, eyes narrowed, "How many of these paintings do you think Ms. Hendrix can make?"

Chapter 10

Wren had read somewhere that life was about loss. She knew about loss. Her mother was gone, she had never known her father, she had given up on lovers and had lovers give up on her, and her work had given her plenty of opportunity to experience rejection over the years. The smoldering wreckage she and Julia came back to after dinner, however, was different — something she could never have imagined or prepared for.

Julia kept her arms wrapped around Wren and watched the firefighters packing up their gear. The Fire Chief walked over to them, reeking of smoke. The acrid air made everyone's eyes water.

The Chief took Wren's hand. "I'm sorry about this, Ms. Hendrix. It looks like arson. There's a lot of evidence. They didn't even try to be clever."

Wren looked beyond the Fire Chief to the blackened, dripping mess that had been her studio.

"Do you have any idea who might have done this?" the Chief asked.

Wren shook her head and swallowed hard to keep from screaming, *"It's that fool Billy Joe Bobb and his band of freaks, The Repentance Undeviant Tabernacle! They phoned me, they vandalized the place, and now they burned my studio and my art!"*

But she didn't say it. She stood still, her arms folded across her chest. Julia held Wren tighter.

"OK," the Chief continued. "If you think of anything, just call me, OK? The good news is that the house might smell a bit smoky, but it didn't take any damage." He started to walk away and then turned back to Wren. He spoke to her in a whisper. "I think you should know that we noticed something kind of odd. When we got on scene the fire was going full tilt. The roof was down already because there was so much volatile material, so much fuel. Well, we looked as thoroughly and quickly as possible because we thought that maybe somebody was inside. It sounded like people were singing in there. What do you make of that? Did you leave a radio playing or something? It didn't sound like a radio to me…"

Wren just kept looking at the studio's remains, puddles and ashes still popping and sizzling.

"…It must have been the wind," the Chief filled the silence after a minute. Clearly, he sensed that there was more going on here than an ordinary fire, but Wren was too distraught to even attempt to fill him in. She nodded absently, her mind slow with the thickness of shock.

"Call me, Wren." The Fire Chief picked up an air tank and walked to his official Fire Department SUV.

Wren walked around the edges of the disaster while Julia stood near the car. The sounds of the firefighters packing equipment and shouting to one another came through, vague and meaningless, as if she were in a narcotic stupor. She thought she might like to lie down and sleep for days, right here on the blackened ash of her paintings. Was there even a word for this kind of loss?

The diesel engines faded into the night as the fire trucks roared down the road toward the station. Then the air was still.

"This certainly is a significantly fucked-up situation," Julia called to her from her perch on the car.

The jarring juxtaposition of formality and vulgarity in Julia's speech made Wren laugh, and she turned away from her sorrow and walked back to Julia. They stood together and listened to the waves touching the shoreline, louder than the hissing of the hot embers.

"Julia, remember when we got those awards from the Mayor?" asked Wren as she looked at the ruins of her studio.

"Sure. My plaque is prominently displayed under a pile of unread mail on my dining-room table."

"I was thinking about the boat that exploded. I read later that it was caused by gasoline fumes. That can happen, I guess. But I remember feeling strange. You're going to think I've got a mental problem, but, well, here's the thing: It felt like an omen. I remember standing in the rain, watching the boat burn, and thinking, 'this is an omen.'"

Julia tilted her head and regarded her friend. Her eyes were kind, and she reached out and gently touched Wren's arm. "You do know that that is complete bullshit, don't you?" she said.

Wren shook her head slowly, looking down at her shoes. "I love your compassionate insight."

Julia pulled Wren close in a sisterly embrace.

"OK," Julia said softly, "come back to my place. I'll rent you my guest room for the night."

Otters and whales rested peacefully, but Wren fell into a sea of nightmares even with the aid of a sleeping pill and a shot of Aberlour. At three o'clock in the morning she gave in and got up.

Wren took a walk around Julia's living room — a familiar place, but not in the middle of the night. The room was filled with art. There were paintings by Alden Mason, Christopher Mathie, and, of course, Wren Willow Hendrix. Tip Toland and Patty Warashina ceramic sculptures and a Justin Novak "Disfigurine" were displayed prominently on shelves. Near the front door a whimsical beaded sculpture by Sherry Markovitz hung next to a contemporary Navajo rug.

One of her favorite pieces, a Chuck Gumpert painting from his "Departure" series, reflected enough light to catch her eye. The painting was an abstract in blue, depicting ghostly figures stepping into, or out of, a bright light.

Wren went into the kitchen and was making herself a pot of coffee when Julia appeared with the Seattle paper under her arm, puffing on a Havana Honey.

"You, too, eh?" Julia grunted.

Wren forced a little smile, "Yes, me too. I think I prefer the real and present nightmare to the ones that sleep was giving me. Got any bread?"

Julia nodded toward a cupboard. Wren toasted four slices of bread and sent mounds of butter melting into them. She offered two violent sneezes and waved at the smoke.

Julia crushed out the burning tobacco. "Sorry."

"This almost feels normal," Wren ventured, "like normal people starting a normal day. Here I am smearing strawberry jam on toast, chatting with you and choking on your cigar smoke while you scan the newspaper. We're like old married people. 'I hope you have a nice day at work, honey. Don't forget to stop at the grocery on the way home.'"

She put down her spoon, bit the corner off the slice of toast and jam and set the rest on her plate. She covered her face with her hands while she chewed. "I'm probably going to gain twenty pounds. I eat when I'm upset. I *am* upset." She finished off the toast. Sipping coffee, she leaned back into the chair, staring at the crumbs of toast on the tabletop. "When there's enough daylight, I need to go have a closer look at the damage," she said.

Julia folded the newspaper and laid it on the table. "I'll come with you. You shouldn't have to face that alone."

"Thanks. I owe you one."

"No, you don't. Hey, it's a good thing you gave in to me and brought those five paintings over here."

"Yes... at least I've got the five."

"Hmmm... seven. Don't forget the two I stole from you the other day, the day I went to Bangor."

"Right. OK... And there's one more. I gave one to Jeanette Perdot at Huxley-Lavelle."

"What? She's showing it?"

"No, just keeping it safe. It's hers, though. I figured she'd know what to do with it."

Julia poured more coffee. "OK, eight paintings currently exist. I'll make some space for you in my studio and you can get to work... When you're ready, of course."

As Julia set her cup on the table next to the paper, a tiny headline caught her attention. She had folded the paper so that page eight was facing out. She snapped up the newspaper so fast that she sent her cup and its contents rolling across the table and onto the floor. The empty cup spun around and around and around in a swirling lake of coffee.

"You OK?"

Julia read the item. "Well, this article by Eliot Stern says that the Reverend Billy Joe Bobb and his Repentance Undeviant Tabernacle will be picketing the Fremont Solstice Parade. Reverend Bobb says God hates Naked Bicyclists just as much as he hates gays, Jews, Blacks... and probably kittens and puppies. And artists, of course."

"That's the guy my neighbor Mrs. Enquist mentioned. She's a believer, and Bobb is the... I guess you'd say, cult leader." The room was so silent that Wren could hear the blood rushing through her veins. "I think Billy Joe Bobb burned down my studio as some weird act of perceived retribution for my evil paintings. What do you think?"

Julia accidentally kicked the fallen cup across the kitchen floor as she stood. "What do I think?" Her usually low alto voice climbed a couple notes. "I think this slimy bastard slithered out of the dark ages, and I think I've got a plan."

"Oh, dear," Wren whispered, "I don't know if I want to hear this."

"I'm going to take one of the smaller paintings to the Fremont Fair, and I'm going to confront the Reverend Billy Joe Bobb." Julia leaned in close to Wren and added, "I think he may become a different man after he spends a couple minutes with one of your 'evil images straight from Hell'. I think it's worth a try."

Wren wanted to protest, but yawned instead. "I'm sure I can sleep peacefully now, comforted as I am by your detailed and plausible plan."

"Ha," Julia snorted. "You laugh now, but you'll see. You can't deny that when people look at those paintings, *really look*, it changes them."

"OK," Wren acquiesced.

Julia took the newspaper and stretched out on the couch in her living room.

Wren turned off the kitchen light, took a last glance at the Chuck Gumpert painting, and shuffled off to the guest room, wondering where the mysterious figures were going. As she fell asleep, she felt herself traveling with them, then fell into an odd dream about a moth.

Wren and Julia stood beneath a leaden sky of frenzied low clouds that flung daggers of rain at the earth. In spite of the rain, a sour odor rose from the ashes of Wren's studio.

"It looks worse in the daylight," Wren said.

Julia nodded in agreement. She could see nothing that resembled a canvas, a jar of paint, or even the discernable remains of a building. "Are you OK with this? Maybe we should just go back to my house."

Wren walked into the middle of the ruins. "No, Julia, I have to be here. I need to see this." Pushing at a mound of soggy ash with her foot, she turned to Julia and said, "Do you know what this feels like? It feels like I'm the last leaf of autumn, clinging alone to the end of a branch." She kicked at a clump of debris. "Goddammit. The world's too big." A sob caught in her throat.

Without my work, she thought, *I feel like I'm too small to even take in breath.* Hot tears escaped her control as she jammed her hands into her jacket pockets and stomped around in the ashes. She pulled her sleeves down over her palms and wiped her face with them.

"I'm so fucking angry! I'm so fucking angry!" Wren screamed into the rain, raising her arms toward the sky.

She kicked at a blackened pile of debris, and as anonymous bits flew into the air, she heard the light tinkling of a bell. She kicked at it again, and once more heard a high note tinkling on the breeze. The rain eased and Wren stood still, wiping raindrops and tears from her face with both hands. She turned and saw that Julia was smiling, and, to her amazement, she was smiling, too.

"I'll get you some tissues," Julia said, and walked toward Wren's house.

Wren was kneeling down, pawing through the mess trying to figure out the exact source of the bell, when she heard a car crunching up the gravel driveway. Looking up from the ashes, she could not think of anyone she knew who drove a black GMC Yukon.

Homeland Security Agent Levi Bitters sat alone at the counter in the crowded diner. Reading the news on his laptop, he pushed scrambled eggs around with a fork through a puddle of ketchup. The diner served up a desperately acidic cup of coffee that packed a walloping caffeine punch. A waitress with a diamond stud in her nostril winked at him and refilled his mug. Agent Bitters attempted a friendly smile and winked back, though he worried that in his current preoccupied mood the whole thing looked more like a wince.

He straightened his tie, smoothed it down his shirt front with his right hand, and went back to his laptop.

Levi Bitters believed that reading the local news gave him a sharper perspective on the behaviors of a community. This was a habit he had learned from his father, a now-retired FBI agent. Even his grandfather had been in the service of the FBI, albeit as a janitor. Levi Bitters had learned from these men to be dedicated, patriotic, and loyal, and so he had leapt at the opportunity to join the new Homeland Security team.

Sipping his coffee, he clicked and typed on his laptop. He was particularly interested in the columns referred to as "police blotter", "911" or "crimes". Today, amid the usual assortment of car wrecks and domestic brawls, an item about a fire gave him pause. He read it twice:

Famed local artist's studio burns down — arson suspected.

Bitters closed his laptop and drank more high-octane coffee. He straightened his tie again, paid his check, and left a dollar under his coffee cup. He would call the local Sheriff's Department and find this artist. There was no evidence or logic to support it, but Agent Bitters felt in his gut that this incident was connected to the painting that had shifted his world at the submarine base. Bitters had to admit that seeing that painting was like diving into a hypnotic fog. The fuzziness had cleared about an hour after the encounter with the wild-haired woman who was holding it, but something in him was changed. He was still sharp, still focused...but still, somehow, he felt soft around the edges. It seemed that in some way he was more aware, that he was a truer version of Levi Bitters.

Opening the door to leave the diner, he pulled the collar of his trenchcoat up around his neck. The rain was coming at him from all directions, pushing its way into his skin. Bitters wondered why the rain in the Pacific Northwest was exempt from the laws of gravity. Rain dripped off his coat and puddled on the car seat as he tapped his cell phone. The Sheriff's office answered the call as Agent Bitters started the car to get the heater running. As soon as he got the address, he pulled away from the curb and splashed down the street toward Wren Willow Hendrix's studio.

Bitters drove his car off the paved road and down Wren Hendrix's gravel driveway. As he crunched to a stop, he saw a copper-haired woman kneeling in the debris of a burned building. Closing the car door behind him, Bitters reached into his jacket and produced his identification card and badge.

"Excuse me, ma'am. I'm Agent Levi Bitters, Homeland Security. I'm looking for Wren Willow Hendrix." He pitched his voice at its most reassuring, a low smooth rumble.

The woman stood, wiping her hands on her jeans. Bitters walked closer — but sensing that she had a protective emotional wall around her, he stopped about six feet away. The woman looked directly into his eyes, and it chilled him that her dark eyes appeared to absorb light rather than reflect it.

"I'm Wren Willow Hendrix," she said, showing a hint of a smile as she briskly wiped her hand again and extended it to him. "Sorry about the dirt."

Agent Bitters shook her hand. This woman did not even remotely resemble the woman he'd encountered at the Bangor Submarine Base. He kept his countenance still, not daring to reveal his consternation, and proceeded with his mission.

"Ms. Hendrix, first I'd like to say that I'm sorry for your terrible loss. I enjoy art, particularly painting, and I know this must be a difficult time." He wondered why he was blathering on like this. Frankly, he wouldn't know the difference between a Rembrandt and a Rothko. Bitters glanced at the hand that had shaken Wren's, but could not detect any changes. *Get your head straight, Levi*, he thought.

Wren seemed to sense his uneasiness, and, oddly, her own tension appeared to dissipate. Agent Bitters looked at the ground near his feet and took a little sideways step, steeling himself to again become the hard-edged, tough-minded defender of his country.

"Ms. Hendrix, we — that is, I — would like to talk to you about the risk your paintings pose," Bitters plowed forward.

"Risk? What are you talking about?"

"There was an incident at a peace demonstration at the Bangor Sub Base involving a woman holding a painting, and we believe the painting may have been one of yours. Look, I realize now that it was not actually you who brandished that painting at the demonstration; the point is, the painting elicited extreme responses from the persons who viewed it. They became different. They were softer, kinder, pliable. Agreeable and calm. Peaceful. I think you can see the problem here."

Wren failed to contain a little chuckle. "I see. Yes, that must be a terrible danger, having a world full of calm, gentle, peaceful people. I can see that my paintings present a risk to the concept of conflict as the normal state of humanity. There could be a real danger that peace and harmony could break out all over the place."

"Well, yes. That's it exactly."

"But how can that be a bad thing, Agent Bitters?"

"Ms. Hendrix, you obviously don't understand the world economy and its relationship to the military-industrial complex. Without a certain more or less constant level of conflict, some very important elements of the global economy would fail. Commerce feeds the world, so we don't wish for those businesses to collapse. Do *you*?" Bitters narrowed his gaze and his jaw tightened. "Your paintings are dangerous."

Wren looked out toward the water, standing silently, uncertain whether to laugh or to run and hide under her bed. As she looked back toward Agent Bitters, she thought she spotted Julia peering out from the edge of the mudroom doorway, scrunched down near the floor. The door was ajar and Agent Bitters' voice was resonant, so her friend was probably hearing every word of their exchange.

Wren made a grand sweeping gesture with her arm, indicating the burned pile that used to be her life's work. "Dangerous paintings? I'd say that's hardly an issue now. Wouldn't you agree?"

"Ms. Hendrix, I know there are more of your paintings out there. I personally saw one, and I know what they are capable of. I wish you wouldn't make this unnecessarily difficult."

"You wish. *You wish?* Really? Well, here's what *I* wish. I wish to be left alone!" Wren's voice was hard and dark. "My paintings hurt nobody. Nobody! Nobody gets hurt…except me. I've lost everything—all of my work, all of my tools, pieces of myself I can never get back. Gone. So leave me the hell alone! Leave me alone to grieve and try to decide if I can somehow rebuild my life." Wren's voice found its full volume, and her sorrow and anger were now pointed sharply at Agent Levi Bitters.

Bitters seemed stung by her attack. "OK, Ms. Hendrix, then consider this," he said softly. "You have an appointment at the Seattle Homeland Security office this Tuesday afternoon. Be there. Please." He held her gaze and handed her an envelope. "This appointment is not optional." He sounded sad and oddly conflicted as he added, "I *am* sorry for your loss."

Wren watched Bitters turn and walk toward his car, her shoulders sagging from the weight of his request. She had liked his voice at first. It reminded her of James Earl Jones in "Field of Dreams"—golden tones, rich and thick like warm honey. But now she revised her opinion of his James Earl Jones voice—it was more like Darth Vader.

Once Agent Bitters was at least a couple of miles away, Julia emerged from her leg-cramping listening post. Wren was still standing, looking out toward the road, when Julia came up beside her and put an arm around her shoulders.

"I heard everything. You absolutely can't go to the Homeland Security office on Tuesday. They'll arrest you. Hell, they'll probably dissect you to figure out what it is you're doing and how you do it. Then you'll be put in some secret prison-laboratory-atelier compound and forced to make weapons-grade paintings."

Wren frowned at Julia. "I think you're exaggerating a little. I don't think there is such a thing as a 'weapons-grade' painting."

Julia shook her head and said, "OK, but get in the house and pack two suitcases anyway. We'll leave your van right here at your house. I'll dash home on foot and get my car. I'll tell you where we're going while we're driving."

They looked at each other. Conspirators. Escapees.

"I'll be in deep crap if they find me," said Wren.

"Yeah, but which 'they' — Homeland Security, The Repentance Undeviant Tabernacle, or the press? It looks like you've got a flock of groupies, my friend. I'll be right back."

"Want to take my bike? It's faster, and I don't think anyone will notice it's gone."

Julia nodded, picked up Wren's bicycle, and walked it down the gravel driveway toward the road. With a wave of her hand, she mounted it and wobbled off toward her house.

Wren looked around her home, beginning to wonder if this was the last time she would ever see it. Feeling the urgency of the moment, she pulled two large suitcases from a closet. She crammed them with summer clothing, winter clothing, a favorite pillow, toiletries, three books, and the tattered brown teddy bear her grandfather had given her for her first birthday. She then slid the age-worn wing-backed chair across the bedroom floor and pried up two floorboards. After removing a fifteen-inch dry bag that had been sequestered in the floor space, she replaced the boards and chair and sat on the bed to look inside the bag. Thirty thousand dollars in cash. Would it be enough? For how long? Maybe they could stop at a bank. *Oh, shit,* she thought, *the government will freeze my accounts when I don't show up on Tuesday.*

She heard a car on the gravel and looked out the window to see

Julia's Audi. She felt dizzy. Bumping her suitcases down the stairs, she met Julia at the mudroom door. Not a word was spoken as Wren handed Julia one of the bags. Wren cast one quick sideways glance back at her house as she walked to the car, feeling uncertain of the future.

"OK," Julia said, tucking the suitcases in the back of the car and slamming down the hatchback door, "Get in. Road trip!"

"So I guess I'm Louise and you're Thelma, huh? Well, that's not too scary..." Wren mused.

Julia maintained the speed limit through the light traffic on Highway 3. They were past the exit for Naval Base Kitsap, Bangor before Wren spoke.

"So, where are we going?" Wren asked.

"Port Townsend. I have an old friend there. Her name is Grace and she lives on a little farm. Raises greens, carrots, garlic, that sort of thing. I think she even still has some chickens and a couple goats. You'll like her."

"Does she know we're coming?" Wren frowned in Julia's direction.

"Oh. Good point. Hand me my cell phone."

Wren shook her head, grinning. Julia thumbed the touch screen on her phone, disregarding the laws prohibiting the use of cell phones while driving. She evidently felt that the rules had changed for her and Wren now. Wren could hear the phone connecting.

"Hey, Grace." Pause. "Yeah, me too. Look, I'm coming up your way with my friend Wren." Pause. "Today, in about an hour. OK? Good. I'd like to leave her with you for a little while. I'll explain when we get there." Longer pause. Julia laughed and said, "Great. That's wonderful. See you soon. Thanks."

Julia ended the call and tossed the phone into the back seat. Wren stared at her and asked, "How long do you think I'll have to stay with your friend?"

"Oh, I don't know. A week, a month...maybe until Hell freezes over. What do you think?"

Wren sat silently, looking out at the scenery blurring as they sped by. She felt like she had a fever. "I don't think I'm ever going back to my home," she said softly. She stared out the window a moment before adding, "I don't think I can ever go back to my life."

The Audi's tires sang against the bridge decking, filling the silence as they drove on the floating span across Hood Canal. The huge expanse of the fjord was flat, calm. Looking out across acres of deep silver-blue water, Wren felt too defeated even to look for whales. Two sailboats rocked a lazy rhythm in a barely noticeable breeze. Her gaze settled on a twenty-foot long cedar log, wallowing aimlessly. In silence she commiserated with the log, sharing the reality that they were both simply adrift.

At last, Wren spoke again. "You've never mentioned Grace. Why not?"

"You and I lead busy lives, my friend. We've got deadlines. We are consumed by the making of art. We parade in public with paint on our clothing. Grace has a very different life. She's extremely private and rarely leaves her home turf. She is a captive of the earth's cycles, the seasons, the needs of her animals."

"…What else?" asked Wren.

Julia squirmed a bit, trying to figure out if she wanted to say more. "You can ask Grace. She'll decide how much she wants to tell you. I will only say that she leads a quiet life because of some unfortunate incidents in her past."

"Is she a criminal?"

"Not in my opinion."

"Oh, boy."

"Hey, you're the one Homeland Security is after. You're the one a group of wing-nuts is attacking. Just saying — you need to embrace some perspective about other people's little issues." Julia tapped her fingers nervously on the steering wheel.

Silence filled the car like a fog. Wren thought back to the exact moment all this started, the moment she saw the streak of paint on Julia's painting. Or was it the moment of the explosion in the harbor? Whatever it was, she half-wished it hadn't happened...but also warmed to the idea that this *thing* would have found her anyway, sometime, somehow. Now she was headed for...for what?

The heavy gray clouds were now in a hurry, retreating in the direction of Wren's old life. The sun reflected dangerously off the wet pavement as they turned north. A small single-engine airplane circled above them in its approach to the county airport, then disappeared from view as the Audi entered a long tunnel of Madrona trees.

While Julia was transporting Wren away from danger, the planet continued to plummet through the galaxy. People lived their lives, some making plans for good, some planning trouble, and some simply sitting and drinking coffee.

Homeland Security Agent Levi Bitters sat in his usual diner. He felt he stood at a crossroads. He stirred a full teaspoon of sugar into his third cup of this witch's brew of coffee. Three cups of the diner's blend would make any other mere mortal attempt to flee their own skin, but Agent Bitters sat ramrod straight and still, staring out the window like a man in a trance.

Examining the broader picture — training, oaths of loyalty, and his own integrity regarding his commitments — it was obvious to Bitters that he was a true believer. However, since his encounter with the painting and his conversation with Wren Willow Hendrix, something had changed deep within his being. The essence of Levi Bitters was shaken, and now he stood on emotional and intellectual ground liquefied by the quake of seeing the painting and meeting its maker. He felt the need to speak with Ms. Hendrix again, and promised himself that he would do exactly that when she came to the Homeland Security office on Tuesday. Certain she could answer the questions that had arisen since he saw the painting, he felt his confidence return. He straightened his tie and ordered a cheeseburger and a glass of tap water.

Chapter 11

Wren was too nervous to enjoy the scenery passing by. She worried about imposing on Julia's friend Grace, and wondered what sort of person she might be. Obviously, she was generous enough to take in a stranger in need. Nevertheless, Wren felt like a piece of unclaimed luggage. She fidgeted with a button on her blouse until it came off in her hand.

Thirty miles behind her, Delbert Florian Bobb was also fidgeting. Inside a slightly beat-up travel trailer, Reverend Billy Joe Bobb sat with his dull-eyed nephew. The travel trailer was Reverend Bobb's parsonage, parked in the truck loading area behind the nearly dead strip mall that housed The Repentance Undeviant Tabernacle.

"Delbert, you have done the Lord's work admirably," said Reverend Bobb, handing an open can of sugary cola to his nephew while he pushed unruly strands of his stringy hair away from his eyes.

"Thank you, Uncle Reverend," Delbert said, pulling at the seat of his pants.

Billy Joe Bobb regarded his deceased brother's only child with narrowed eyes, two cold steel marbles, as he opened his own can of soda pop.

"Delbert, I think you can just call me Uncle. Now drink up."

"Yessir, Reverend Uncle. Uncle. Yes, Uncle."

Delbert pulled down three deep gulps of the fizzy drink.

Billy Joe Bobb curled his lips into a thin, sinister smile, and with a loud sigh, he settled into the sagging orange and brown plaid couch. His smile turned to a frown as he regarded Delbert standing there — *standing in the shallow end of the gene pool*, he thought.

In a soft pastoral voice Billy Joe Bobb said, "I think you know there will be investigations about the fire. Trouble, son, trouble. So what we're going to do to keep you safe is send you out to do some missionary work." Billy Joe Bobb paused. He smiled broadly and said, "You're going to bring the Word of the Lord to the heathens in Venezuela."

Delbert Florian stopped mid-swallow, choking, sending cola out of his nose and down the front of his white shirt. He looked into his uncle's stern visage and felt a chill crawl down his spine like a spider.

Billy Joe Bobb went on, "Missionary work, boy. I'm giving you a one-way ticket to Caracas, and enough money to get you settled in, get you on your feet. I'll wire you some more in a month." Grinning a toothy yellow smile, Billy Joe Bobb reached into his desk and brought out a manila envelope and handed it to Delbert. "Now, your cousin Buddy Sol is waiting outside in his car to take you home. Go pack your basic needs in one suitcase, and then Buddy Sol will take you directly to the airport. Your flight leaves five hours from..." Billy Joe Bobb looked at his wristwatch and raised his eyebrows, "...now."

Delbert Florian Bobb looked like a boy who had just slipped down a rabbit hole. Venezuela? He wasn't even sure where that might be. Why couldn't he just hide here, or maybe go to Idaho or Louisiana? The only good thing, he figured, was that just about everything he owned would fit in one suitcase. But Delbert Florian didn't say a word. No one ever questioned Uncle Reverend Billy Joe Bobb.

His uncle shook his hand, patted his shoulder, and pushed him out the door. The door closed against his back before he was even completely over the threshold.

Billy Joe Bobb knew in his heart of hearts that he was a low-life snake-oil peddler, but he figured this was probably going to be his worst deed. Cousin Buddy Sol would not be taking Delbert Florian to the airport. There would be no trip to Caracas, no need for a packed suitcase.

"Hey, Cousin Buddy, how come the seat's covered with plastic?" Delbert asked before getting into the car.

"I'm reworking the upholstery," Buddy Sol lied in a steady monotone voice. His oily black hair fell across his right eye as he turned to glare at Delbert, "Get in, let's get outta here. You gotta get all packed and make your flight."

Sitting in Buddy Sol's car, Delbert began to feel dizzy and clammy. He thought it was probably from the shock of his unexpected travel plans. He turned to say something to his cousin when his eyes flew wide open and he choked on a gurgling cough. His head slammed back against the seat as Cousin Buddy Sol sped onto the freeway headed for Oregon. Delbert's chin dropped to his chest, pink foam bubbling from his mouth as the poison in the cola did its work.

He was stone cold dead before they'd gone twenty miles. Buddy Sol winced at the sudden unpleasant odor as Cousin Delbert Florian's bowels performed their last act. He opened the windows, giving himself a pat on the back for having had the foresight to wrap the passenger seat in plastic. Leakage contained, first part of the job done. In three hours Delbert Florian Bobb would be securely tied and weighted and his body would slide softly into the mighty Columbia River, with any luck never to be seen again.

Chapter 12

While Wren held her breath and stamped on an imaginary brake pedal and Buddy Sol kept just below the speed limit and took his turns gently, Eliot Stern was gloating as he sat at his desk in the newsroom. He had enjoyed himself for a while, riding the wave of accolades for his article about The Repentance Undeviant Tabernacle's funerary activities. Now he began to daydream about his acceptance speech at this year's local journalism awards banquet, basking in imagined adulation.

He quickly snapped back into the moment as he read an item from a county newspaper about the arson at Wren Willow Hendrix's studio.

"Oh, Christ, it's her! It's the painter that caused the whole mess in front of the art gallery," Eliot shouted. He stood up so quickly he banged his knee hard on the corner of his desk, forcing him back down, wincing, into his chair. Several coworkers turned to look at him, and he shook his head at them, "Nothing to see here, everything's OK." A star reporter never gives away a good scoop.

Eliot sat, rubbing his knee and trying to invent a course of action. He pulled his car keys from his desk drawer and limped down the stairs to his Smart car. Checking the dashboard clock, he saw that he had time to make the ferry if he ignored enough red lights and speed limits.

Eliot didn't see anyone moving around the Hendrix property, even though the rusty white Econoline van he'd seen leaving the chaos at the art gallery was parked in front of the house. The place was quiet and smelled of burnt wood and gasoline. Water from the fire hoses still puddled all around, and rain splashed into the puddles while little brown birds chittered curiously from the surrounding shrubbery.

Eliot grabbed his black porkpie hat from the passenger seat, tugged down the brim, left his car, and walked around the property.

The birds stopped talking; they had nothing to say to the press.

He knocked at the door of Hendrix's house. He rang the bell. No one answered. A breeze rustled up from the bay, carrying the strong scent of the tide. He noticed the silence — even the birds had suddenly vanished. The lack of any sounds of life gave him an odd feeling, like he was intruding into a sacred place, and he felt as if he were being watched. He walked carefully through the remains of the studio, occasionally reaching to pick up a bit of charred and unrecognizable debris. Shuffling through the middle of the blackened ruins, he kicked at a mound of ashes in frustration. Bells tinkled faintly.

"What the hell was that?" Eliot said aloud.

Laughing nervously, he walked to his car, looking back twice and nearly tripping over a piece of singed lumber. Safely in his car, hands trembling, he scrolled through his phone to find the number for the Huxley-Lavelle Gallery. What the hell was her name…?

The phone connection was made and a woman said, "Huxley-Lavelle, this is Jeanette Perdot." Perfect.

"Ms. Perdot," Eliot ventured, "I need to speak with you about Wren Willow Hendrix. I am looking at the charred remains of her studio at this very moment, and there is something peculiar out here. What can you tell me about her?"

The silence went on so long that Eliot thought he'd lost the cell connection, "Are you there?"

"Mr. Stern, I don't want to discuss this topic over the phone. I'll be waiting for you at the gallery. The door will be open. Please lock it behind you when you come in."

Eliot felt a flush of excitement as he slipped his phone into his jacket and drove back to the ferry dock.

The Huxley-Lavelle Gallery was dark and looked as though it was closed. However, when Eliot tried the door it swung open; inside, blue lights glowed dimly from ceiling-mounted tracks in the two large gallery rooms. He closed the door and cringed at the grating, metal-clawing-at-metal sound as he turned the lock.

The air inside smelled like dust and linseed oil and stale — but expensive — perfume. Eliot stepped through the room, quiet as a thief, ignoring several extraordinary paintings and nearly colliding with a pair of elegant figurative sculptural pieces. Drawn to a brighter light at the back of the building, he had that odd feeling again, of being in a holy place. He walked toward the light.

Now he saw dark paintings, looking like huge rectangular holes, looming around him. "Hello?" he called out. He tensed, a little prickle of fear touching the back of his neck. He rounded a partition and bumped into a life-size bronze statue of a nude woman holding a small bird to her breast. He squeaked a little "Oh!" and turned around. He walked hurriedly down the narrow hallway he found.

An unseen door to his right burst open and Jeanette Perdot, the Goth woman, stepped out. He thought he might have a seizure.

She thrust her hand out toward him, her gleaming black nail polish startling him. Eliot instinctively took her hand in his.

"Eliot Stern, right? I'm so glad you came, I was beginning to give up on you," she smiled.

"Traffic, you know."

"Well, yes, I know about traffic, but what I don't know is where Wren Willow Hendrix is. Did you go to her house, or did you just sniff around in the ashes? …Still, I can't imagine she'd stay there after the fire."

"Yes, I did check. I went there, to her house, and there was no one around." Should he tell Jeanette about the bells? He thought not.

"Since you are here, Mr. Stern, I have something you need to see."

She started to walk, but stopped and studied Eliot Stern with a critical eye.

"Are you ready to open your mind?" Jeanette grabbed both his upper arms and looked into his eyes. She looked down at him, as her five-inch platforms increased her already considerable height.

"I suppose I am," he said casually, with a toothy grin.

It only took him a second to pick up on the seriousness in her demeanor and, losing the grin, he said, "Yes, I'm ready."

"I certainly hope you are."

She was so abrupt, so brusque and direct, that he momentarily felt his sharp journalistic footing slip.

"Wren left a painting with me. You know, the day Mr. Lavelle kissed the sidewalk? Anyway, this is a unique painting, Mr. Stern. Are you interested in art?"

Eliot cocked his head and managed a tight-lipped grin. "Frankly, Ms. Perdot," he confessed, following her formality, "I have no real interests other than chasing down a story — and, in all honesty, I am extremely good at that."

She narrowed her eyes, then took his arm and led him to a storage room just off the kitchenette. The room was cool and bathed in a soft, dim, golden light. Floor-to-ceiling racks of paintings lined the walls. A dark wooden cabinet containing twenty large two-inch-deep drawers probably held hundreds of archival drawings. A desk lamp, some ceramic bowls, and an army of little carved fetishes cluttered the top of the waist-high cabinet that ran the length of the wall. Eliot noted that the room was climate-controlled to the point of having no discernible odor, and in a momentary flash of synesthesia he perceived the darkness as an aroma. What to call that aroma, he couldn't say. Jeanette led him to a four-foot-long brown leather-upholstered bench that stood in the center of the room.

"Mr. Stern, this is the painting I want you to see. I don't know if it will help you find Wren. I don't know if I *want* you to find her." Jeanette turned her head a little and squinted at Eliot. "But maybe it will give you some insight. I've been exploring different ways of viewing this painting, and I'm going to show you the simplest way first. Sit down here."

Pushing him ungraciously onto the bench, she used a remote switch in her pocket to turn on a spotlight at the far end of the room. Eliot felt his heart race as the spotlight illuminated a black wall with a large canvas leaning against it, hidden by a sheet of black velvet. Jeanette glided over to the canvas, and as she whipped the black velvet shroud away and heard the reporter's sharp intake of breath, her face softened with a knowing smile.

Eliot Stern gasped when he saw the painting, then he smiled, hummed a little tune, wept, and smiled again. He could not contain his emotions. His deepest feelings were all upon him at once.

"What the hell is this?" he inquired, dabbing his eyes with his sleeve.

Jeanette gently turned him so his back was to the painting.

"I have no idea what the painting is doing or how it works" she said, "but there is more. Are you ready?"

Eliot nodded, feeling more than a little apprehensive, and Jeanette handed him a pair of sunglasses. "These are polarized lenses. They enhance the effect. Put them on now."

He put them on as commanded, and she turned him to face the painting again. Immediately Eliot saw flowers raining down from a cloudless sky all around him. He held out his hands to catch them. He captured one beautiful dark-red rose in his hands and brought the fragrant bloom to his face. He breathed the scent and studied the flower at length. He counted thirteen petals, and saw a single black and gold bee inside the blossom. If he could have seen inside each rose, would he have seen the same bee in each one?

Now there were many bees flying around him, thousands and thousands of bees. He felt them bumping his body, hitting his face, and he saw all of them, each of them so vivid. The buzzing was deep and sonorous, almost deafening. The air that had at first been odorless and cool on his skin was now suffocating, humid, heavy, and much too warm. The fragrance of roses and honeycomb was so thick, so cloying, and the movement so dizzying, he worried that he might be sick. At that moment a gentle breeze allowed the air to become lighter, and he felt better. Eliot reached out his hand to touch one of the bees and was surprised, but not shocked, to see that his own hand was a translucent wing. He was *with* the bees; he *was* a bee. Eliot laughed out loud as he gave gravity the slip and flew effortlessly, joyously with them.

He was barely aware of Jeanette pulling off his glasses. She draped the black velvet back over the painting and stood, watching him.

"My God," he said, rubbing his face briskly, "did you somehow give me LSD? Or maybe psilocybin?" He sat looking back into the boundless depths of this surreal experience for a few minutes, the room so still he could hear his heart pounding, his breath coming hard as though he'd been running.

"I was free. I was flying. More than that, I was flying with beings that were *with* me. I mean, it felt like I was part of some great community. ... No, wait, that's not it... I was part of some great, huge, enveloping being, and I felt deeply loved and cared for, as if no harm could come to me. I was so happy..."

Eliot sat on the bench and sobbed into his hands like a child. Jeanette placed a comforting hand on his shoulder.

"I don't know what to make of this," he said raggedly. "Have you seen it?"

Jeanette sat beside him on the bench. "Repeatedly."

Eliot scrutinized her while he wiped his eyes with his handkerchief. "Well, you don't seem any worse for wear. Is it always the same?"

Jeanette smiled a little, nodding. "Are you ready for the grand finale?"

"Oh no — there's more?" he asked uncertainly, running his hands through his hair.

Jeanette turned off the white spotlight using the remote, and lit a brilliant blue spotlight instead.

"Eliot, I'm a little nervous. I've never shown this view to anyone, but I do know that it is powerful. I'm fairly certain that even Wren Willow Hendrix isn't fully aware of the power and extent of her painting's reach." She paused a moment, her gaze centered in some middle distance. "I wonder if all the recent paintings she's done have this effect, and I wonder if each painting sends a different…what?…Hallucination? Vision? That would be some serious mojo."

"Ms. Perdot," said Eliot, touching her hand, "I think I'd like to see the last act of this show."

Pulling his hair back from his forehead, Eliot turned to face the painting while Jeanette walked to the far end of the room and stood, waiting.

"It's not going to be like anything you've ever experienced."

He laughed and said, "And the past few minutes were?"

Jeanette waited for him to gather himself and settle.

"OK. I'm ready," he said, exhaling audibly. He put on the polarized sunglasses.

Jeanette revealed the painting once again.

Eliot's eyes opened wide and his pupils dilated to their maximum. At once the floor fell away from under him and he was floating, weightless, amid a sea of stars. He saw the earth, blue and green and white below him, then, somehow, above him.

For a moment Eliot thought he would not be able to breathe and flailed his arms in panic, like a man drowning. His fright was instantly replaced by euphoria as sunlight warmed him, and the fragrance of lilies overwhelmed his senses. He didn't even try to wonder what was happening, to wonder if he was losing his mind, because his mind was no longer his own to wonder about. The painting had taken him, and he went along willingly.

Comets, novae, planets, and stars all streaked through this new sky, so close he could hear them, a sound like thunder or a rushing river, roaring to eardrum-bursting volume. Colors flew around him, vivid and intense in deep-hued blue that tasted like blueberries, red that looked like blood and smelled of copper, yellow that made him think he had tasted the sun. Many miles distant, a black shape hung in the sky, like a ball or a face. Eliot was compelled to watch the shape as flames shot out from it in all directions. The flames raced toward him, time and distance collapsing, and he was certain he was about to be burned to death. But when the fire was only inches from his face, it stopped, immobilized in space. The flames, now motionless, looked sculptural, like blown glass, and Eliot could tilt his head from side to side and see around the flame-shapes. There was a silence so deep that it pulled at his inner ear with a painful pressure. Eliot saw movement in the sculpted shapes. Fissures were now crawling along the frozen flames, emitting high-pitched metallic sounds. A deep, resonant *whump* rolled a massive sound wave through the air around him, and the frozen fire burst apart. Fracturing into red and green and blue translucent crystals, the fragments floated all around him with a faint tinkling sound. Eliot thought it was the sound of a thousand champagne flutes touching, a toast in some grand celebration. And then he began to hear actual flutes, receding into the distance but leaving an echo deep inside him.

He began to be somewhat aware of his body again, still hovering, but now turning. He was certain he was still drifting among the stars, but felt something against his back, and thought he was lying in the grass.

A face formed gradually out of the infinite darkness. He knew this face: Jeanette, the pierced, tattooed, black-nailed Goth art goddess. She seemed to be floating above him and he felt her warm breath, felt her touching him, and he could see her fingers. They looked like the flame-crystals that had been suspended in space with him.

Jeanette turned off the spotlight with the remote and the room fell back to a soothing golden dimness. Eliot gradually allowed his conscious mind to resume control. He was lying on the leather bench in the middle of the room, his arms folded protectively across his chest. Jeanette was perched on the edge of the bench near his shoulder, removing his sunglasses for him as a conspiratorial smile curled at the corners of her mouth.

"My god, I... I..." he whispered. "That was..." He broke off, completely losing his train of thought.

He sat in a daze, not daring to ponder aloud what had seen. Eliot swung his feet to the floor and tried to stand, but lost his equilibrium and dropped hard to the bench. Sitting beside Jeanette, his mystery-trip guide, he wondered if she'd seen it, too.

As if she had read his mind, she said, "Yes, I was there with you. In all of it."

"What do you think it is? I have to know what this is about."

"I doubt we can ever know what this is about...but as near as I can tell, it's about energy, about the senses." Jeanette paused a moment, biting her lower lip, "I think it's about seeing the beginning, the beginning of everything, with a complete absence of fear."

Jeanette was glowing and speaking faster and louder with each word, her voice climbing in pitch. Eliot was a curious yet pragmatic man, not an easy mark for New Age nonsense, but he could not deny there was a pulsating blue glow surrounding Jeanette. When he looked at his hands, legs, and arms, he was forced to accept his *own* blue aura. He hoped radiation was not involved, and then felt ashamed for thinking such a thing.

They sat in silence as Eliot considered how long he had been held in the painting's spell. It felt like five minutes and it felt like five hours. He looked at his watch. Forty minutes had elapsed since he had walked through the gallery's front door.

Eliot stood up, staggering like a drunk, straightening his clothing and running his hands through his hair in a futile attempt to put himself together.

"I have to go," he said haltingly, "I've got a deadline."

Jeanette led him back through the gallery.

"I need to meet this painter," he said, trying to regain his normal assertive nature. He still felt shaken. "And we need to talk about this...this experience."

Jeanette stood in front of him at the door and touched her finger to his lips. "No. We don't," she whispered.

Opening the gallery door, Eliot stepped out onto the rain-slick sidewalk. Looking up at the normal Seattle sky, he blinked away raindrops and tried to remember where his car was parked. He still had no leads to where the artist might be, but Eliot Stern, Tenacious Journalist, *would* find Wren Willow Hendrix. He decided that the search would commence immediately after some serious consumption of scotch and about ten hours of sleep.

I wonder how much more of that painting trip I can get? he thought.

He should have been asking how much more of it he could take.

Chapter 13

*J*ulia fiddled with the car radio, scanning for something soothing but not somber. She settled on a Chopin piano etude and returned her full attention to the road.

Beside her, Wren watched houses, farms, meadows with sleeping cows, pastures with grazing horses, spandex-clad bicyclists, and road-kill raccoons blur into a plotless movie that she viewed with an empty heart.

No place in her imagination held the idea that she could recover from the violation of her private life and the loss of her studio. Miles rolled by, colors and shapes swirled, and paintings began constructing themselves, pinballing around her synapses while Wren thought of nothing.

Arlen Divine woke up on the floor of his dented, rusty 1984 Winnebago. Opening one eye, he assessed his situation. It was wet under his cheek, and he felt a little relief in discovering it was only drool. It was not uncommon for him to wake up in worse circumstances.

He tried to sit up. The room swam around him, and he stretched out his arms and gripped the tattered couch cushions to steady himself. Slowly, he brought himself to a kind of upright posture. Arlen sat like that for half an hour, a reclining crucifixion. He opened his bleary eyes and looked down to see what he was wearing. Gray, greasy, food-stained sweatpants, and a black Iowa Hawkeyes sweatshirt, more holes than fabric. At least he wasn't lying there in his baggy briefs like that time he woke up in Gasworks Park. He never did find his pants… Arlen ran the fingers of his right hand through his dense black and gray beard, still gripping the couch with his left hand. Gaining a little equilibrium, he listened to the cars slushing by on the rain-wet street and pulled himself up onto the couch. He stank of beer. He carefully turned his throbbing head, with the certainty that with one wrong move he would vomit. A metallic banging on the Winnebago's door yanked Arlen sharply out of his agony.

"Open," he growled, his head sagging into his hands.

His old friend Steve opened the door and stepped inside. They had known each other since Kandahar. Steve's life was everything that Arlen's was not. He had a successful business — a store dealing in rare vinyl recordings — a beautiful wife, and three great kids. Steve owned the building the record business occupied, as well as the fourteen-space parking lot behind it.

Arlen, on the other hand, possessed only a rusting Winnebago RV and a powerful drinking problem.

"Hi, pal," Steve said softly. "You've got to move your Winnie. The city's starting to clear the streets for the Solstice Parade and all its attendant mysteries." Steve paused and assessed his friend's condition. "You sober?"

Arlen looked up, "I don't know." He tried to stand, but fell back hard to the couch.

"OK, here's what we'll do. You don't mind me driving her, do you?"

Arlen winced as he shook his head. The room spun and his hands trembled.

Steve took the keys from the dinette table and sat down in the booth facing Arlen.

"Arlen, I'm going to drive you over to my lot. You can stay there for a week. Nobody'll bother you. Now, you lay down, pal, and I'll drive to the pump-out, get your tanks fixed up. OK? You battened down?"

Arlen looked at Steve and a tear escaped his sorrowful eyes. "You don't have to do this for me. I'm in this fix all on my own accord."

Steve stood, put his hand on Arlen's shoulder, and let out a deep sigh. "Arlen Divine, I owe you my life. There is not one breath I take — not one — that I don't think, 'Damn, if that dumb bastard Arlen Divine hadn't been such a tough motherfucker, I would not be taking this breath.' There were other guys with us that day, but when I took that sniper fire you were the one who came for me. *You.* My guts may be patched up and sewn together, and the whole pipeline may be a little shorter than when I started this life, but I doubt that anybody has more real guts than you, Arlen Divine. So, for Christ's sake, just sit there. It's only a pump-out and a parking space, not a new yacht and a winning lottery ticket."

Steve dropped into the driver's seat, turned the key and the ancient engine sparked to life.

The pavement ended and Julia bounced the Audi gingerly down a two-track gravel road.

"At least it isn't raining," Wren said flatly. She was beginning to feel the initial shock of losing her studio and its store of irreplaceable paintings recede, revealing a thick layer of dull despair.

The sky had been reflecting her state of mind, but now the clouds scattered and they were driving through brilliant sunlight. The dense forest opened on a pasture, and when she put down her car window Wren could smell the salt mist rising off the nearby Strait of Juan de Fuca. Something was tugging at the edges of her conscious mind. What was it? As she breathed in the salty air, she found a name for the thing she felt. It was hope. She found it rather strange and surprising.

Julia drove up a steep incline surrounded by madrona trees and stunted wind-blown firs. As her friend turned sharply to the left into a wide driveway, Wren exhaled. "Oh, wow," she said, as they looked out over a lush little valley of well-tended rows of vegetables, blueberries, and an orchard of fruit trees.

Julia turned off the engine and they got out of the car. Walking toward the small, stuccoed house, Wren realized she could see right through the living room and out across the Strait, a breathtaking view. A side door flew open and a wiry woman with an Einstein hairdo so white it looked electrified came hopping down the stairs.

"Julia Burlow, it has been too fucking long!" the woman shouted, seizing Julia by the shoulders and wrapping her in a bear hug. "I saw that little PBS show about 'The New American Art Scene'. You did a nice interview, but I don't think they showed examples of your more interesting work. Well, what can you do, eh?"

"Grace, even merely adequate media coverage about art is better than the usual zero. In art school you get whole courses on how to survive being ignored."

The two friends laughed heartily, and then Julia briefly informed Grace about Wren's plight. Wren studied Grace all the while, observing her well-muscled arms and the way she moved — like her name, gracefully. Although Grace was thin, she looked like she could pick Wren up and toss her easily into the back of the old red truck that was parked next to the barn.

Grace's age was impossible to read — somewhere between forty and sixty, Wren guessed. Her eyes were an almost unnatural green, like the valley her farm was set in; and though there were laughter lines at the corners of her eyes, Wren detected a soft, distant, but permanent sorrow in her face.

"Apparently Julia's not going to formally introduce us. You have to be Wren," Grace said, pulling Wren to her in another spectacular bear hug. Wren blushed, unable to imagine why she should be blushing.

"Yes, that's me. So, you are the amazing Grace." Wren blushed a deeper shade of beet red, feeling like an idiot for her choice of modifier. "I mean, Grace, it's so good to meet you. I'm graceful, that is, I'm grateful to you for letting me spend a few days here."

Grace frowned. "A few days? My dear, I think you'll be here some time longer than that, given the attention that's gotten pointed your way."

Wren could scarcely pull her gaze from Grace's. She felt something a little odd, like vertigo.

"Anybody want to help unload the car?" Julia asked as she walked away.

Julia began pulling suitcases from the car and marching them into the house. Grace and Wren followed, burdened with grocery bags and more suitcases.

"I'm making coffee," said Julia. "Where are the beans?"

"I've only got pre-ground. Spring is too damned busy, no time to waste grinding coffee beans."

"Savage. Heathen," Julia scoffed as she set up the coffee maker.

Wren wandered around the living room looking at photos of Grace at the helm of a sailboat, Grace sanding the hull of the boat, Grace laughing and swinging in a bosun's chair from the top of the mast. She looked young in the photos, maybe twenty-five or thirty years old, and Wren wondered who had taken them. There were also books on a variety of topics filling a floor-to-ceiling bookcase, more books stacked on their sides on top of the neatly shelved ones, and still more books piled up on end tables. Wren followed a row of books about goats to the end of the shelf, a few inches from the window that opened out to the water. She looked out at the magnificent view.

"Hypnotic, isn't it?" said Grace as she walked up beside Wren. "I've lived here for twenty years and it never gets old."

"Yes," Wren said, as if in a trance, "it's different from where I live, right on the water. We're so high above everything here."

Gleaming white seagulls carved self-portraits through the sky below them.

Grace touched Wren's arm, "It's a calm place, a good place to work things out. I think it's starting its work on you already."

"Hey, coffee's ready," Julia called from the kitchen.

Wren looked into Grace's startlingly green eyes and felt something akin to the feeling her paintings created. She thought she caught a glimpse of the threads of commonality, like streams of paint, weaving themselves around her, around all of them. She named her feeling: It was wonder.

In the kitchen, Julia had poured the coffee and was putting a cigar in her mouth.

"Whoa, girl, don't you light that goddamn thing. Your little cigars smell like the devil farting," Grace grumbled. Snatching the cigar away from Julia's lips, Grace smiled and, eyebrows raised, said, "I've got something much sweeter for us to smoke."

The three women went out to the yard to take in the sight of a passing ship in the Strait, and then sat back in Adirondack chairs, sipping their coffee. Grace lit a generous joint and passed it to Wren.

"Legal now. Civilization, ho! Never thought I'd see the day. It makes you wonder what the hell sending some of my friends to prison in the 1970s for doing this was supposed to accomplish," Grace said, while attempting to hold in her toke. She exhaled what little smoke was left, closing her eyes. After a few seconds she smiled, opened her eyes, passed the joint to Wren, and said, "Julia says you've got the Homeland Security jokers interested in your newest work, along with a merry band of asshole religious maniacs. I'm guessing it's not all about the aesthetics of the art."

Wren pulled in a shallow hit and shook her head vigorously as she was overcome by a combination coughing fit and laughing attack.

Julia puffed on the cigar she had rescued from Grace and spoke as she let out the smoke, "The government people are probably the biggest problem for her, but the religious nuts are less predictable. We'll have to figure out something long-term, but I think Wren will be safest here for a while. You can put her to work pulling weeds."

The joint came to Julia, and then went around again, and the three fell silent. It was so quiet here, like the whole world was resting. The wind rising up the cliff face, the rustling trees, songbirds, all accompanied the waves rolling onto rocks and sand eighty feet below the smiling trio slouching in their lawn chairs. Gulls suspended on air currents called out, and gulls waddling on the beach squabbled over food, squealing like rusty garden gates. From behind her, Wren heard Grace's hens muttering to one another in low voices as they prowled for bugs.

"So if you'll be here for a while, would you like the grand tour?" Grace asked Wren.

"Sure. I'd love it."

The three women walked around the house and into a small orchard that ran out to the west for a hundred feet, following the cliff about fifty feet back from its edge.

"It's a manageable size," Grace said as she closed the gate behind them, "apples, pears, and figs."

"It's completely fenced in, even has netting above," Wren observed. "Why?"

"That's so all those sweet little birds, lovely delicate deer, and charming raccoons don't help themselves to snacks. They'd eat the whole orchard down to twigs, given the opportunity," Grace replied.

Julia lit another cigar.

"All right, OK… Just stay downwind of me with that repugnant thing," Grace said, flapping her hands in front of her nose. "Let's go down to the garden."

Out of the orchard, away from the cliff's edge, and away from the effects of wind and water, the temperature rose. They hung up their jackets on fence posts, while the grass made a shushing sound as their feet slid through. Wings pushed the air and birds chittered as they tried to keep pace with hungry hatchlings. A single-engine plane passed low overhead with a droning vibration that caused Wren to feel like she had fallen into a dream. There was an arms-wide-open sensation of immense space around her. She sat down in the warm grass beside a row of cabbages, then lay on her back and watched clouds floating across the sky like cotton balls. She closed her eyes and imagined she was levitating above the land and water. She was flying high above her burned-out studio, far away from her pursuers, toward infinite possibility, as bright strands of color and light streamed past her.

Grace examined a few plants, assessing their health, then looked at Wren stretched out in the grass. After a moment she smiled and softly said, "We'll leave you here to absorb your new surroundings."

Grace, it seemed, had a solid understanding of loss and the value of solitude.

Turning to Julia, Grace said, "I've got something in the barn to show you."

As they walked away, Julia turned back to see Wren lying in the grass. She felt certain that the image would stay with her forever, like a painting. Crushing her cigar butt under her heel, she followed Grace into the barn. It was cool and dry, and shafts of sunlight pierced even the darker spaces. Time seemed to slow, and Julia felt a prickle of anticipation.

"I think she'll be all right here. It will just take a little time. This farm is good at soaking up all kinds of shit and using it for fertilizer," Grace said.

"Are you OK with this?"

"Oh, definitely, of course. Are you staying a few days, too?"

"I'm sorry to say I'm going back this afternoon. I've got some things to organize for the Solstice Parade."

Grace set her jaw. "OK, fine — although I have no idea why you could possibly want to get involved with something like that."

"I'm sorry, Grace — I have my reasons. I promise I'll come back up for a few days after my work at the parade is done."

Julia walked around the cavernous barn, studying the place with a frown. "Hey, what happened? Your barn is completely empty."

"That's what I wanted to show you. Last week I suddenly got this weird idea that I wanted a big empty barn. I hired a couple local teenage hooligans to help me move stuff around, get rid of junk I didn't need, and sweep the floor. I'm amazed at how well it cleaned up, but I've got no idea what to do with this space now that I've got it."

"I worry that you'll miss all the old car parts," Julia quipped as she ran her fingers over a row of hubcaps hanging on the wall near the door.

Grace stepped to the far side of the barn. "*Regardez, ma chérie.* Organization!"

Julia gaped at an entire barn wall packed with various automotive parts. There were fenders, hoods, windows, door panels, and two engine blocks, along with hundreds of smaller bits.

"Alphabetized, Grace?" Julia raised an eyebrow.

"Yes, well, you'd better tell your friend Wren that you're about to abandon the poor dear, alone on a farm, with someone who arranges truck parts using the Dewey Decimal System," Grace said.

"I'm not that dense, you old vixen. I don't think this is going to be much of a hardship for either of you."

Grace smiled, her eyebrows jumping, and patted Julia on the shoulder. "Well, you know I'm here to help however I can."

Julia looked around the huge, nearly empty barn, "This *is* a big space, and it's got some halfway decent light. Maybe Wren could paint in here…"

"That," said Grace, nodding, "would be an honor."

Wren and Grace stood beside the Audi as Julia put a bag of fresh chard and peas on the back seat, and a cold soda in the cup holder. Julia hugged Grace, thanking her for everything. Wren and Julia embraced and Julia said, "I'll be back after the Solstice."

Wren smiled and said, "Ha — that sounds like a comment from someone in my mother's old commune. Don't worry about me. This is good. I've got some thinking to do, and about ten acres of weeds to pull for Grace. You, on the other hand, need to be careful in your mischief-making. Stay out of the newspaper."

Julia drove away in a cloud of dust, waving out the window until the farm was no longer in her rearview mirror.

Chapter 14

*A*rlen Divine's Winnebago was neatly tucked into an official parking space, guaranteed by his friend Steve to be safe for the week. No cop would pound on the side of the RV at five in the morning shouting at him to *move the vehicle, sir, move the vehicle.* He had taken a hot shower and put on reasonably clean blue twill pants and a matching shirt with "Frank" embroidered in red script in a white oval above his heart. He looked like an auto mechanic, albeit not one you would want fondling your fuel injectors.

The whole Fremont neighborhood was frenetic with preparations for the Solstice Parade. A woman was at the far end of Arlen's parking lot releasing three-foot wide soap bubbles into the breeze. They writhed like alien creatures trying to shrug their way out of a birth membrane, then hung in the air, wobbled, and floated into the trees.

Arlen could hear the hammering and banging that announced the construction of several live-music stages. He figured if he stayed sober enough to climb onto the roof of his home he could watch the whole shebang, from clowns on stilts right down to the last bouncing titty and wagging pecker of the Naked Bicyclists.

Arlen sighed as he admitted to himself that this happy scenario was probably not going to play out. Staying sober was not all that high a priority. Even as he watched the bubble-woman, he felt himself slipping down the hole of despair. Arlen was overwhelmed by memories of his son, Dave, as a toddler — chasing bubbles, jumping, trying to catch them, trying to bite them, squealing when a bubble disappeared in his clapping hands. Sweat poured down Arlen's face, and — stricken with a sudden vertigo — he fell backward onto the floor of the RV. He clutched at the refrigerator and pulled out a cold bottle of Labatt Blue. He was trembling as he twisted off the cap and gulped the fizzing elixir, pulling down the entire contents of the bottle in four long swallows. Some relief followed, but another bottle sure would help things along. The memories were harsh and they were intense, and he needed to silence their noise. He needed to forget. But he could not forget. He remembered his life, his family, his war, and he remembered the night he attacked his wife.

Arlen had really meant no harm when he pinned his wife in the corner with their bed. He was just protecting his men...and at that moment, she was the enemy. He had no idea now how this could have happened, but right then he was absolutely sure that a Taliban sniper was impersonating his wife to gain a position at the bedroom window that night. There had been a rare lightning storm over Puget Sound, and the flashes and rolling, window-rattling thunder had wakened him from a long and vivid dream. Awake, deep in the hot, dry hill country, he was wearing full battle rattle, huddling behind a rock. The lightning flashes became tracers lighting up the sky, and the thunder was the sound of mortal danger. Sweat poured from him and adrenaline pumped. He believed his response was the right one; it was what he needed to do to protect his men, to survive.

So he pushed his enemy/wife onto the floor and grabbed her by the hair, shoving her into the corner. In his battle-mind he had saved his men by pinning her hard with the whole weight of the bed. He had meant no harm to his wife when the heavy wooden headboard broke her jaw. He was just immobilizing this T-man, this enemy.

Lightning flashed again and he took his pistol from the night table and fired six rounds out the window at the trees. He was so certain that those trees were Taliban. The nearest neighbor, a retired Seattle policeman, lived a quarter mile away through the woods, and intimately knew the sound of pistol fire when he heard it.

The phone call was made, the Sheriff arrived, and Corporal Divine was subdued and handcuffed. The ambulance arrived, too. Arlen's wife, blood spraying through her broken teeth, shouting "You fucking devil bastard," lay strapped to the gurney to keep her from leaping at Arlen. She came back to the house only one more time — with her sister standing guard — to get her clothing, leaving behind furniture, trinkets and every single photograph of her life with Arlen. She spat on the floor as she walked out the front door. It seemed like a talisman against the awful error she had made when she married Arlen Divine.

He had been an iron worker after the war, welding beams that became the bones of skyscrapers, then pipes in power plants to transport cooling water, and, finally, odd-job welding for neighbors, who mostly felt sorry for him. Arlen had been using alcohol since the day he landed back in the United States, his first day home from Afghanistan. Self-medicating, he called it. Just easing the pain a little, he said, and there was a lot of pain — enough to share around.

Arlen's drinking gained new heights and reached its apex the month after his wife left him, when his son died in a commercial fishing boat accident. The floodgates of sorrow opened, and the booze flowed in.

Dave had fled the Divine household at sixteen, lying about his age to get a fishing job. His father's drinking binges and fights with his mother had been too much to bear. He was a sensitive kid, and he knew he had only himself to rely on for salvation.

Arlen had taught him to weld when the boy was just twelve. Dave loved watching the metal, so solid one moment, subtly shift color as the magic happened. Impenetrable, unbendable, indestructible metal became a flowing liquid — red hot, white hot, blue hot puddles that cooled and caused separate pieces of cold, hard metal to become fused into one. As the boy grew to be a young man he began to see that alchemy as religious, or at least sexy.

The terrible irony was that Dave was killed when an imperfectly welded joint snapped and two tons' worth of kinetic energy was released in the form of a cable aimed directly at his skull. This was fodder for a year's worth of brand new nightmares for Arlen.

After Arlen's wife left, the silent house became unbearable, and Arlen had simply walked away from it. He took up residence in the driveway, in the old Winnebago he had bought ten years before. His son, his wife, and his former self had enjoyed several camping adventures in it. Dave had decorated the RV's front grillwork, welding "W I N N E B A G O" to it in individual letters, telling his dad that the mere painted words were not cool enough. The boy just wanted to show off what he'd learned from his father.

Arlen had come to understand that a heart could break more than once, or even twice. One night, a year ago, malicious frat boys pried off and stole some of those letters while he lay passed-out drunk beside the Winnie. Now the welded tribute read, "W I N   E B A G". It was a true statement, to be sure.

One day, when he still lived outside his big empty house, he began to imagine he was made of glass. He stood naked before the bathroom mirror watching his dark hair gradually graying, plucking the two or three white whiskers appearing in his bushy black mustache. Arlen had studied his reflection and was curious, but not surprised, that he could see clear through himself, right past the bone and muscle, past the place where his heart had once been, clean through. Clean through. He felt so fragile and breakable, and so hollow.

Sorrow stacked upon sorrow stacked upon sorrow stacked upon sorrow eventually makes a man of glass crack and shatter. And that is what Arlen Divine did.

His brother came up from California and sold the house for him. Arlen's ex-wife, wanting no part of it, pretended the last twenty years had just been a weird, bad dream.

She would keep pretending, with no success, for the rest of her life.

Arlen packed a few clothes, some photos, and the contents of the refrigerator into his Winnebago. He would have left his pistol behind if the Sheriff had not already confiscated it the night Arlen broke his wife's jaw. He didn't need the gun anymore, and he did not want to remember that part of his life. He left the front door of the house wide open, got in the RV, and drove away. His brother had put the money from the sale of the house into the bank, and with that, along with his disability pension, Arlen had enough money to survive on. At first, he lived in the RV at a state park beside the ocean. But the silence there became too overwhelming. Hoping the urban hum would be louder than the pain of his memories, he moved to Seattle, drifting from parking space to city park to construction zone to abandoned-building parking lot. On the rare occasions when he was sober, he drove to the mountains for a week of high-elevation alcohol consumption.

Arlen skated back over the border of the real world often enough to keep the RV running. The oil puddles, rust, and dents simply came with the scenery.

Hammering, shouting, warning beeps from trucks with roaring diesel engines... the sounds of Solstice Parade preparations brought Arlen back to the moment. He began to tremble again, and opened the refrigerator for another beer. Empty. He locked up the

Winnebago and hurried out to a nearby bar.

Some of the wildly colorful and eccentric parade floats were receiving final preparations in parking lots and on side streets. The air carried the sweet fragrance of marijuana, and music and laughter wafted along with it.

Arlen walked briskly to a little bar a couple blocks from his parking space. Stepping inside, he stood still a moment to let his eyes adjust to the dimly-lit tavern. Planting himself on an elegantly curved electric-blue plastic bar stool, he ordered an icy draft lager from the bartender. When the beer arrived he drank it in swift gulps and ordered another.

"Hard day today, Frank?" asked the bartender as he set the second mug of golden liquid in front of Arlen.

Arlen stared at the bartender, his mind spinning. Who the hell was Frank?

The bartender pointed to Arlen's shirt. Arlen craned his neck around to get a look at the embroidered name there. He was Frank all right.

"Yup, hell of a day," Arlen said sadly.

The bartender went on to another customer, and Arlen picked up a newspaper that was lying on the bar near him. He sipped his mug of pain relief and read a headline about a fishing boat accident. He muttered "Oh, shit, no," softly, and swallowed half the contents of his mug. Arlen turned the paper to the sports section. The Mariners were on a losing streak again; even the Chicago Cubs, miraculously, had whipped them in inter-league play. There was some drivel about soccer and a photo of a golfer grinning stupidly at the little white ball he was holding.

Someone had folded the paper like origami and had mixed the inner pages of the front news section in with the sports. As he was tossing the paper aside, a brief article with a small photo — a story about a fire at a painter's studio — caught his attention. The accompanying photo had been taken earlier, at an incident in front of a Seattle art gallery, and showed part of a strange abstract painting leaning against the artist's van.

Arlen could not pull away from the photograph. Even in black and white, the picture of the painting spoke to him. He had never understood abstract art, never cared for it, so he surprised himself when he found that he could not put down the paper.

Arlen Divine put a handful of crumpled, sweaty dollar bills on the bar, folded the page with the article on it, tucked it into his shirt pocket right below "Frank", and walked, without staggering, out of the bar and back to his Winnebago. For the first time in a long while, Arlen Divine was smiling.

Chapter 15

Eliot Stern sat drumming his delicate fingers on the steering wheel of his Smart car as he waited at the Fremont Bridge. The bridge deck was split in two, opened wide like gaping jaws pointing at the clouds waiting for some unsuspecting prey to drop into its maw. Automobiles, bicycles, and pedestrians waited and watched as a sailboat's tall mast glided between the deck sections. This was the waterway from Lake Union leading to the Ballard Locks, which allowed boats access to the salt water and, by extension, the entire globe.

Eliot was an urban land animal. Concrete skyscrapers, paved streets, and bars purveying single malt scotch were his habitat. While he supposed the tourists found the boats and drawbridges to be colorful elements of his city's scenery, he thought of them as irritants.

Seattle was a maritime town, and, as such, the terminology of bridge position favored the boats. So when a drawbridge was raised high above the waiting line of cars it was said to be "open", meaning it was closed from Eliot's point of view and open for tall-masted boats to pass through. When the bridge was "closed", it was really open — open to cars and trucks and regular people. This confusion grated on Eliot every time he had to wait for an "open" bridge to "close" again. He continued drumming a tattoo on his steering wheel.

The Fremont Bridge finally settled into its mated posture, and Eliot scooted across into Fremont, Center of the Known Universe.

Once a whimsical home to aging hippies, Fremont was now a curious juxtaposition of slick software businesses, pricey upscale coffee shops, a statue of Lenin, sushi-pizza-Greek-Thai-teriyaki-hashbrown-hummus restaurants, a rocket, coffee shops, food co-ops, a shoemaker, coffee shops, pubs, bicycle stores, ice cream stores, and, amazingly, yet more coffee shops. Eliot wondered how Seattle managed to keep its reputation as a slow-paced, laid-back city when there was a coffee pusher on every corner catering to the caffeine junkies. He sipped his coffee with an ironic smile, and pondered how the annual Solstice Parade now seemed to be the single day of the year that old Fremont rose up and let its freak flag fly.

Eliot parked his car on a postage stamp and fished through his briefcase for the card with the address scrawled on it. He was meeting with the director of the parade for an interview, getting a feel for this year's extravaganza of clowns on stilts, floats decked out to look like flying dragons, and, of course, Naked Cyclists. He pulled out a small card that he hoped had the address, but instead he'd found the business card for the Huxley-Lavelle Gallery. His heart began pounding. He could see his shirt buttons tap dancing on his chest. He smiled to himself, nodding and wondering if Jeanette Perdot would consider showing him that painting again.

Inside the dramatically lit Huxley-Lavelle Gallery, Jeanette Perdot sat, smiling slightly and humming the third movement from Beethoven's Seventh Symphony as she attacked the paperwork on her desk. She had just sold a beautiful painting, a six- by four-foot realistic landscape of mountains and waterfalls. It was the last landscape painting by Wren Willow Hendrix that she had — probably the last one she'd ever have.

However, one more of Hendrix's paintings was waiting for her in the storage room, and *that* one she would never sell. She had shown it to only three people so far, and at first wondered if even that had been unwise. She worried that the reporter, Stern, would want a repeat performance, but she had heard nothing from that quarter. Ultimately she had dropped most of her concerns about the politicians when she realized they were incapable of agreeing or deciding upon anything. It saddened her to know that these people had a wonderful tool for doing good things within their grasp, but chose to bump around in the darkness, waiting for an impossible consensus.

The front door opened, and a nattily dressed couple eased in. Jeanette stepped into the kitchenette, prepared two cups of coffee and set them on a tray with sugar cubes and a tiny pitcher of cream. She closed her eyes and waited two more breaths, then, carrying the tray, stepped into the main gallery to greet her clients.

In a strip mall devoid of any obvious trace of spirituality, the Reverend Billy Joe Bobb labored in the sanctuary of The Repentance Undeviant Tabernacle. The fluorescent lighting gave Reverend Bobb's face an unearthly green glow, and his yellowed teeth appeared nearly orange. Electric staple gun in hand, he was helping two of his congregants put the finishing touches on placards they would be taking to tomorrow's Solstice Parade. The signs shouted the usual Repentance Undeviant Tabernacle epithets about fags, Jews, Blacks, heathens, heretics, and the United States of America in general.

Billy Joe Bobb was excited about the additional debauchery of the Naked Bicyclists. Surely, God was cosmically pissed off with people who painted themselves purple and rolled down the public avenues with their privates exposed.

The Repentance Undeviant Tabernacle planned to stand as one, holding their placards high and shouting their greatest-hit slogans — plus maybe a prayer or two — at the top of their lungs. The heathens would have to take notice.

One of his followers lit a candle, not as a spiritual act, but to use the flame to seal off the end of a length of nylon rope. Billy Joe Bobb turned to look, grimacing as he imagined the rope tying his nephew, the arsonist Delbert Florian Bobb, to a cinder block at the bottom of the Columbia River. The moment passed and Reverend Bobb smiled beatifically, as he shifted his mental image to Delbert resting happily in the arms of the Lord.

"So much better for him than this life," he whispered. "Better for all of us."

Homeland Security Agent Levi Bitters was distressed. He sat at his bulky gray metal desk twisting and untwisting the ends of his necktie. A pile of papers lay before him, higher than the short stack of pancakes he'd had for breakfast that morning. He regarded the paperwork with trepidation and antipathy.

Wren Willow Hendrix had failed to appear Tuesday for her appointment. Now there was hell to pay because his superiors believed that Bitters had lost her. *In the wind,* they said. His imagination awakened to that, and he pictured Wren scattering into the sea breeze like the ashes of her burned-out studio. This unnerved him because, until quite recently, he had been utterly certain he did not possess an imagination. There was so much more going on here than was discernible at the surface… How had he lost her? Where did she go? How could he find her?

Bitters switched from twisting his necktie to twirling his pen, but it escaped his grasp and skittered across the floor, coming to rest against the shoe of a naval officer who had just quietly entered the room. Bitters recognized the man as an officer at Naval Submarine Base Bangor.

"Oh," Agent Bitters inhaled sharply, "excuse me. Just dropped my pen."

The officer continued through the long room without a word, and Bitters picked up the pen and returned to his desk to consider the problem of Wren Willow Hendrix and her paintings.

Suddenly he stood, grabbed his trenchcoat, and left the building. *Bangor.* In his mind's eye he saw the woman with the weird painting at the demonstration in front of the gate at Bangor. *That was it.* If he could find her, he could find the painter. Bitters *would* find her, too, because he had her license-plate number and the whole of Homeland Security Intelligence behind him. Agent Levi Bitters smiled and confidently straightened his tie.

It was like standing under the center of a beautiful celestial donut. The sky above Wren was brilliant blue with a few white gauzy clouds; but all around that cerulean opening, dense gray clouds full of rain hovered like an augury. Wren ignored the dark clouds and smiled up at Grace. The light had turned Grace's shining white hair into a halo. They were pulling weeds from the cabbage patch as they knelt in a spot of sunlight, supplicants before the altar of agriculture.

Grace stood up and stretched, her hands on her hips as she arched her back, "Ahhh! Don't stay down there too long. You'll become a feature of the landscape."

"Would that be so bad?" Wren asked as she looked around, taking in the gardens, the orchard, the mountains and forest in one direction and the saltwater Strait of Juan de Fuca in the other.

Grace didn't seem to find any disagreement with that thought. Wren pulled some weeds, then pulled some more. Finally, she spoke. "Tomorrow is the Fremont Solstice Parade. I'm worried about what Julia might do with that painting. She could get into trouble, cause a riot, or maybe even start a stampede. I don't know, but I don't feel right just pulling weeds while Julia is in danger."

"What danger? She's just going to flash a few old hippies your painting and give them a free trip. Harmless. Really, Wren, what could possibly happen?" Grace noticed Wren's alarmed expression and looked abashed at having let that last sentence escape. She paused with her lower lip clenched between her teeth. "...OK," she said, "look — Julia is a tough girl. You know that, and I could tell you some stories from our student days that would ease your concerns." Grace paused again, no doubt doubting the wisdom of sharing any of those stories just now. "Well, at any rate we can't do much from here, and we definitely can't be there with her. The universe will just have to flow on as it will. Julia *can* handle it — rough seas or smooth sailing."

Wren looked into Grace's eyes, found the comfort she sought, and said, "Hoist the jib, matey." They both laughed a little, albeit nervously.

Chapter 16

Wren's painting leaned against the wall, painted side safely hidden, next to the front door. Comfortable, loose clothing was laid out on the chair near the bed — all black fabrics, hip Seattle-ninja style. Hiking boots stood on the mat. Julia figured that she might have to walk, or run, some distance tomorrow — maybe the whole parade route. She felt none of the apprehension that Wren felt; she was simply eager to do the work.

Julia took her glass of red wine out to the sunroom overlooking the bay, leaned back in her minimalist Scandinavian recliner, and lit a Havana Honey cigar. She imagined presenting the painting to Reverend Billy Joe Bobb, watching as he forever abandoned his hateful ways. She imagined his followers weeping with joy and pleading for redemption.

Julia finished the wine, stubbed out the cigar, and went off to bed. Sleep came easily, but her dreams were odd and she awakened twice, soaked in sweat. At last she dreamed that she was sitting in a wagon in Grace's orchard and a tall man with a thick, dark, bushy mustache stood beside her. The dream had them flying over the land and over the water; and looking down, they saw Wren and Grace on the deck of a sailboat. Wren and Grace waved up at them, and in a wink the boat and the two women vanished.

When Julia awakened in the morning — the morning of the parade! — she lay beneath the warm covers for a few minutes, pondering her dream. For some reason, it made her feel strangely happy; and smiling broadly, she stepped out of bed and into a very big day.

Delibertus quirkus — freedom to be peculiar — in the center of the known universe: Seattle's Fremont neighborhood was buzzing, humming, clanking, bagpiping, whistling, and pulsating.

Inside the old RV, Arlen Divine was about to peel his naked body from his sleeping bag when he heard someone shout, "Daddy, there's a man in there!" Leaning up on one elbow, he looked toward the window and came eye to eye with his unwanted visitor: a boy perhaps nine years old, who was clinging to the window of the Winnebago. Arlen quickly wiggled deeper into the sleeping bag.

"Get down from there before you fall. Get away from that thing!" a man, presumably the boy's father, called. "He could be dangerous."

Arlen sat up and watched as the boy slid down the side of the RV and ran to catch up with his mother and sister out on the sidewalk. The boy's father looked back at the RV, seemingly worried about whether the man inside would break into his car. He put a hand reflexively to his pants pocket, perhaps feeling for his wallet, and went on to join his family. Arlen shook his head. Pointless fear and persistent vigilance over one's possessions... The saber-toothed tiger had been replaced by the stranger in the street, or the man in the house next door. Paranoia was the constant companion of the modern man.

Arlen dressed and made a cup of instant coffee. He put on his green army fatigue jacket, slick with the stains of a decade's misadventures, and started toward the door. Then the folded newspaper on his table grabbed his attention.

Arlen Divine sat at his tiny dinette table in his rusted Winnebago in his safe parking space in his generous friend's parking lot. He gazed at the photo in the newspaper. Only the smallest corner of Wren Willow Hendrix's painting showed in the photo, and the black-and-white halftone rendering should have eliminated the possibility of projecting any unusual effects of that painting — but Arlen was susceptible, and Arlen was hooked. He smiled and wiped at a rime of instant coffee that had formed on his formidable mustache. He gazed at the photo a little longer, then stood up to leave, took one last look at the photo, and tapped it three times with his index finger. Stepping out of the RV and locking the door behind him, Arlen drifted into the gentle chaos of the Solstice Parade celebration.

The gathering crowd was already packed from sidewalk's edge to the walls of the storefronts for whole blocks. The Fremont Bridge was gaping open to the water below, reaching for the clouds above, and the clouds were in abundance. Thick gray masses, dense with the threat of rain, swung around in the sky above the revelers. It was nearly noon, as a banjo player on a tent-covered music stage plinked his final note. The small crowd of his dearest fans clapped briefly but exuberantly, then ran off to find a good spot to view the parade.

Arlen strolled to the intersection and leaned on a post supporting traffic signals, now all flashing red. The sky darkened further, threatening rain, but Arlen felt oddly light. Stranger still, Arlen Divine was sober and was not even thinking about a drink.

Without fanfare, five men and women on stilts materialized from their hiding places in doorways and alleys. The crowd "oohed". The stilt walkers were costumed in rainbows and moons and stars, wearing masks that gave them three-foot-long faces on top of their ten-foot-tall stilted bodies. High top hats crowned their precarious glory. The crowd sighed, "ah!" The stilt walkers careened back and forth across the street with gossamer pink, white, and purple scarves flying as they moved on down the parade route.

The crowd erupted in cheers, a wave of sound rolling up the street, as a twenty-foot-wide banner appeared at the far end of the street. Two male elves and two female fairies carried the huge message against the wind: "DELIBERTUS QUIRKUS". Their faces were painted as the embodiment of the solstice, a radiant yellow sun. Following at a respectful distance, a marching band played a sparkling rendition of "The Age of Aquarius" on an odd collection of horns, drums, glockenspiel, cowbells, cymbals, and a solar-powered theremin. The band was immediately pursued down the street by a forty-foot long inflatable Trident nuclear missile controlled by members of Ground Zero, pulling on ropes to keep the missile from becoming more than symbolically destructive. Other members of the group threw flowers to the assembled celebrants.

A woman wearing a rainbow dress, her rainbow wig spreading color above her head, her face painted half blue and half yellow, led a group of two dozen six-year-old children. They were variously costumed as stars, suns, moons, and pea-pods. One sun held a vivacious puppy on a leash. The dog wore a black sweater and had a hat tied to its head with white stars on long springs wiggling above its ears. The rainbow woman picked up the dog occasionally to give it respite from the long walk. The crowd clapped, cheered, and made "Oh, they're so adorable!" comments.

Two or three minutes passed before a large float appeared in the distance. Its base was draped in black cloth covered with great swags of golden stars and moons. A fire-breathing dragon made of rip-stop nylon fluttered in the wind above the float, a grand illusion that made the dragon appear to be flying on its own. The float carried a string quartet, four women wearing long black dresses with silver face paintings of glittering wings spread across their noses and around their eyes. They had magically distilled the "Summer" movement of Vivaldi's *The Four Seasons*, and the crowds could only stand in awe as this musical float glided by. Arlen heard a man standing near him remark dreamily, "The world is large and I am so very small!"

A woman in a dark body suit followed the Vivaldi quartet. Her face was painted white, with glued-on rhinestones twinkling from it. She swept quickly and gracefully across the street wielding an eight-foot long PVC pipe painted periwinkle blue and festooned at the end with broad twenty-foot long striped ribbons. As she moved her arms in rhythm to a melody only she could hear, the ribbons jumped and dived in glorious silent flight. Tiny abrupt jerks on the pipe caused the ribbons to soar in long sinuous loops. All other days of the year she might have been a coffee barista, a banker, or a surgeon, but today she was an enchantress, ensorcelling the hearts of the crowds all along the route.

A float bearing several drummers, with an entourage circling the float playing cowbells, moved along a short distance behind the rhinestone-encrusted sorceress.

Julia Burlow jostled her way through the crowd. She wore a large dry bag on her back. It looked like she was carrying a folded lawn chair, but it was Wren's painting inside that bag. She looked to her right but could not see where Reverend Billy Joe Bobb and The Repentance Undeviant Tabernacle had set up shop. She twisted and wriggled her way through the crowd and onto the street. She found herself walking beside the Gay Pride float, joining many others who surrounded the float and threw chocolate kisses to the crowds. For a moment she thought that she recognized her ex-husband dancing on the float wearing only a hunter-orange jockstrap, but her search for Billy Joe Bobb kept her moving forward and she did not look back.

At the next intersection, Julia slipped away from the marchers and bounced roughly into a crowd of spectators, surveying the terrain, seeking out the Tabernacle hate group.

Arlen turned to see what had jostled the crowd ten feet away from him. He saw a woman with a wide pack on her back, and could not turn away. He hadn't bothered to look at a beautiful woman in more years than he could remember. Seeing her made him feel the same spark of wonder as the strange photograph in the newspaper had.

The parade crawled onward, enthralling the eclectic neighborhood with more dancers, a salsa band on a float pulled by twelve shirtless bodybuilders, and a stream of tattooed people in costume, throwing candy.

Just up the hill, things were less festive. On all other days, the street below would be part of the land tour of the Ducks, Seattle's fleet of amphibious tour buses — or boats, depending upon location — but not this day. The driver of this particular Duck had parked his Duck-load of tourists at the top of the hill to wait for the parade route to clear. He sat beneath a bright yellow hat adorned with a white-feathered, yellow-billed duck on top. He was eating a granola bar and chatting with the passengers, his bright red, long, curly hair waving like a flag from under the duck hat when the wind ruffled it. They all wanted to see the famous sculpture, *Waiting For The Interurban*. He was proud to be showing off his beautiful city to the tourists, and at $27 for an hour-and-a-half tour, he wanted to give them the best view possible. The happiness and gratitude of his passengers was the best part of his job.

They were just a five-minute land trip from the boat ramp where he would drive them straight into Lake Union. He always loved the squeals and screams of delight and amazement, and that little tingle of fear as the tourists reacted to going from land to water in the same vehicle. The driver noticed an opening in traffic and decided to move down the hill a little, in hopes they might catch a glimpse of the Naked Bicyclists. He squeezed the bill of his duck hat to make a quacking sound, and the passengers laughed and made quacking sounds at pedestrians as the Duck sped past.

The driver put his foot to the brake pedal and the brakes squealed like a startled cat. Then the pedal hit the floor. There were no brakes. There would be no stopping. The Duck continued to roll toward the festive scene at the bottom of the hill.

The Solstice Parade had been moving along nicely until a group carrying the banner "Atheists and Free Thinkers" reached the block just after the bridge, where The Repentance Undeviant Tabernacle stood with their signs. A Tabernacle member was waving a sign proclaiming "God is glad you have AIDS" when a sudden gust of wind overpowered her, causing the sign to whack a Free Thinker in the face. The sign was too light to do serious harm, but it was enough to give the Free Thinker a spectacular nosebleed. His fellow Atheists leapt to his defense, fists swinging Freely.

While some marchers and spectators struggled to restore calm, others seized the moment to wrest signs from the hands of The Repentance Undeviant Tabernacle members and jump up and down on the despicable words. A priest stood shoulder to shoulder with a man in a T-shirt proclaiming "Your God Loves Atheists" as they both tried to separate the brawlers.

The long-awaited Naked Bicyclists were bearing — or, more accurately, baring — down on the scene, oblivious to the flying fists and shouts ahead of them. Parade spectators previously distracted by the fight were now equally distracted by painted naked bodies on bikes. Heads were swiveling right and left.

Eliot Stern had, until now, been finding this whole event to be a bit of a bore; but it had suddenly transformed into a journalist's paradise, and he began rapidly snapping photos, recording video, and jotting notes. He regretted his earlier whining that being assigned to cover the parade this year was beneath the professional dignity of a hard-hitting star reporter. (His editor had countered that a reporter who wrote about what was likely to happen at the parade could damn well show up and see if he'd gotten the story right.) He was grinning now as he ducked to avoid a "God Hates Fags" placard swung at his head.

Arlen crossed the street to get a better look at the fracas, and lamented that there had been a time in his life when he could have single-handedly put every one of these miscreants in their place. He kept one eye on the lovely woman with the backpack, who was also approaching the brawl.

A few yards away from where placards and fists were flying, Julia observed the situation and knew that this was the moment — absolutely the right moment. She crossed the street in front of three bicyclists — two orange and blue striped penises and one set of voluminous green breasts — riding around in a tight circle. Time slowed as Julia pulled out Wren's painting, hanging the empty dry bag over her shoulder. Her heart was pounding louder than the taiko drums thundering from around the corner. She held the painting at shoulder height and waited for a reaction. At first people seemed to see her as some sort of performance artist, and some applauded before they had any idea what they were clapping for. Someone tossed candy at her. Turning, holding the painting high above her head now, showing it to everyone looking in her direction, Julia was elated to see people stopping in their tracks.

The effect was almost instantaneous and complete, as though a soothing blanket had been spread over the crowd. Some people held hands, some wept, some laughed…and people on the fringes, unable to see the painting, looked confused.

The Reverend Billy Joe Bobb had been approaching his flock when he became aware of the shift in energy. He cut his eyes in a sidelong glare at the tall woman and the painting she was displaying. Following some wicked instinct, he pulled on a pair of dark glasses and pushed past people, shoving them and cursing them. He lunged for the painting; the woman stepped to the side, and Billy Joe Bobb fell into the street onto his hands and knees, sprawling like a large grotesque spider. He stayed down a moment, rolling onto his back.

He closed his eyes and called out, "Lord, help me put an end, once and for all, to all the works of the Devil."

The Reverend Bobb opened his jaundiced eyes to find a bicyclist parked beside him.

"Hey, man," the cyclist asked, "You OK? Can I help you up?"

Billy Joe Bobb heard some laughter in the crowd as he surveyed the Good Samaritan. The man had a three-foot long neon-pink rubber penis strapped to his body and draped forward to dangle limply across the handlebars of his bicycle.

Billy Joe Bobb was in a rage of disgust and humiliation. He pulled himself to his feet as the woman with the Hell-painting surged closer to him. He wanted to grab the bicyclist and fling him to the street, but the painting concerned him more.

He stepped toward Satan's artistic minion and screamed, "Your painting is pure evil! Look what it's doing to people!"

People standing near the scene looked at each other and smiled. Members of The Repentance Undeviant Tabernacle were holding hands with the Atheist group; others were swaying and nodding to the beat of some secret music.

"Yes!" shouted his Adversary. "Look what's happened to your followers. They're behaving like actual Christians for once! One John 4:21 — you're supposed to know that one, asshole."

A gust of wind came out of nowhere, rustling the woman's wild hair. As she stood there, shoulders back, holding the painting proudly in front of her, she reminded Arlen of a 1930's WPA-era statue — the strong leader of the revolution, a goddess in human form. Or at least an updated version of Rosie the Riveter. This was Arlen's vision as he emerged from the throng, and he was thoroughly smitten.

Arlen collected himself and moved closer to the painting, certain it was the same one he'd seen in the newspaper photo. He was about to position himself to look directly at it when the Reverend Billy Joe Bobb made his move. The wiry, sandy-haired cult leader pulled a knife from his pocket, unfolded it, and threw himself toward the woman, slicing a gash in the canvas from the top center down to the lower right-hand corner.

The crowd gasped as one, and the woman staggered. Some might have thought she'd been stabbed, but no one came to her aid. Everyone was riveted, unable to move, as waves of sound washed over them. At first it was a little tinkling bell, high-pitched and faint. Then a deeper bell tolled loudly, like a great cathedral bell calling the faithful. Other bell tones joined in — haunting, round mellow tones and jarring brass clangs filled the air as the volume built on itself.

Julia could scarcely hold the injured painting as the bells became so loud and insistent that she had to cover her ears — yet she dared not set the painting down. The bells were cacophonous, ringing, pealing, tinkling, great cascades of notes and pitches tumbling over one another, underlaid by a deep, deep bass roaring that caused the ground to shake. The painting vibrated, jumping wildly in her hands as she leaned her head to one shoulder in an effort to protect her hearing in at least one ear.

The driver of the Duck-load of tourists had no way of knowing what mayhem was going on down the hill. He didn't know for certain that he was about to create a special kind of mayhem of his own. He did, however, know that his Duck had no brakes and there was a parade in its path. Only much later would he learn that his ex-girlfriend — herself a former Duck driver — had sabotaged his vehicle as an act of revenge. She had been fired for assaulting a woman whom she had caught fellating *her* boyfriend, our dear driver, in the rear of his Duck, as a special thank-you for the superb tour he had just finished conducting.

Now the driver shouted to his tourists to crouch down and hang on tight as he sideswiped a line of parked cars in a desperate attempt to slow the momentum of six tons of amphibious fury. Metal screeched, people screamed, and gravity had its way as the Duck rolled onward toward the bottom of the incline. These amazing amphibious vehicles had once seen military action at Guadalcanal, Normandy, Incheon...and now this one was attacking Fremont. *Delibertus quirkus* indeed.

Julia Burlow stopped worrying about her hearing when she saw the Reverend Billy Joe Bobb reach for the painting. Each holding tightly to the canvas, they began a tug of war; Bobb gave a hard yank, and Julia slipped and went forward with it but kept her grip. Billy Joe Bobb dragged her around as she clung, impossibly, to the torn painting. She regained traction and leaned back with a vengeance. Billy Joe Bobb pulled again, but Julia held tightly, anchored to the ground. The bells were subsiding, but still rang loud — too loud for the two combatants to hear the screeching metal and screaming tourists. The bells rang too loudly for them to hear the warnings of horrified onlookers.

"Duck, Duck!"

Of course, some people covered their heads and crouched toward the ground, but they were lucky enough to be shoved out of the way by other people who understood the true noun-hood of the trouble racing toward them. The white hull of the amphibious craft loomed larger and larger as it thundered down the hill toward the crowd. Standing on the curb with her back to the street, Julia gave a sharp tug on the painting. The Reverend Billy Joe Bobb slipped (later, some swore they had seen a banana peel) and fell backward onto his bony backside. He let go of the painting, and Julia, singularly focused and still pulling with all her strength, fell backward into the street. Directly in the path of the rampaging Duck.

The Duck driver gave a last, desperate twitch to his steering wheel, and the amphibious vehicle came to an abrupt halt, impaled on a fireplug. Passengers moaned and inspected themselves and one another for injury. A geyser of heavily chlorinated city water spouted fifteen feet into the air and rained on the parade. Reverend Billy Joe Bobb, leader of The Repentance Undeviant Tabernacle, rolled onto his belly and then, like the snake he was, slithered beneath the Duck. Emerging on the other side, he left the chaotic scene behind and ran.

Julia had fallen uphill from the fireplug. The Duck hit her just before it met its own nemesis.

Arlen tore off his jacket and ran toward the dead Duck. Covering the woman who had entranced him, he instinctively knew he should protect the painting, too. Clutching the torn painting to his chest, now only one deep and mournful bell tolling faintly from it, he leaned close to her face. He could hear sirens approaching and was glad, because he could tell she was in bad shape. Her arms and legs were bent in places where no joints existed; blood trickled from her mouth and sprayed a pink mist when she exhaled. Her breathing was shallow and quick, and her jaw was hanging askew. This was not the worst he had seen, not by far, but it was so unexpected here, today, on this street, that he had to swallow hard to keep from puking and to focus on helping this woman. Her eyes were begging him to listen, but her mangled jaw would not let words take shape. So, there in the midst of chaos and tragedy and spurting water, Arlen began a guessing game.

"Take 'hainting," Julia gasped, motioning with her eyes toward the sliced painting. Her attempt at speech came as liquid hisses and staccato clicks.

Arlen wanted to touch her, but could not find an undamaged place where touch would be painless. He answered, "Take the painting with me? Blink once if that's a yes, two for no." He felt like he was repeating some stupid cliché movie script, but he could think of nothing better. Julia blinked once. He sensed she had something urgent to tell him before the ambulance came to take her away.

"Tort Townten. Tort Townten," she whispered through her unmoving jaw.

"Oh, Port Townsend. Yes? Port Townsend?"

Julia blinked once. Arlen smiled a little and nodded.

"Gray Tharn." The 'y' and the 'th' came out as a gurgling hiss.

Arlen was beginning to panic, "Gates, grate, grays..."

The woman blinked frantically and Arlen thought she might be seizing, but he realized she was trying to tell him that he'd gotten the first word.

"Grays — a color?"

Two blinks. Wrong. "'Ercy."

"Grays, not grays...oh shit. Mercy. Mercy..." Arlen smiled broadly and whispered, "Mercy and Grace...it's *Grace*. It's someone's name."

Julia blinked once and a tear slid down her broken cheek.

"Second word is her last name." He was so panicked and excited that he was rocking back and forth on his knees.

Julia blinked twice. No, not her name.

"A place?"

One blink. One tear.

"Tharn, tharn." Arlen tried to think of what letters the woman couldn't pronounce. "Barn, parn, farn, marm, farm."

Julia blinked wildly.

"Grace Farm!" Arlen said excitedly.

Arlen nearly jumped out of his skin as someone gently pulled on his shoulder. "I'll help her now. I'm a doctor," a woman said. Completely nude, her blue body paint was now streaked and running, having been soaked from the fire hydrant. A drenched yellow feather boa clung to her back as she got to work.

Arlen drew the painting tighter to his chest, scooted backward on his knees, and without taking his eyes from the patient's, stood up under the spray of water. Trembling, he walked quickly at first, and then began to jog as the dark, lowering sky split open, dropping lakes of rain down on the festival. The wind gusted and blew the rain in all directions.

Arlen squeezed through knots of people raising umbrellas or pulling jackets over their heads. Then, the most rare of Seattle weather events occurred: the sky flashed lightning and thunder shook the ground. People stopped and looked up in wonder, hard rain hammering their clothes and skin. Arlen kept moving, rounding a corner where a small group of people danced in the rain, unaware of the terrible accident just one block away. He trotted past food vendors frantically pulling plastic sheeting over their burritos and baklava, past trinket tents full of soaked souvenirs, and past the covered main music stage where the axiom "The show must go on" was being fulfilled. A performer with a guitar was appropriately singing "The sky in Tacoma's raining razor blades" as Arlen felt the rain biting at his face with every step he took.

Hurrying like a man pursued by wild hounds, Arlen Divine fished his keys from his pocket and dove into his Winnebago. He stood trembling, listening to his own breath, and dripping a puddle onto the vinyl floor. He was still holding the painting against his body, embracing it like a passionate and protective lover. He stood like that for a long time, staring at the wall as lightning flashed, sending surreal shapes dancing in the RV. Blinking raindrops from his eyelashes, Arlen finally relaxed. He looked down at the puddle under his feet. Finally, he sighed and released his grip on the painting, setting the canvas on the floor behind the driver's seat, facing it toward the interior of the RV. He could see it from any position he might take in the RV's living space.

Stripping off his wet clothes, he went to the galley and heated water for a cup of instant coffee. He kept his eyes on the painting. Walking backward toward his bed, he tossed his wet clothes into the shower, never letting his gaze wander. Arlen wondered about this. Was he afraid the painting was going to wrap itself around his throat and strangle him? Did he think it would move on its own around the Winnebago?

Arlen shook his head and gave a kind of snorting laugh as he selected dry, tattered jeans and a faded blue sweatshirt from the pile on the floor beside his bed. Sitting at the dinette sipping his bitter brew, he became sharply aware that he was unsure of everything in this world, except for three things: First, he was unshakably certain that he would do anything to protect this painting. Second, he would push the Winnebago, shoulder to bumper if need be, all the way to Port Townsend to find "Grace Farm". And the last thing caused him a bit of consternation, but he was willing to go with it. He was sure that he was completely in love with the dark-haired woman who had fallen beneath the Duck — a woman who, all too likely, was either dying or already dead.

Arlen sighed and looked at his new companion. The canvas was torn and wet, sagging from broken stretcher bars, but Arlen was content. He wiped at his mustache and smiled at the occasional faintly tinkling bell.

Chapter 17

After a long, mesmerizing time, Arlen began to stir. He had sat for thirty-six hours looking constantly at the painting. He had turned it on its side, turned it upside down, around again, and eventually realized he wasn't clear about which way was supposed to be up. But it didn't matter; Arlen had felt that way about a lot of things in his life.

He took nourishment from beef jerky sticks, a package of hamburger buns, a block of Velveeta, a box of honey-puffed wheat cereal, water, and about a dozen cups of instant coffee. He paused for toilet breaks. He brushed his teeth twice, and dozed off once for twenty minutes.

At O-dark-thirty in the morning, he stood, walked to his bed, and slept for eleven hours. When Arlen Divine finally got up, he took a long hot shower, not worrying, for once, that he might drain his water tank dry. He shaved, except for his magnificent mustache, got dressed, and packed away all loose items in the Winnebago to prepare it for travel.

Arlen had three errands to complete before making the drive to Port Townsend. He walked several blocks to the Fred Meyer store, where he bought three pairs of jeans, a blue plaid flannel shirt and a denim shirt with pearly snaps, briefs, socks, T-shirts, handkerchiefs, and black cowboy boots with not-too-pointy toes.

On the way back to the Winnebago, he stopped for a haircut. Afterward, looking in the barbershop's mirror, he scarcely recognized himself. This man looked good — perhaps even handsome.

He got back to the RV, took the tags off his new clothes and folded them away, and set an alarm for the morning so he could get an early start. He slept another twelve hours.

In the morning he locked up the RV again and went to find a bus headed for Harborview Hospital, Seattle's main trauma center. He figured the woman who had brought the painting into his life had to be there — if she was still alive.

After the ambulance had sped away with Julia Burlow, the soaking wet, blue-streaked, naked physician turned her attention to Eliot Stern. He was beginning to come around.

"Lie still a moment, Mr. Stern," the blue doctor said.

Eliot's eyelids fluttered. "How'd you know my name? Are you an angel? Oh, shit — am I dead?"

She smiled, reached under his shirt, and held up the lanyard with his press ID, name, and photo.

"Oh," Eliot sputtered. "Yes, of course. I should have known."

After the blue doctor helped him sit upright, Eliot leaned against a young man sporting purple hair, a vast array of tattoos, and a skateboard.

"I think you just fainted," said the blue doctor, "but do you have any pain? Did someone hit you?"

Eliot passed his hands over his face and head and gave a thumbs-up gesture. He attempted to stand, and — staggering dramatically — got himself to his feet. He knew exactly what had caused his loss of consciousness: the painting. He could only surmise that his intense encounter with the other painting at the gallery had made him more deeply susceptible to the power of all of Wren Willow Hendrix's work. And then, seeing this one — and especially seeing it, *feeling* it, get slashed by that asshole preacher — he had been completely hammered.

"I'm OK. Thank you for your concern. I really am fine," Eliot said. He suddenly jerked his head back. "Uh... You're naked."

"Oh," she laughed. "Bicycling. Just bicycling. You know. The parade. Good thing you didn't need a tracheotomy, 'cause I would have had to do it with my teeth."

Eliot thought her streaked blue face might have taken on a shade of purple, and he smiled weakly at her. Looking at his watch, he was relieved to see that he would be able to make his deadline.

Reverend Billy Joe Bobb, spiritual guide of The Repentance Undeviant Tabernacle, ran and ran and ran. He had put twenty city blocks between him and the Devil's freak show. He was horrified and panicked by what he had seen — not by seeing the demon bitch run over by the Duck, of course, since she and her painting were hellspawn and obviously God can use any vehicle he wants as His chariot. No, what disturbed the Reverend was seeing his followers dropping their placards, seeing the goofy drugged looks on their faces... And the worst thing was that they touched — *actually touched* — heathens and queers and Naked Cyclists with huge pink rubber penises. How could the Creator of the Universe see fit to crush one enemy, yet allow His most faithful flock to be lured away from Him by Satan's minions and their degenerate "art"? And if God allowed The Undeviant Tabernacle to turn into a bunch of deviants so suddenly, was *anyone* safe from the Lord of Evil? Was he?

Billy Joe Bobb stopped running and leaned against a dumpster, wheezing and panting, his mouth hanging open and his eyeballs bulging. He had done everything right. That demon woman had some nerve thinking that something as insignificant as a *painting* could turn *him* into a babbling, fag-loving, sinning, smiling fool. He looked down at the grease-stained concrete and prayed.

He prayed that God would remove that devil-woman from the world. Then he prayed that he would have sufficient strength to avenge his shame at having been pushed around by a mere female.

An idea was coming to him… God in Heaven Above was blessing him with a plan to handle that woman. Breathing was getting easier.

Huddling behind the dumpster, his thoughts in perfect harmony with the odors emanating from the big metal container, the Reverend Billy Joe Bobb waited until darkness to slip unseen toward his minibus. A minibus that was, to his great dismay, now twenty blocks away.

Chapter 18

A street sweeper roared by the illegally parked Smart car where Eliot Stern pounded out his article.

"There you have it," he said aloud as he hit the Send button. He loved electronic technology when it actually worked. No couriers to trust, no sitting at a desk in a room full of distractions; just a click, and his work arrived instantly on his editor's desk.

Eliot snapped his laptop shut, shoved it into his briefcase, and dropped his forehead to the steering wheel. It was late afternoon, the rain had stopped, and while Solstice activities were still going on two blocks away, the city was working quickly to clean up the accident scene. The Duck had been towed, and the tourists on board had been taken to the hospital to be inoculated against any tendency to litigate. The fireplug had been replaced, and the blood and debris — including an unlit skinny cigar — that hadn't been washed away was being swept up.

Eliot closed his eyes and breathed deeply. He thought again about his fainting spell, and then he fell into a vivid recollection of the whole experience with Jeanette and the painting at the Huxley-Lavelle Gallery. The memory alone was enough to make him feel like he was dreaming, peacefully floating.

A sharp, loud knock on his window evicted him from his reverie. "Hey, Stern! Open up!"

Shocked back to the present, Eliot jumped, banging his bruised knee on the steering wheel. Wincing and swearing, he let down the window to take in the full funk of a junkie named Richard. In spite of being in a fog most of the time, Richard watched the streets closely and noticed things that most people were too preoccupied — or simply too dense — to see. Eliot occasionally paid the guy for information. Knowing there was no way he was going to rehabilitate Richard — and it was not his job, in any case — Eliot felt no remorse about the certainty that any cash he gave the man was headed straight to the pocket of Richard's dealer.

"Hello, Richard. What do you know?"

"Well, that'll cost you," Richard laughed, his white mustache taking the shape of a seagull poised to fly up his nose.

Eliot passed a twenty-dollar bill through the window and was immediately rewarded.

"Hey, you seen that poor gal get run over? I seen that sleaze that was fighting with her over that weird picture. I seen him run off."

"Yes, yes," said Eliot, impatient for more, "I saw that, too."

"Yeah? OK. Well, so, I seen that other guy. Took the tore up picture and run away."

"OK, that's something I missed. Tell me more."

Richard stopped his story and looked around the street. "Stern, high quality dope is sure getting expensive."

Eliot stared at Richard, thinking *fucking extortionist*, but handed over another twenty.

Richard looked relieved and excited, the mustache bird flapping its wings. "Tall guy. Dark hair, big mustache. I know where he run to."

Eliot could not suppress a grin. "…Well?"

Richard lit a cigarette, shifting his weight from one foot to the other, exhaling a billowing, acrid cloud into Eliot's car. Jerking his head and pointing with his cigarette, he said, "He run off to that parking lot on the alley."

Stern followed the gesture and saw a lone RV in a big empty parking lot, sitting like the carcass of a hulking prehistoric animal.

"Richard, you are a true and loyal friend," Elliot said, rolling up his window so fast it nearly clipped the end off Richard's cigarette.

Eliot Stern parked at the corner of the lot, as far from the RV as he could. There he sat and watched and waited. The first night, he saw a dim light flicker inside the RV and was certain he heard someone shouting and sobbing.

In the morning he had to take a chance and leave his post. Bodily functions required attention, and food needed to be acquired. Upon returning to his tiny car, Eliot ate a breakfast burrito while staring at the Winnebago. Hours passed. He wondered if the guy was dead. The day dragged on; cars came into the lot, cars left the lot, and attendants removed cash from the "Pay Here" box. By early evening on the second night of his vigil, Eliot began to play the phrase "Marathon of Boredom" over and over in his mind, even attaching a dirge-like melody to it. His thoughts drifted and his body felt lighter. He fell asleep. Time passed.

Eliot jolted awake. Pulling up his sleeve to look at his watch, he was horrified that three hours had gone by. The RV was dark. Had the guy gone out? Was he sleeping, too? He watched carefully and saw the RV rock slightly, a sure sign someone was moving about inside. Eliot sighed with relief and eased back into the seat, stretching as much as he could inside his miniature car.

In the warm afternoon of his third day watching the RV, something extraordinary happened. The door opened and a man with a large mustache stepped out and walked away.

Eliot quickly abandoned his post to snoop around the RV. Short of breaking in, there was nothing to learn, except that someone had once welded the letters "W I N N E B A G O" onto the front grill, and several had fallen off, leaving the word "W I N   E B A G".

"Bizarre," Eliot mumbled and walked off to get something to eat. It felt good to move around and stretch his legs, and he felt fairly confident he wouldn't miss anything. He also felt like he would go raving mad if he sat in his car any longer.

He walked to a local grocery, bought a turkey sandwich and coffee, and returned to his car in time to see the mustachioed man enter the RV carrying a couple of shopping bags. Eliot jumped into his car, ready in case the fellow drove away. But nothing happened — after a while the lights in the RV went out and all was still. Eliot settled into the driver's seat, sipping his coffee. He could easily wait some more, he thought. Like a snake stalking a rat, Eliot moved in on his sandwich.

At 7:30 in the morning, the man with the mustache left the Winnebago again. Eliot went to get some breakfast and stretch his cramped legs. He couldn't take too much more of this — but he had a feeling he wouldn't have to.

Arlen stepped out of the elevator and into the hallway. In this hospital, in one of the rooms on this floor, he hoped to find the woman who had struggled with the weird militant preacher and had fallen under the raging, doomed Duck — the woman who had awakened his heart. He held his breath as he approached the nurses' station, the nerve center of this ward. He needed to know — but was afraid to find out — if she was alive. A round woman with stiff dyed-black hair looked up from her computer screen with an expression that could have seared his flesh from the bone.

"May I help you, sir?"

"Uh. Mm, I was wondering if you could direct me to the room of the woman who was brought in from an accident. Uh, an accident at the Fremont parade. She fell under an out-of-control Duck."

The nurse scrutinized him suspiciously and said, "Just a moment. I'll have to check if you have clearance. What's your name?"

Arlen was wary and his guard reflexively went up. He gave her a name. "Morrison. James Morrison," he said.

The nurse picked up a phone, turning her back to Arlen as she spoke barely above a whisper. He sensed big trouble when he overheard, "James Morrison? No, not on the list."

The nurse held the phone, listening, casting a quick glance down the hall.

"OK. Should I call the guard that's outside her door, or just buzz security?"

Arlen heard that question and, stealthy as a cat, slipped silently around the corner. Turning around and looking toward the far end of the hall, he saw a huge man in a dark suit sitting on a metal folding chair. Arlen watched as the man stood up and stretched, revealing a shoulder-holstered pistol as his jacket fell open. The guard sat down and returned to his newspaper, looking calm but fully alert. It was a look Arlen knew well: This guy had seen his share of combat and was not to be trifled with.

A blonde nurse carrying a tray of blood samples was hurrying toward the guarded room when Arlen heard the loudspeaker announce "Code Blue, 512." The nurse turned toward him and time froze as they made eye contact. Arlen stopped in his tracks. The nurse seemed strangely startled, too. He blinked, and the nurse turned back toward the guarded room. He was certain he would never forget the electric-green eyes that had peered from behind her dark-framed glasses. He drew back quickly around the corner of the hall intersection. Then, like any ordinary visitor, Arlen calmly stepped into an elevator and left the hospital.

He was elated. *She was alive!* He walked to the bus stop with a jaunty gait, but his mood turned darker as he pondered the armed guard at her door. That guy looked expensive, or even official — not some bargain-basement rent-a-cop. Was the guard there to protect her, or to prevent her from getting out? Escape didn't seem too likely, if Arlen was still any judge of injuries... Maybe they were looking for someone specific, and that someone would be expected to come running to her side? He figured he'd caught a lucky break getting in, finding out at least a little, and getting out again, although he was also a little mad at himself for failing to learn the injured woman's name. He had only "Grace Farm, Port Townsend" to go on, and he was unsure how to begin a quest based on such a thin clue.

As the bus moved through city traffic, Arlen looked at the other passengers, but avoided direct eye contact. He looked out the window, but shrank away from the glass whenever a pedestrian or car passenger looked up at the bus. He snorted, feeling like a kid who'd just seen his first scary movie. "Caution will serve you, paranoia will kill you," Arlen whispered to himself. He'd learned that from a wise old sergeant, and it had stayed with him.

He got off the bus at his intended stop and walked a block in the opposite direction of the RV. When he was certain he was not being followed, Arlen went back to the Winnebago, started the engine, and drove the lumbering machine toward the ferry terminal.

Eliot had dozed off again. He heard a noise — a gunshot in his dream — but as the haze of sleep began to clear he realized it was the big Winnebago backfiring. The mustachioed man had started the old RV and was driving out of the parking lot.

Eliot spilled cold coffee in his lap and smeared day-old salsa all over his pants and shirt in his attempt to sop up the coffee. Finally, giving up and throwing everything into the footwell on the passenger side, he started the car and zipped down the street behind the RV. His nerves were jittery and it felt like ants were crawling through his clothes, but he easily kept sight of the RV — it was a big, obvious target. It was going toward the Fremont Bridge. He'd catch up to it as soon as the stoplight turned green.

Eliot sat at the stoplight, waiting, watching the RV cross the bridge, and listening to the alarm bell that signaled that the bridge would now "open" for boat traffic to use the canal. Eliot pounded on his steering wheel like a toddler throwing a tantrum as he sat, stranded, at the bridge. The RV had made it across the bridge and he saw it at a stoplight, saw the light turn green, saw the RV take the street that ran toward Fisherman's Terminal.

When the bridge deck finally dropped for cars to cross, Eliot shot through traffic, squirting around every car in his way. Sweat trickled down the sides of his face. He lost sight of the Winnebago, and now he was stopped at another red light. Jittery, tapping the wheel, pulling at his hair... Then there it was, in the rearview mirror: the battered old RV was at a gas station. Eliot, cutting off a bicyclist who yelled something about the circumstances of Eliot's birth, spun the little Smart car in a U-turn and squeezed it unbelievably between a tow truck and a Cadillac. Without slowing, he bounced into the gas station's parking lot. Stopping just around the corner of the station, he sat and watched Mustache Man. Ten minutes later the RV was on its way, with Eliot's car so close behind that it looked like the Winnebago was blowing a Smart-shaped balloon out its exhaust pipe.

Eliot Stern flew into a red-faced panic when he realized the Winnebago was headed for the ferry dock. Mustache Man could lose him there. Which boat — Bremerton, or Bainbridge Island?

Rows and rows of cars were waiting to board the huge vessels. Automobile engines spit and growled to life, and the loading began. A long, slow, steady stream of motorcycles, bicycles, trucks, and cars took their positions aboard the floating behemoths. Eliot watched with clenched jaws as the Winnebago driver purchased a ticket and drove down the dock toward the line of cars headed to Bainbridge Island. The old RV rocked ominously from side to side as it rolled onto the ferry. Eliot now knew which ferry to board.

Fumbling for his wallet, he bought a ticket and followed, only three cars behind the RV now. Car after car drove across the ramp and into the gaping maw of the ferry. He began to doubt there would be room even for his tiny car. He stopped and he waited, his tapping fingers on the steering wheel sounding like a drumline of woodpeckers. A member of the deck crew pointed at Eliot and made a grand sweeping gesture with both arms, inviting him to drive aboard — the last car they let on. His car zipped across the dock and onto the boat, filling a space that would never have fit even a Beetle, with Eliot managing a little smile at the knowledge that now he had his target in sight for at least the next hour.

The man with the big mustache stayed inside his RV the entire ferry ride. At one point Eliot thought he heard bells jingling, tinkling, and clanging. He rubbed his face, sure that fatigue must be screwing with him. Yawning, Elliot leaned his seat back and fell instantly asleep.

Chapter 19

When Julia didn't call them after the parade, neither Grace nor Wren was too concerned — Julia was not exactly known for paying rigid attention to details and precise schedules, and who knew? She might have met an interesting Naked Cyclist at the parade. They saw the news about the Duck of Doom, of course, but the TV news said that the only injured pedestrian had been treated at the scene.

The next day, though, it was obvious that something strange was going on. Even Julia at her most free-spirited should have been in touch by now. Calling her number just went to voice mail. Wren and Grace kept their phones charged, paced, fed the animals, paced some more, tried Julia's number again and again, and tried not to think about what could be keeping Julia out of contact.

By the third day, both women were certain that Julia was in some kind of trouble. Had she been abducted by Billy Joe Bobb and his crazed Undeviated followers? Was she stuck somewhere in a painting-induced trance? Had she and her Naked Cyclist wheeled off into the sunset? They checked every news website they could find, watched TV news, listened to radio news...nothing. They discussed filing a Missing Persons report — but how do you do that when the last thing you or your missing friend wants is to have cops sniffing around?

*A*gent Levi Bitters sat in an unforgiving wooden chair in his superior's office. Fiddling with his tie, he listened as his boss gloated about catching the maker of those "weird-ass" paintings. "That wraps this one up," she said. "Couple weeks from now, this will be someone else's problem."

"But it isn't her!" he said. "You've got the wrong artist. Worse still, if you hadn't suppressed the story, the real creator of those 'weird-ass' paintings might have shown up at the hospital to check in on her friend. Now we've lost two full days!"

Director Polly Ramsey leaned toward her desk, took out a long, filtered menthol cigarette, and lit it. "Look, Bitters," she said, "the woman had one of those things in her possession at the demo and at the parade. There was no evidence of paintings like it in that other artist's burned-out studio. Just accept it. Sometimes things are not that complicated."

Holding the smoldering cigarette in her right hand, Ramsey gripped the arm of her leather chair with her left. She leaned back at an angle, a posture that always reminded Bitters of the cocksure attitude of a mob boss. Smoking wasn't even allowed in this building; but if Bitters brought this up he was certain she would simply narrow her eyes at him and snarl, "Bite me."

Bitters sighed. Apparently, for Homeland Security to look strong and efficient and worthy of its budget, they needed swift arrests, a bird in the hand being worth billions more than the truth. "OK, Director. I'll just go write up my report, and send it over. May I know who's going to be taking over this case, and where the artist is being transferred to?"

"Need-to-know, Bitters," the Director said. "Strictly need-to-know."

Agent Bitters nodded. He wondered at how calmly he was taking all this. It wasn't like him at all. Nor, for that matter, was the sense of rebellion he was carefully keeping away from his face and body language. He wondered about that, too.

Ramsey blew a jet of acrid smoke in his direction. "Tell you what," she said in her smoke-charred voice. "Just to humor you, I'll take the lid off the story tonight, let all the editors know they can go ahead and report on Burlow's injury. Maybe catch us an accomplice or two. Meanwhile, I've got things to do — and I'm sure you do, too."

Bitters straightened his tie, stood, nodded to Director Ramsey, and left her office. *Need-to-know...* Well, he had his own reasons for needing to know. What's more, he had his own ways of finding stuff out. So yes, he had things to do, alright...and among them was a quick visit to the hospital. Orders or no, Bitters was determined to find the real painter of those enigmatic paintings, even if he was slightly foggy about exactly *why* he wanted to find her. Inexplicably, he felt the need to protect her rather than arrest her.

Chapter 20

Wren Willow Hendrix knelt in Grace's carrot patch pluck-ing weeds from the soil as though they'd personally offended her. The sun was about to clear the tree line and it was not yet six in the morning. Summer had officially arrived, and it had rolled up to Wren and Grace with a shock; but this time the shock wasn't the usual one of warm days and sunshine in a part of the world that never really expected them. Far less pleasant news had arrived the previous evening.

Wren and Grace ate avocado-onion sandwiches and cold beer while watching the evening news. The announcer seemed quietly outraged to have to reveal to his viewers that the "treated-on-the-spot" pedestrian from two days ago had indeed been treated on the spot — but was in fact seriously hurt, and had been taken to Harborview Hospital where she remained in "critical but stable" condition. The victim's name was Julia Burlow.

"Critical but stable" wasn't enough to reassure Grace; she paced around the living room anyway, muttering, "Oh, God, she can't be dead."

Wren felt her insides go cold, her legs useless rubber bands...but her mind remained focused and clear. "Grace, sit down," Wren said firmly.

Grace, stunned by Wren's sudden rock-solid, stern assertiveness, sat.

Wren called Harborview Hospital and asked the condition of her friend Julia Burlow. The operator checked her computer and replied curtly that no information on this patient was authorized to be given out over the phone.

Wren hung up and sighed. "I can't go into town," she said sadly, "but maybe you could go to the hospital to see how she is?"

A gust of wind rattled an upstairs window. Grace massaged her face with both hands as though trying to get some warmth into her cheeks, or possibly to rub away the numbness of shock. "I don't know...I never go to the city."

Several seconds ticked by as Wren absorbed this revelation. "Ever?" Wren asked, surprised.

"That's right. I just don't go there."

"Well, why?"

"Too much traffic going too fast. Too many people...I can almost hear them thinking. The city distresses me, reminds me of things I don't care to remember, OK?"

A ponderous silence thickened in the living room. Wren moved to sit side-by-side with Grace on the worn brown leather couch. Their touching shoulders seemed to pool their energy and slowly dissipate their fear as they looked through the window glass to the spectacular view beyond. After a while, Grace stood and walked to the window, fingertips to the glass.

"It's a good view. There is something mystical about the way the water and sky move together, like they are dancing."

Wren came to Grace's side, seeking some of that magic, and said softly, "Yes. Look how far you can see, how far. Wow! You can see until there just isn't any more *far* to see."

Grace turned to look at Wren and surprised them both by laughing at Wren's remark. The murkiness in her expression was beginning to clear. "Yes, it is indeed that far. Give me a couple hours. I'll think of how best to check in on Julia. That's all I know right now."

Wren squeezed Grace's hand and said, "Good. That will work."

Neither let go of the other's hand as they stood at the window watching the day fade into darkness.

Now, in the warming morning, Wren stood in the midst of hundreds of carrots, hoping the work of weeding could steady her nerves. Grace stepped into the garden wearing blue nurse's scrubs and carrying an oversized tan purse.

"My," said Wren, "don't you look professional. What else have you got?"

Grace opened the purse to reveal a blonde shoulder-length wig and a pair of generic black-framed glasses. "I don't know if the cloak-and-dagger business is really necessary, but I've got a hunch, an intuition, that it's probably not good to be recognized. I'll be back tonight. Meanwhile, don't feel like you have to pull every weed in the county."

Wren felt a little worried, but stood tall. "Grace, you've done this before, haven't you? I mean the wig-and-glasses thing."

Grace looked sad and said, "Hmmm. I think we'll have to talk about that later. Here comes my driver. This is our neighbor and occasional hired helper, Gordon."

Gordon smiled at Wren, raising a two-finger wave from the steering wheel of his green and yellow 1959 Rambler station wagon. "While I'm in town, you might want to go to the barn and have a look around. Julia thought you might find it suitable for painting in. See you later. No worries, girl."

One quick hug and a wave and Wren was standing alone, her hair lifting on the wind. She listened as the old Rambler chugged a little, crunched across the gravel, and rolled out of sight.

A hummingbird whirred by her head on its way to a flower. Wren went inside to make coffee, to worry, and to think about going to check out the barn.

Chapter 21

Grace moved through the hospital corridor with purpose, playing the part of the harried nurse to perfection. She carried a clipboard, an iPad, and a tray of tubes for the collection of blood samples.

More than a little familiar with hospitals, she walked briskly through the assault on her senses. The air felt as dry and hot as a sauna, and her wig felt like a sleeping peroxide badger draped over her head. Aromas from strong disinfectants, bedpan products, and the disturbingly unhealthful lunch cart mingled in an olfactory stew. Down the hall, the elevator chimed delicately, adding its musical voice to the hospital's orchestra of beeping monitors, chirping phones, moans, shouts, and the frequent loudspeaker pages for Dr. Graham, Dr. John, Dr. Robert, Dr. Benway.

"Code Blue, 512. Code Blue, 512," an urgent voice intoned from the intercom. Nurses and doctors appeared at doorways and raced down the corridors to the emergency in Room 512. Grace saw her opportunity and made her way towards the door with the guard sitting beside it.

A few steps from the guarded room, she turned to see if any of the hospital staff were watching her — and locked eyes with a tall man sporting the thickest black mustache she had ever seen. Grace momentarily froze, then forced herself to turn to check the corridor behind her. She took a quick look back to where the tall man had been, but he was gone now — so she resumed her steps toward Julia's room. The guard looked like a block of granite stuffed into a suit, and Grace imagined he could bench-press a refrigerator without breaking a sweat. He was scanning a newspaper, his gray, ball-bearing eyes scarcely looking up at her. She figured that by now he had become lulled into carelessness by the constant comings and goings of people dressed in scrubs — he wasn't guarding against hospital staff doing their jobs. Grace breezed past him without a glance, pushed open the door, and walked right through.

Inside the room, Julia lay on a narrow bed, both legs encased in plaster and suspended by cables from an intricate metallic modern sculpture bolted to the ceiling. Her right arm was also in a cast, slightly bent, and her left arm was bandaged from wrist to shoulder. It was Julia's jaw that made Grace's stomach lurch. A metal cage surrounded her head entirely, and wires emerged from punctures in her jaw, running like tiny tightropes to their attachment points on the cage. Her eyes were closed in a peaceful narcotic sleep. Grace unconsciously rubbed at her own jaw and then leaned down close to Julia's ear.

"Julia," Grace whispered, "can you hear me?" She paused hopefully.

Julia made a soft, whispered groan, and her eyelids fluttered. She finally kept her eyes open and looked at Grace. Grace was uncertain what she read in those eyes. Was it fear, or surprise, or a smile?

"Julia, Wren is fine. We just had to know how you are. I can see that you won't be able to talk. Can you touch letters on my iPad?"

Grace held the pad so Julia could touch the screen with a finger of her bandaged arm. With great effort Julia tapped the iPad screen. Bandages, casts, and heavy drugs made this a painfully slow process; Grace sent out good vibes to the patient in Room 512, hoping they would live so the nurses would remain occupied there for a good while and not walk in on this confab.

Julia closed her eyes and Grace read what was on the iPad screen. "thx homlandscurty moveme 2wx"

Grace absorbed this information and made an instant decision. "Julia, my dear old friend, we will get you out of here. You need to heal a bit more" — possibly the understatement of the century — "but we'll get you out before then. In the next ten days. I promise."

Grace touched the exposed fingers of the bandaged arm and Julia returned the pressure and drifted back into morphine's benevolent embrace.

Grace hurried out past the guard, looking official with her tray of blood-filled tubes. She returned the tray to the cart she had taken it from and grabbed her purse from the vacant visitor's lounge. Then she stepped into the lady's room, pulled off the glasses and wig, and jammed them into her purse. Smiling a little, she walked from there directly into an open elevator car.

As she stood on the sidewalk waiting for Gordon, she wondered how she was going to get Julia, legs and all, out of this hospital. She looked around, calmly scanning the crowd for the man with the big mustache. She would know that face if she saw it again, but Grace did not see him now; and with an abundance of relief, she hopped into Gordon's car.

"Gordon," Grace said quietly, "please drive us away from this place, away from the city."

Gordon jerked the car away from the curb as Grace looked solemnly out of the window at Seattle. Sitting in silence as Gordon bumped his old Rambler station wagon along toward the ferry terminal, she ran her fingers through her hair and eased back into the ancient upholstery. She closed her eyes and searched her thoughts, trying to formulate a plan to make good on her promise. Nothing. This would take a little time, a little effort, and a lot of wine.

Grace, Wren, and Arlen weren't the only ones interested in Julia. The Reverend Billy Joe Bobb was almost as intensely concerned about her as her friends were, but his intentions were far less benign. And he was fairly certain that his demonic quarry would be right here, in the best trauma center in the city.

Billy Joe Bobb strutted right through the front door of the hospital, a well-picked-through Bible in hand, and marched up to the main desk, demanding "to pray at the side of our dear battered sister who was cruelly run over by a misguided Duck." The desk nurse looked him over. His disheveled appearance and yellow teeth put her on red alert.

"Sir, there are no visitors allowed for this patient at this time. I'm afraid you'll have to leave."

"Certainly, ma'am, certainly," Billy Joe Bobb bowed and smiled, sneaking glances all around, trying to spy out where his quarry was being kept. When no clues appeared to guide him, he slunk away.

But Billy Joe Bobb was as persistent as an unreachable itch. He would try again at a different entrance, this time without mentioning his true objective until he had breached the first line of defense. He slicked back his stringy hair and held his Bible to his chest, gold cross gleaming from the cover of the book. He wanted everyone to notice him and see that he was in the Lord's service.

At the ICU a nurse informed him, in a truly unpleasant manner, that the patient he sought was no longer in her care and had been moved to another floor. He correctly deduced that she was not going to tell him where that might be. Billy Joe Bobb walked toward the elevator, and on his way happened upon a janitor mopping the floor in a waiting room.

Holding his Bible a little closer to his collarbone, he met the janitor's eyes, "Sir, I do not wish to disturb your work. Cleanliness is, as you well know, next to godliness, and is so crucially important to ministering to those whom Our Father has afflicted." Reverend Billy Joe Bobb cast his eyes toward the ceiling.

The janitor paused, left hand on his hip and his right hand on the top of his mop handle. He was as big as a tank, and towered over Billy Joe Bobb. His head was like a concrete altitude marker at the top of a mountain. He scowled at Reverend Bobb, but upon seeing the Bible, the janitor's expression softened into a gentle smile. In the highest, squeakiest voice Billy Joe Bobb had ever heard from such a big man, he said, "How can I help you, brother?"

"Well, dear brother, it seems that one of my beloved congregants was in a terrible, terrible accident. She was brought to this hospital, and by God's mercy her condition improved enough to be moved from the Intensive Care Unit to a room on another floor — Orthopedics, or perhaps Trauma, I imagine. Our dear sister is in great need of spiritual guidance and succor. Have you seen her? She's the woman who was run over by a Duck at the Parade of the Holy Solstice."

The janitor looked up at the ceiling for a minute. Billy Joe Bobb was worried that the fellow had lost the thread of the conversation and was instead now searching for cobwebs.

"Pastor, I ain't sure this is the sister you're looking for, but there's a room on the fifth floor with an armed guard who's even bigger than me. I heard a nurse sayin' the woman there got run over by a Duck. Dunno what she needs a guard for. She sure ain't leaving any time soon — not with legs and arms all in casts and a weird-looking wire cage around her head."

Billy Joe Bobb placed his free hand on the janitor's shoulder, "Thank you, brother. Let us pray."

Reverend Bobb cleared his throat and said, "Jeezuz, hallelujah, God bless this lowly laborer for his kindness. Amen."

The janitor scowled at being called a "lowly laborer", but bowed his head in prayer anyway.

Rather than risk an unpleasant encounter with hospital staff in the elevator, Billy Joe Bobb ran up the stairwell, taking two steps at a stride. Wheezing at the door to the fifth floor, he waited to catch his breath before he stepped through the doorway into the bustling hallway.

Bolstered by the janitor's generous gift of information, Billy Joe Bobb decided that the direct approach would probably work best. He walked briskly to the door of the guarded room and stopped in front of the guard. "Brother, I humbly beg you to invite me in to bring the word of the Lord to my dear, wounded warrior of The Repentance Undeviant Tabernacle," Reverend Bobb announced.

The guard lowered his magazine and raised his eyes to meet Billy Joe Bobb's. Reverend Bobb felt his spine dissolve.

"I don't know what the hell you just said, but I would like to *invite* you to get the fuck out of this hospital."

Every good preacher — and every competent bad preacher even more so — learns to recognize very quickly who is reachable and who is not. Only saints and idiots waste their time preaching to the unreachable. Billy Joe Bobb faltered, stepped back a little, and squeaked, "Well, then, God bless you, good sir. Bless you."

This would be only a temporary setback, he was certain.

Chapter 22

Grace had been gone less than an hour and Wren was already feeling jumpy. What if Grace got into trouble? Would Grace be arrested? What was Wren supposed to do then? How could she get to Julia? What if Homeland Security came here and found her? What if it rained? What if slugs ate the whole vegetable garden? What would Julia say to her if she saw her in this state of near-panic?

Wren spoke loudly in the lowest pitch she could manage, her best imitation of Julia: "Holy shit, Hendrix, get a grip on your nervous little self."

Wren laughed, but the laughter subsided as she remembered Grace's suggestion to check out the barn. The air felt heavy, thick, as she walked through the gate and out of the garden. Closing the gate behind her, she paused, feeling the sun warming her skin. A white-crowned sparrow sang to her from a hedge, and the floral-scented breeze sounded like a gentle exhalation as it touched her face.

It was beautiful here, but as she looked at her unfamiliar surroundings, Wren wondered how she had gotten to this moment. What misstep had she taken that she should lose so much? She had long ago come to think of life, the universe, and the entirety of what she knew and didn't know as a flow of energy, like a river. She had felt the paint flowing from her brushes just like that river. Now Wren felt like a river of time and a river of space had converged in a strange confluence, pulling her along in the current, conspiring to dump her mercilessly into an ocean of sorrow.

Wren pushed open the door at the narrow side of the barn and stepped in. The air was cool, but dry, and a little dust floated and spun in the golden shafts of light coming in through the high windows. She stood with her hands jammed into the pockets of her worn jeans and turned in a slow circle, seeing everything. She felt the familiar intrusion of a presence behind her, pushing her out of herself and onto the canvas. But there was no canvas here — there was only a wall. The whole of it was around forty feet in length and twenty feet high up to the beams. She searched the barn for old cans of paint and a ladder. Wren found a twelve-foot stepladder lying on a tarp; when she dragged it over towards the empty wall, the tarp snagged and came along, revealing at least fifty cans of paint underneath. A smile dared to play at the corners of her lips. It was a peculiar assortment of colors, and Wren's skin tingled at the possibilities. Opening the unwieldy stepladder at the middle of the wall, she climbed up with a full gallon of "Barn Red". That seemed like an appropriate color to start with…

From her teetering, precarious position on the final step at the top of the ladder, she threw the paint directly from the can in an arc that pumped through space like arterial blood and splashed onto the old barn boards, dripping down like a backdrop from a horror movie.

Back on solid ground, she hurried to scoop the last possible drops of paint from the can with a stiff brush she'd found on the floor. Wren pulled thick lines of red horizontally across the wall even as the drips were overtaking these new strokes of color.

In her studio, Wren would often wait for layers to dry, but today, on this wall of thirsty wood, she kept up the assault. She opened a five-gallon bucket of what the manufacturer had named "Sea Breeze". Wren pronounced it teal, and poured some into a more manageable gallon pail. She went up the ladder again and threw the teal paint with such force that it bounced and skittered across the wall.

She ran across the barn to the workbench, rifling through screwdrivers and old bent nails to find the roll of duct tape that she knew had to be there. Now she stretched duct tape across the wall as a mask at varying angles, so the paint wasn't all flowing downward at gravity's whim, but each drop had to find its own way.

Picking up the stiff brush, she dipped it in the paint cans, changing colors as she moved across the wall, throwing and spreading paint as she walked. She repeated the process from a perch six feet up the ladder, and again at twelve feet. Sweat ran from her forehead and she smeared paint across her face in her effort to wipe the perspiration away — her war paint! — as she engaged in battle with the unseen force that propelled her deeper into the work.

Wren opened a window and a reviving breeze floated in. She stopped moving paint and assessed her work. The painting was overwhelming because it was so big — twelve feet high and twenty feet along the wall's length. And, because it was so large and engulfing, the "effect" was immediately overwhelming.

Wren sat on the floor in front of the massive work. She looked up at it.

"That," she said, uttering her familiar mantra, "does not suck."

Time passed; the sun shifted; the light dimmed, went blue as a cloud passed over. The paint was gone…well, not gone, merely transformed. The artist, too, had been transformed. Wren stood before the painting and experienced the by-now-familiar feeling her new paintings always delivered. She felt happy and began to laugh. Feeling a little too giddy, she put her dark sunglasses on and was able to assess the quality of the new work without the mental alterations. The layers were thick and deep, contrasting colors lying beside one another to produce a feeling of motion that was superbly dizzying. This painting was beautiful all on its own. The euphoria was an added bonus.

It was now a little too late to think that Grace had suggested she paint *in* the barn, not on it!

Wren turned sharply toward the door when she heard gravel crunching under tires. *Grace must be home already.* Wren hastened to wipe paint from her hands onto a paper towel, forgetting the streaks of color that ran across her right cheek and forehead. She pulled the door open...and after a quick look outside, quietly shut it again.

Leaning on the dark green door, heart pounding, barely able to breathe, Wren tried to process what she had seen. Not Grace. Not Grace at all, but a tall man with a heavy black mustache standing beside an ancient Winnebago camper. She opened the door an inch, and with one eye watched the man walk toward Grace's house. Wren dared to feel relief as she sensed that he was not from Homeland Security — unless the old camper was a brilliant disguise. And this certainly was not Reverend Billy Joe Bobb. Wren noted that letters had fallen off the camper's grill, and what once must have said "W I N N E B A G O" now read "W I N   G". Wing... From where had this fellow flown?

"Oh, crap," Wren whispered to herself. He was walking toward the barn! She dashed to the far end of the barn and hid herself behind a stack of truck tailgates.

As the stranger opened the door, he called out, "Hello? Anybody here? I'm looking for Grace. My name is Arlen Divine."

The man was sauntering through the barn, but soon came to a stop. Wren realized he was looking at the twelve-foot by twenty-foot wall she had just painted. He began to chuckle, then to laugh out loud. When Wren came out from her hiding place, Arlen was sitting on the floor holding his knees to his chest and rocking as tears slid down into his mustache.

"It's all right," Wren said calmly, handing him her sunglasses. "Put these on. You can look at the painting without..."

She wondered if she should just let him have the full experience, but he reached for the glasses, wiping his face with a handkerchief. He put them on, then blew his nose loudly.

A minute passed in silence.

"I know this painting," he said, finally.

"How?"

Arlen exhaled raggedly. "I saw a smaller one that made me see things. See things clearly ... and hear things. I saw it at the Fremont Solstice Parade." Arlen turned toward Wren and took off the sunglasses. "You're the painter," he said. "You made this painting and the one I saw in Fremont, didn't you?"

"Yes, I am the painter," Wren answered. She reached out and held Arlen by his wrists. "The Fremont painting — did you see a woman carrying it?"

"Not only did I see her, I saw the whole scene. I saw some madman preacher slice the painting with a knife. I heard bells and thunder coming out of the painting. I saw the woman fall. I saw that damned amphibious Duck-wagon rolling down the hill toward her. I covered her with my coat." He paused a moment, then added, "I think I fell in love with her."

Arlen was speaking rapid-fire now as he told Wren the whole story of that day, of his life, and how that painting had remade him.

"I thought I had left most of my true self back in Afghanistan, and the rest of it died with my son years ago. There's something in your paintings ..." He spoke softly. "What is it? Where's it coming from? How are you doing this?"

Wren shook her head, unable to even imagine an answer.

"Well, whatever it is has caused me to reunite with my true self. Something strong and sweet is living in those colors," he said, gesturing with a nod toward the massive painted wall.

Arlen's story was interrupted when they heard a car arrive. *Grace!*

She came out of Gordon's car like a sudden thunderstorm, running straight at Arlen as he and Wren emerged from the barn.

"It's you! Who the hell are you? Why are you stalking me?" Grace growled.

Wren put herself between Grace and Arlen, holding Grace by her upper arms and hoping she was strong enough.

"I'm not stalking you or even following you. You're some kind of nurse…what are you doing here?" Arlen spoke calmly. If warm maple syrup had a voice, this would be its sound.

"Well, shit, Mr. I-keep-turning-up-but-I'm-not-a-stalker, I live here. How about you?"

Thunder rumbled in the distance, moving closer.

Wren entered the discussion: "Grace, this is Arlen Divine. He was with Julia when she was hurt at the parade, and he's trying to help her now. Julia sent him here."

Grace looked like she had swallowed a bug. She adjusted her collar and tugged on the sleeves of her blouse. "Oh. Okay, sorry, Mr. Divine. I'm a little edgy." Grace tugged at her hair, making it stick out from her head at odd angles. "Did you see Julia in the hospital, too?"

"No," Arlen answered, "I couldn't get past Attila the Desk Nurse…and then there was the small detail of the Incredible Hulk in a suit sitting outside her door."

"Grace, I take it that you did get in to see Julia? Arlen, I guess you're not quite as clever as the inscrutable Miss Grace," Wren said, looking hard at Grace.

Softening, Grace said, "Clever? Not overly clever. I'm quite humble, really. My ego is just big enough to enable my true self to accomplish wonders."

Wren felt a cosmic window fly open when Grace said *true self.* She felt something almost solid enough to grab. She felt completely and absolutely present.

The three were standing together in silence when Gordon called out from his car, "Hey, Grace, can I go home now?"

Grace startled, having forgotten all about the poor fellow. "Gordon, I'm so sorry! Why don't you come in for a little dinner?"

"Thank you, Grace, but I've got to get home and feed my dogs."

Grace walked to the car and tried to press two twenty-dollar bills into Gordon's hand, but he raised his hands in refusal, looking more like he'd just been arrested than like he'd been offered cash. Grace returned the money to her scrubs pocket and shrugged. Gordon favored them all with a smile. With two front teeth missing, one from the bottom and one from the top, he looked older than his thirty-five years.

"See you later, pretty lady," he said, and drove away.

Grace, turning to Arlen and Wren, said, "And that's Gordon: simple, honest, kind, and, for the record, frequently very stoned. I'm starving. Let's cook something, and then I want to hear your stories. Arlen, how did you find this place?"

Arlen smiled, tipping his head a little sideways. "You just have to be polite to the right waitress in the right diner. Ask, and you shall receive; seek, and you will find."

Arlen, Grace, and Wren walked toward the house and never noticed the tiny car parked across the road in the deep shade of towering fir trees.

Eliot Stern, meanwhile, felt he had stumbled into something big, something to do with the incident at the parade. Maybe he had even found Wren Willow Hendrix. He drove to town and checked into a private cottage at a charming tourist hotel. Surely this little tourist town had to have a decent whisky bar . . .

"Who needs a glass of wine?" Grace inquired while pulling glasses from the cabinet.

Arlen asked for orange juice, and explained that until he had spent a couple of days with Wren's damaged painting, he would have happily consumed all the alcohol in the house, pissed in the potted plant in the corner, passed out on the couch, and later barfed all over the carpet.

Grace squinted at him and said, "Right. Orange juice it is."

In the kitchen, Grace washed vegetables and Arlen cut up potatoes. Wren, exhausted from her work, fell into a short but deep nap on the couch.

She woke to her shoulder being gently shaken.

"Food's ready, Wren," Grace said softly. "You were sleeping so beautifully that I almost didn't want to wake you."

Wren had been having a strange dream. She was running from Agent Bitters. He was running awkwardly in overlarge yellow clown shoes while trying to straighten his necktie. It didn't seem like the kind of dream that was going to lead to any great insight if it ran to its conclusion.

Wren blinked and stretched and smiled at Grace. She was happy to be away from the dream, happy to be here in this place, and very happy to be looking at Grace.

By the time they were halfway through eating the perfectly steamed potatoes covered with Parmesan, along with brussels sprouts and artichoke hearts with olive oil, balsamic vinegar, and basil, they were beginning to learn about one another. Soon it felt like they had known one another for many years, as they told stories of their lives.

Arlen described his life again for Grace as he had done for Wren. "I don't know what there was in that torn painting that made me change everything. How the hell does a painting make the sound of bells? *Something* sure as hell reached deep into me, though."

Grace leaned toward Arlen and asked acidly, "You didn't find God, or get born again, or tripe like that, did you?"

"No, Grace." Arlen's maple-syrup voice was now sliding down a spectacular stack of metaphysical pancakes. "It was bigger than that, and a whole lot less easy to describe. More abstract than the long-bearded daddy god of the fear-based religions. I'll let you know when I know what to call it."

"More abstract? I'm getting a mental picture of Salvador Dali presiding over melted pearly gates," said Grace. "Ready for coffee?" She got up, then stopped and turned toward Wren and Arlen.

"You know, it occurs to me that I am the only one around here who has yet to see one of these paintings."

Arlen stood up and took Grace's right hand. Wren took her left, and they walked her directly to the barn.

The old barn's dark-green door creaked on its rusting hinges as Wren pushed it open. The space was somehow different from earlier, the late afternoon sun giving the interior of the barn the aura of a cathedral or ancient ruins. The drying paint hung a bitter fragrance in the air.

Wren put a hand on Grace's shoulder and said, "Grace, this is going to be unlike anything you have experienced while looking at art — or doing anything else, probably. Okay? I'm going to turn you around to face the painting now."

Grace allowed Wren to turn her toward the painted wall and she could not contain her surprise. "Oh!" Grace gasped. An impossible silence came over them as the painting held them all spellbound. The only sound was Grace's quick and shallow breathing. Then Grace collapsed to the floor, out cold.

She regained consciousness almost immediately, laughing softly as she came around to the sound of Wren and Arlen arguing. "No, raise her feet above her heart!" "No, you're supposed to keep her head up!"

Grace mumbled, "Nobody ever gets that right. I'm OK, you two, I'm OK. Wow. Just...wow."

Arlen and Wren sat on the barn floor with Grace as she remained reclining, trying to absorb and understand what she had seen. She tried to tell them what it had done to her, tried to grasp and express the phantoms of detail. She rubbed her palms across her face as they helped her sit up.

Finally, all she could say was, "That was different."

Still sitting, they all turned their backs to the painting — not daring to look again right now, all struggling to understand their own reactions to the painting.

"So?" said Arlen, "How do you feel now?"

"I feel," Grace answered uncertainly, "like I just touched something I'm not sure I was supposed to touch...or, maybe something I should have been touching, holding close to me, my whole life. It's beautiful. I feel deeply content and peaceful. You're right, Arlen. It's big and difficult to name. This is going to take a little time to digest. Now I understand why Homeland Security and Billy Joe Bobb want to get their hands on you, Wren. There's some big, strange, impenetrable energy here."

Wren and Arlen helped Grace to her feet, and they walked out of the barn toward the house without even a glance back at the painting.

Grace brewed coffee, moving as though in a dream, and said, "We should make a plan to spring Julia before they haul her off somewhere she'll never be able to get out of."

"Really? 'Spring'? Have you been watching old gangster movies?" Wren grinned at Grace.

"Rescue, then. Bust out. Liberate."

Arlen poured coffee into three cups and said sternly, "More like kidnap, in this case. Someone set a guard outside her door, and hospital security is acting like a hound dog sniffing out rabbits. And then there's that wacko preacher; I wouldn't put it past him to try something. So whatever we do, we should do it soon. Anybody got any ideas?"

Wren was grinning like a cat that had just devoured the proverbial canary.

"OK, Wren," said Grace, "it appears you have a thought."

Wren took the cup of coffee offered by Arlen.

"I have many thoughts," Wren said with a grand sweeping skyward gesture of her right arm, "Sometimes my thoughts are like meteor showers: just a whole lot of fireworks zooming through the darkness and then, poof! — burned out. Sometimes, however, they make it through the atmosphere and light up the whole landscape." She stopped talking, arms still outstretched, hands spread wide to the heavens.

Wren sat back and drank some coffee. She looked up from her cup to see Arlen and Grace frowning at her. Wren smiled a mischievous tight-lipped grin. "The idea I have for rescuing Julia is one of the latter. A real rock-'n'-roll light show."

Grace's farm became a construction zone. Arlen borrowed Grace's pickup truck and drove to town to buy lumber and screws. Wren quickly sketched out the last missing details of her plan. Grace hurried into town after Arlen returned, buying uniforms and dis-guises for the three of them.

They were concentrating so deeply, working so diligently, they never noticed the little red Smart car driving by, not too fast, not too slow. They did not see the driver hunched over the wheel, watching them. They simply prepared for their mission.

After three days of preparation, they were ready.

That night they ate dinner in silence until Grace spoke. "Gordon will be here with his Rambler at dawn. He'll stay with the car, so he'll be ready to haul us away quickly and won't be involved in the abduction if something goes haywire."

"That's good. I sure hope the desk nurse has forgotten that James Morrison stopped by before," Arlen said through a mouthful of sautéed asparagus spears.

"At least you didn't tell them you were Elvis," Grace chided.

"I almost called myself Sonny Bono 'cause of the 'stache — last time I was sober, he was still alive."

Wren vigorously shook salt on her potato salad, paused, then shook some more. "You know," she said casually, "even if they haven't forgotten you, we've got our disguises; and we'll have the one thing that people who have to work long hours on their feet can't resist…" She suddenly dissolved into giggles.

Grace smiled at Wren, shaking her head. She raised her water glass and declared, "Let's drink to humankind's insatiable appetite, and a successful kidnapping."

Glasses clinked musically and the conspirators drank the sweet wine of optimism.

Chapter 23

Eliot Stern picked absently at a stray whisker he'd missed while shaving that morning. To be fair, it had been well before dawn, and he'd lacked the will to face the laser beam of the bathroom's fluorescent light. Leaning forward in the seat of his tiny car, he anxiously watched for signs of life at the farm. Eliot had parked at a safe distance — about fifty yards up the adjacent road. He felt that he was invisible enough on this semi-rural hillside with its sparse traffic and deep shadows.

The three people he was observing were so intent on their project that they never spared a glance for any passing traffic.

Eliot sipped at a cup of evil gas station coffee. He winced, and leaned back in his seat. *Nothing is going to happen this early*, he thought, and reached to start his car.

A light came on in the house. Eliot froze. Farmers get up early, so this was probably no big deal. More lights. He watched as the man from the RV came out of the house with three duffle bags and set them on the ground behind the old pickup truck.

The road and trees lit up, illuminated by headlights as a vehicle came up the road toward the farm. The headlights bobbed and swerved and flashed through Eliot's car. Fearing he had been spotted, he involuntarily tensed and held his breath. The car swung into the farm's driveway and the headlights went dark. Eliot was able to breathe again. A man got out from behind the wheel, opened the back door of the car, and then returned to the driver's seat. The sky was light enough now that Eliot could see that the car was an ancient station wagon, yellow and faded green and rust. From all appearances this could have been a classic car if it had been carefully preserved instead of being left outdoors and used constantly — but instead, it was a bonafide living junk heap.

Mustache Man came out of the house dressed in navy blue coveralls, loaded the duffle bags and some other stuff into the station wagon, and got in the front passenger seat. Five minutes later two women came out of the house and got in the back seat. Eliot observed that both women were also wearing dark coveralls, and he was pretty sure that one of those women was Wren Willow Hendrix, painter of the bizarre painting Ms. Perdot had shown him at the Hux-ley-Lavelle Gallery and the other one he'd glimpsed briefly at the Solstice Parade before blacking out. The old car came to life with a loud whinny, backed out of the driveway, and rambled down the road whence it came.

"OK," Eliot whispered to himself, "I guess it's time to go exploring."

He waited to see if any more courage was coming his way, then gave up and drove right up to the barn. Turning off his engine and lights, Eliot sat looking around at the farm buildings and then got out of the car. The peaceful silence was almost too much for him — completely unnatural. He went around the back of the barn and nearly pissed himself from shock as three large goats charged toward him. He coughed out a laugh once he realized there was a sturdy fence between him and his horned attackers.

He strolled up to the house as though he had been invited. Trying the door, he found it locked. He wasn't surprised, and he had a journalist's hunch that what he really wanted to see was in the barn, anyway. As he turned from the house, sunlight pierced through the tall trees, nearly blinding him, and he staggered backward.

Donning his polarized sunglasses, Eliot walked toward the barn. He stopped a moment, bending to smell the perfect red roses growing along the path. As he cupped his hand around a bloom, a swirl of images flooded his memory. There were roses raining from the sky...a magnificent rose in his hand...his body freed from gravity, flying with the bees. It was the painting. He stood up straight again and slid his hands into his pockets, as though afraid the roses might clutch at him. Eliot looked up at the clear azure sky, and then quickly back again at the roses.

"Hmph," he grunted, frowning a little — and then his lips formed a slightly confused smile. His mind might be doing strange things after his visit to the gallery, but so far, at least it seemed to be doing rather *nice* strange things.

Thus fortified by the Ghost of Paintings Past, Eliot swung open the barn door. The huge space was filled with beams of clear bright light and deep shadows that were almost impenetrable with his dark sunglasses on. His head was bathed in a shaft of sunlight, and the raised board of the threshold was in shadow; Eliot tripped inelegantly over it, falling to his knees on the barn floor. He turned to his right as he stood up, raising his sunglasses to better scrutinize his pants and tailored shirt. His shades fell back down to his nose as he cursed and brushed dirt and sawdust from his expensive clothing. Eliot was blowing dust from a sleeve when he picked up the unmistakable odor of fresh paint. He paused with his right hand still holding his shirtsleeve and turned to his left, toward the sunlight, toward the painted barn wall. He looked up at the huge painting and his eyes opened wide.

"Oh, oh. I, wow, I...aaaahhhh," Eliot stammered, and then released a yowling scream that tapered off into a sigh as he slowly collapsed to the floor.

After Jeanette's demonstration at the gallery, Eliot Stern would have known that if he had only removed his sunglasses he might have met with a completely different outcome; but he'd had no way of knowing that Wren Willow Hendrix had broadened her canvas beyond...well...beyond canvas. The polarized lenses magnified the

arcane power of Wren's paintings, and this was a painting of Brob-
dingnagian proportion. Perhaps his episode with Jeanette Perdot
in the Huxley-Lavelle Gallery's back room had primed his cranial
pump to extra sensitivity, or maybe it had pushed his cerebral cortex
off axis just enough to make him ready to topple over.

Some would say he snapped. Some would say he lost it. Some
would say the dude tripped out, or just went ape-shit crazy. What
would Eliot say? From now on Eliot Stern, the former master of
expository prose, would not have all that much to say at all — and
in any case he didn't seem to feel he had any problem that needed
to be talked about.

While Grace, Wren and Arlen were on their rescue mission, this
was the scene at the barn: After Eliot hit the floor, he sat looking
beatifically at the huge painting. Each thread of paint pulled him
farther out of his mind, each splash of red alarmed him, and each
arc of blue awakened every sadness he had ever known. Eliot cried
out and wept, purging all sorrow. He took his sunglasses off and
threw them at the painting. He pulled off his blue and gray striped
necktie and dabbed his eyes with it. Buttons popping as he pulled it
off, his starched white shirt became little more than a handkerchief
fit for Paul Bunyan.

Eliot reclined on the barn floor and gazed at the painting for the
first time without his polarized lenses. It was too late...too far in,
too far gone, or too far out, it no longer mattered to Eliot how he
viewed the painting. Had he and the painting somehow merged,
become one? The barn was heating up as the sun's warmth inten-
sified. Eliot peeled off his eight-hundred-dollar Burberry trousers
and flung them onto the workbench atop two greasy screwdrivers
and a pry bar.

Eliot Stern happily rolled, just like a child rolling on a grassy hill,
from one end of the barn to the other and back, stopping frequently
along the way to look into the depths of the painting.

With all his awareness of sorrow, frustration, outrage, and anger removed, the painting now went to work on filling those spaces in Eliot's psyche with absolute joy. Sometimes he would break into great gales of laughter, then settle and watch the painting for half an hour before rolling along for a few more minutes.

Then, of course, there was the music. Only Eliot heard it, unless maybe the goats and the chickens outside did too — nobody asked them, and they didn't volunteer anything. At first it was the tinkling little bells that he had heard before, then a resounding pealing of bells of every pitch and tone. Great brazen chords assailed his eardrums and filled his mind. After some time passed — Eliot had no idea how much — the bells modulated and became the sweet airy lilt of wooden flutes.

"Flutes," Eliot grinned up at the painting. "Flutes!"

If you could have seen his eyes you would have been amazed. All the colors from the painting were swirling, lifting, falling, softening, blurring, sharpening, dancing in his eyes.

A reflection? Maybe. Maybe not.

Chapter 24

Gordon waited at the back of the hospital, right beneath a sign that read "NO STANDING". He was not a city dweller, and he figured he was safe because he was clearly *sitting* in his old green and yellow station wagon. He was completely clueless about the mission Grace and her friends were on, but he was content because he had a box of assorted donuts to work through while he waited for his passengers to visit someone at the hospital.

He had to admit that he thought *something* about this trip was a little odd. Grace and her friends had loaded his car with duffle bags and some bits of painted plywood, and one piece that looked like a home-made backboard, straps and all. Gordon knew that those were for serious accident victims...but he was just the driver, so he didn't ask any questions.

Then he drove the group to Seattle and they stopped at Rings of Saturn Donuts. Donuts were good and normal, but he was surprised to see Arlen, Grace, and Wren walk out of the store each carrying three double-dozen boxes. Gordon thought getting so many donuts was pretty weird, until Grace announced that one box was his — an entire large box of fresh assorted donuts just for him. He broke the speed laws on the way to the hospital. With so many donuts in the car, he could smell their greasy, sugary goodness right through the cardboard boxes; the air had enough fat molecules to coat his nostrils as he breathed. Gordon could have sworn there was already sugar on his lips as he licked them. Those donuts were a siren song.

Things got *really* strange, in Gordon's opinion, when they arrived at the hospital. Grace pulled the backboard out of the station wagon and laid it on the sidewalk. Gordon got out of the car to watch as Arlen opened two of the duffle bags and pulled out several pieces of shiny painted plywood, assembling them into a large box right there on the sidewalk — a box that fit perfectly on top of the backboard and was the same color as a pink frosted donut with multicolor sprinkles. Wren draped the box with an elegant lace-edged table runner and set all the donut boxes on top of it. Except, of course, the box reserved for Gordon. He was drooling like his dogs.

Grace opened the third duffle bag and took out wigs, glasses, makeup, and cans of Colorista hair spray. The threesome transformed before Gordon's eyes as he ate his first donut: He started with a nice, traditional raspberry-jelly-filled. Finally, as he eyed a cruller as his possible next victim, his passengers peeled off their coveralls, revealing that underneath they were dressed like waiters, in black pants and white shirts. Gordon bit into the cruller while he watched Grace and her friends transform into whatever it was that they were becoming. It was like watching a movie.

"OK, Gordon. Wait here. If you have to move the car, come right back here as soon as you can," Grace said, giving him a serious look and grasping him by the shoulders.

Gordon nodded, wide-eyed, a little powdered sugar dusting the left corner of his mouth.

"Don't worry," Grace continued calmly, "we're just delivering donuts to the staff. From a grateful patient."

"I've got it nailed," Gordon said confidently, not realizing that he was expected to be worried. "I'll be right here."

Grace slung the third duffle over her shoulder and ran to hold the door while Wren and Arlen walked through carrying the board and the plywood box laden with donuts.

Gordon got back behind the wheel and smiled down wistfully at the delectable mother lode of fat and sugar in the box on his passenger seat.

Grace quickly found a gurney. Wren and Arlen went to work fitting it with the backboard/box/donut delivery system. Then they wheeled it along the hospital corridors, calm and steady and smiling. Assailed by the usual unpleasant hospital smells — perhaps the most offensive ones were those emanating from the kitchen — each member of the rescue team held their own memories conjured by those odors.

Arlen was shaking a little, but said, "Keep smiling, gals. We're going to have some happy customers."

Riding the elevator up to Julia's floor, Wren looked at the donut boxes. "Man, I could eat a whole box of those things myself," she said.

Grace and Arlen glared at her.

"When I'm nervous, I eat, remember? I just don't get nervous very often — it's fattening."

"Huh. I get that. I used to drink when I got nervous. Or when I wasn't nervous, for that matter," Arlen grinned.

The little elevator bell chimed and the doors opened with a *whoosh*. They pushed the gurney out into the chaos of the hospital floor. Observing that the guard was still at his post in front of Julia's room, they rolled the gurney in that direction.

Grace shook a tiny bell that had been a Christmas-tree ornament in its previous incarnation, and to the accompaniment of its shrill metallic tinkling she called out, "May I have your attention, please."

All movement stopped. All eyes turned to Grace. Other than her big smile and her bright-green eyes, she looked utterly nondescript in her disguise. Perfect.

"We are here with a gift from a grateful former patient. He wants to remain anonymous, but I'm sure you all know who he is."

Ahhh, the hefty power of suggestion… The staff exchanged giggles and nods and knowing looks. Each of them mentally revisited memories of particularly irascible recent patients, and each was certain they knew who the mysterious benefactor had to be. Without ever saying a name, they all seemed to come to a silent consensus about the grateful patient's identity; they chattered on and on about how wonderful a person he really was, despite all their earlier gripes about his being a total fucking pain in the ass.

This woman's a genius, Wren thought.

Arlen was opening boxes with the help of two middle-aged nurses eager to get down to business with the powdered, jelly-filled, custard-filled, chocolate-covered, frosted, sprinkled, maple-bacon — and, of course, plain glazed doughy delights. Wren began surreptitiously placing opened boxes of donuts on horizontal surfaces farther from Julia's room as Arlen inched down the hallway, rolling the gurney toward the armed guard. Wren caught Grace's eye and gave one sharp nod.

With banter and smiles still going, Grace walked toward Julia's room as if it was the next thing the donut crew was supposed to do.

"Hey, officer, you look like you could use a tasty treat," Grace called to the guard. "What's your favorite — jelly? Chocolate glazed?"

Looking up from the morning newspaper at the sound of Grace's voice, the guard tensed, showed them his permanent practiced-in-the-mirror tough-guy scowl, dropped his paper to the floor, and stood up. He was a six-foot-five mass of muscle with a waxy blonde crew cut, wearing a shiny gray suit cut loose around his broad shoulders.

"Seriously," Grace went on without a pause, "they're fabulous donuts, and if you want one you'd better take one before the voracious hordes down the hall vacuum them all up."

Wren and Arlen arrived with the gurney and the promised donuts. To their absolute amazement, the guard smiled and looked into the box, obviously debating between custard and glazed. As he reached for a custard-filled, Grace set her duffle bag on the floor, unzipped it, and pulled out the painting that Arlen had brought to the farm after taking it from Julia's hands. It was a scarred veteran now, a proven performer even when it was torn and battered; and Wren had made careful repairs, tested it on herself, and pronounced it ready for battle. Grace held it up so it would be at the guard's eye level as soon as he took his eyes off the donut box.

Looking up from his unexpected bonus directly into the painting, the guard froze, custard dripping down the front of his suit jacket. As his gaze remained riveted on the painting, the carbo-hydrate-pushing kidnappers could see his muscles relax and his expression soften from mere ravenous hunger into sympathy and compassion. Then a twinkle of absolute joy lit his eye, and his donut fell to the floor.

Arlen stepped forward, took the docile guard's arm, and led him into Julia's room. "Come with me, pal," Arlen purred. "Every-thing's going to be beautiful."

Grace moved with them, keeping the painting always in the guard's sight. Wren checked behind them to make sure no one was watching, then hurried the gurney through the door and scooted it up to Julia's bedside. She closed the door behind her.

Wren looked at her friend and was horrified by all the tubes and wires and casts. She wondered how they were ever going to be able to move Julia without causing her enormous pain or severing some important IV fluid line.

Julia opened her eyes. Even though her broken jaw was wired tightly closed and attached to a metal cage, she somehow made her eyes smile at Wren. Wren blinked away tears and smiled back. Behind her, in the bathroom, she could hear Arlen ripping off long strips of silver duct tape.

Grace began deftly checking wires and tubes, deciding what could be left behind and what was needed for the trip. She grumbled about the wires in Julia's jaw and the medieval torture device around her head. "Later. Deal with it later," she growled to herself. She motioned with her head to Wren, and the two of them lifted the box from the gurney and set it on the floor.

Grace leaned close, her lips about three inches from Julia's ear. "Julia, I'm going to give you a little extra pain relief, OK? Then we're going to slide you onto this backboard and hide you under the donut table and get you the hell out of here," Grace whispered hoarsely.

Julia made her eyes smile again and made a sound that was probably laughter, but sounded more like oatmeal cooking.

Arlen came out of the bathroom carrying the painting, and Wren stifled a giggle. The guard, duct tape over his mouth, was securely taped to the toilet, pants around his ankles. Curiously, he looked absolutely contented with his lot. The door's locking mechanism made a metallic "ping" as Arlen pulled it closed.

Arlen hurried over to the bed and put his hands beneath the sheet under Julia's shoulders, her caged and wired head lying vulnerable in front of him. "It is gonna be all right, Julia," he promised, his eyes holding her hopeful gaze.

Wren grasped the sheet under Julia's plaster-casted legs. Grace stood over Julia and swiftly presented the painting. Julia's pupils dilated like a cat's eyes in the dark. Setting the canvas down, Grace got her hands under the sheet at Julia's hips.

"On the count of three, hoist," Grace said. "One, two, *three!*"

In spite of her height and the weight of casts, Julia was light enough (or their adrenaline was running strong enough) that Wren thought they might overshoot the gurney as they lifted her. Grace gathered drip bags, catheter bags, tubes, and wires, and dumped the works unceremoniously on top of Julia and between her legs on the backboard. Wren and Arlen slid the "donut table" over the whole arrangement. The box was lightweight and was open at one end so that Julia could breathe easily. The lacy table runner was draped neatly over the pink-frosted-with-sprinkles box, hiding the open end; and a single remaining box of donuts remained open on the tablecloth as they wheeled the gurney out of the room and headed for the elevator.

Wren pressed the call button, worried that this had all been too easy. The elevator doors swooshed open and she breathed a sigh of relief that the elevator was empty. *Home free!* Wren was thinking, when a man's large hand grabbed the door and held it open.

"Hey," his voice boomed authoritatively, "what have you got there?"

The man's white coat was embroidered "Dr. Charlton, Chief of Surgery". His shiny bald head gleamed as though it had been recently polished. Dr. Charlton walked with a cane and wore a brace on one leg. He was also wearing a heavy air of authority that made Arlen and Wren shrink into themselves, while Grace stood taller, shoulders back.

Wren was paralyzed, and could not utter a word. Arlen looked as though he might lose control of his bladder. But Grace simply smiled and said, "These are all that's left of the donuts sent from your anonymous, but very grateful, patient."

Dr. Charlton scowled, "Hell of a gift from a heart patient, wouldn't you say? Anonymous, my ass... I'll make sure Benway gets a couple of the ones with powdered sugar on them." He laughed a loud, deeply officious laugh, took the entire box of donuts, and left. The door slid shut and they all started breathing again.

The green and yellow 1959 Rambler station wagon sat idling near the hospital side entrance. Gordon was admiring the creamy texture and enchanting flavor of his fifth jelly donut — blueberry, this time — when a meaty fist pounded on his window.

"Hey, pal, you can't stand here."

Gordon allowed some jelly to escape and it stuck in his beard stubble. He was confused. He was sitting, not standing!

The cop leaned in and growled, "Move the damn car. Now!"

Gordon placed his donut in the box and put the car in gear. As he looked up from his abandoned sugar bomb, he caught sight of the hospital's sliding double doors opening. Grace, Wren, and Arlen were wheeling a hospital gurney quickly toward his car. Gordon was not a particularly deep thinker, but he could move fast and his brain was currently running on 5.5-donut rocket fuel. He snatched up the box of donuts — eighteen tasty gems he now would never get to know intimately — jumped out of the car, and thrust the box into the cop's arms.

The police officer stepped back in surprise, looking at the box.

"My friends are here, and we have to go now. More donut deliveries." Gordon paused a moment, then reached into the box and retrieved his half-eaten jelly donut. "Sorry about that one. I got hungry waiting."

Gordon opened the back of the station wagon and helped the donut crew move the backboard with Julia and her tubes and bags and the box and the lacy table runner. The whole assembly slid easily into the back of the ancient car, the lace snagging momentarily on the rear gate as they got it turned the right way. Grace placed the painting, safely back in its duffle bag, next to the box. Wren closed the back of the station wagon. They abandoned the gurney on the sidewalk, and they all calmly got into the car. Wren waved cheerfully to the policeman as they lurched down the street toward a clean escape.

The cop stood there a moment looking at the now-vacant illegal parking spot and wondered what the hell had just happened. He lifted the lid of the box. He breathed in the sugary aroma, smiled, and reached inside.

Chapter 25

The Reverend Billy Joe Bobb bided his time before returning to the hospital. This time, he would try a different approach; he would go in through the side door, and use stealth — Proverbs 24:6 and all that. The Lord would show him the way to crush these fools, these unwitting tools of the Devil.

And then, miraculously, God made smooth his path (Isaiah 26:7) as he left his minibus and walked around the side of the hospital. That smoothness took the form of a 1959 Rambler station wagon where four people were loading something bulky into the back; it looked like a coffin, except that even in these decadent latter days coffins weren't generally painted like a pink frosted donut with sprinkles. A policeman stood beside the old car, devoting his full attention to a large donut box.

As the Reverend watched, the group slid the box off a hospital gurney and maneuvered it into the back of the car. A lacy tablecloth covering the box caught on something, and for a brief moment the painting-demon's raven curls and metal-framed face were revealed to him.

"Oh, dear Lord," he gasped, "it's that woman with the Devil's painting!"

Self-righteous hatred percolated in Billy Joe Bobb's uneven mind. He would never forget how that woman had humiliated him in front of his followers, in front of the whole world. His fractured concept of reality split further when he realized that the tall fellow with the mustache had also been at the Duck disaster. A conspiracy! A coven! And all the players were here, practically within his anointed grasp. Billy Joe Bobb had just been given a Divine gift.

He ran to his minibus, confident that he could keep up with the decrepit old Rambler. He would destroy these abominations. Surely a castle was being built in heaven for him even now! Reverend Billy Joe Bobb, leader of The Repentance Undeviant Tabernacle, smiled and gloated, immersing himself in the sins of pride and wrath.

Gordon drove at a steady pace. When he asked if they were going to make a regular thing out of this donut delivery service, Grace told him only that their friend was being held against her will and they were bringing her home. There would be no more donuts.

"Don't worry, Gordon," Grace said, "Julia is heavily sedated and will be out of it for a few hours, but she'll be all right."

Wren wondered if that much sedation was safe for Julia, but kept silent. Grace had pulled back the table runner so Julia's head was visible, and her pulse and breathing were easily monitored. She kept a steady focus on Julia's wellbeing as they drove.

Wren was watching Arlen, who sat in the front passenger seat. He kept glancing in the side mirror and was constantly turning around to look at the cars behind them.

Suddenly Arlen turned and said, "Gordon, let's take the freeway up to the Edmonds Ferry. I don't think we'll make the Bainbridge ferry from downtown."

Wren studied Arlen's face. Something was wrong.

Gordon dutifully drove up to the freeway on-ramp and headed north at sixty miles per hour. Arlen's covert surveillance was barely perceptible, but he was clearly tense. His eyes flitted like birds to the right mirror, to the left mirror, then a quick shot over his shoulder, out the back window.

After a few minutes, Wren could no longer stand it. "We're being followed, aren't we, Arlen," she said firmly.

"Yes, Wren, I believe we are," Arlen said, looking straight ahead.

Gordon panicked at that, and sped up.

"Whoa, Gordon," Arlen said quietly, "let's go easy. Let 'em catch up. I want to see who's so damned interested in us."

For fourteen miles they played a game of cat and mouse, with Gordon alternately slowing to fifty-five and then speeding to sixty-five. The Rambler began to shimmy alarmingly at sixty-five, and Wren worried that rods and gears and hoses might come shooting out of the engine like Roman Candles.

Looking back, just as they changed lanes, Wren caught a glimpse of the pursuit: a dented, dirty, light-blue minibus. She couldn't see any passengers in the minibus, and couldn't tell if the long-haired driver was a man or a woman.

"We'll get a better look at them soon if they follow us off the freeway onto the ferry," Grace observed.

The battered minibus and the Rambler station wagon arrived at the Edmonds ferry dock together. Both drivers bought tickets and drove into line. Gordon drummed his fingers nervously on the steering wheel, and Arlen craned his neck to look at the minibus behind them.

"I still can't see who's driving," Arlen said. "OK, a boat's coming into dock. Now we shall see who's so interested in us. Gordon, maybe it's just somebody admiring your car."

Gordon grinned a gap-toothed smile and drove straight down the middle of the boat, parking behind a new Chevy pickup with lots of shiny plastic faux chrome. A black van with "Ed's Bottom Painting" emblazoned on the sides pulled up beside them on the driver's side.

"Boat hulls," Arlen observed. "That's what bottom painting means. The guy paints boat hulls."

"I know, Arlen. Thanks. I have a passing acquaintance with boats, and even their hulls," Grace said, stifling a seaworthy grin.

The minibus rolled into the lane on the Rambler's passenger side, moving past the station wagon just slow enough for Arlen to get a good look at the driver. "My, my," he said with a toothy smile, "If it isn't the Reverend Billy Joe Bobb, head of The Repentance Undeviant Tabernacle. I don't believe it. We can only guess what he's up to."

Wren slumped down in her seat and Grace tensed her jaw.

"Who the heck is that?" Gordon asked.

Wren answered, "He's a slimy snake oil peddler. Billy Joe Bobb thinks the creator of the universe whispers sweet nothings in his ear. Only in his case, the nothings aren't very sweet."

Arlen rubbed his face with his palms. "That bastard is the reason Julia's lying back there in the shape she's in."

As Gordon eased the Rambler into Grace's driveway, Wren watched Billy Joe Bobb drive by.

Arlen chuckled, "Just a guy out for a joyride in the country."

Gordon braked suddenly when he spotted Eliot Stern's Smart car parked in the driveway. "Looks like you've got some company, and they came in a clown car," he said.

The tiniest car Wren had ever seen without a child playing with it sat directly in front of Grace's barn. There was no driver in sight, but the barn door was ajar and a faint blue light streamed out.

Grace pushed the group forward, saying, "We'll investigate that later. Right now we've got to get Julia settled in."

Wren was too tired and too concerned for Julia's health to be alarmed about an intruder, especially one in a car that small.

Julia's friends moved her so carefully that at times the backboard appeared to be floating rather than being carried. The box that had hidden her now lay discarded beside the Smart car. Arlen stashed their duffle bags in his Winnebago before following the others into the house.

With hanging IV bags, tubes, and Julia's spectacular casts and wires providing the ambience, Grace's living room was instantly transformed into a mini medical center. They had rented a hospital bed before driving to Seattle, adjustable in ways reminiscent of origami, along with plenty of IV poles and other gadgets and supplies.

Wren brought a chair next to the bed and sat there, her hand on Julia's arm. "She looks so fragile, so vulnerable," she said softly.

Grace adjusted Julia's plaster-encased legs. "She is indeed vulnerable right now, so we're all going to have to take shifts playing nurse. She's going to wake up and need things — water, kefir through a straw, drugs for pain management. This is not going to be easy, but it's still better than having her taken by some government agency. Fortunately, I've got a friend who is a surgeon, and she's offered to help us over the next couple of weeks, even without knowing all the details. We got lucky on that one."

They all hovered, watching Julia's drug-induced slumber.

Gordon kept looking out toward the barn. When his agitation drew no attention, he said, "Umm… Shouldn't we go out there and see who's in the barn?"

Arlen walked over and put his arm around Gordon's shoulder. "Gordon, I think we've taken enough of your time today. You should get home and look after your dogs. OK?"

Gordon frowned a little, then seemed to digest Arlen's words and smiled. "Yeah. You're right. Well, OK, listen, I'm just glad I could help you all," he said brightly. He said his goodbyes, scuffed through the gravel and got into his old station wagon. The ancient Rambler disappeared down the road with a loud backfire.

Wren said, "I think Gordon was right. Do we have any idea who that is in the barn?"

Arlen shook his head. "I've got no idea." He looked at Grace.

Grace looked at Julia. "She looks fine for now, and she's going to sleep for a while yet," she said.

"In that case," said Arlen, "let's go greet our guest."

Crunching across the gravel path, the trio crept toward the barn door. Grace pushed the door wide open. Avoiding being entranced by the painted wall was easy, because their attention was fully captured by the naked man dancing in the middle of the barn. He was singing "... Wonder Woman saves the day" in a nasal monotone as he spun in slow circles. Then he extended his arms like the wings of a malfunctioning 787, changed his song to "oooh-oooh-oooh", tipped his left hand toward the floor, leveled off as he ran away from the group, tipped his right hand toward the floor, leveled off again and ran back toward the trio, his mouth in the shape of an "o".

As the naked man turned back toward the door, he stopped his imaginary flight and dropped his hands to his sides. He appeared to be trying to work out how these people had gotten into his private universe. He stopped his flying song and his face opened into a broad white-toothed smile.

"Do any of you have a flute?" the nude fellow asked. "I think I might be more of a flute man. Now that I have an audience, it is abundantly clear to me that I'm not a singer." This struck him as extremely humorous and he began to laugh so hard that he choked.

While he attempted to compose himself, Grace spied the man's pants and underwear on the workbench. She handed them to him, inviting him to put them on.

"Who are you?" Wren asked. "What are you doing in here?"

"My name is Eliot Stern," Eliot said as he put one foot into the wrong pants leg. He began to hop in a circle then fell on his derriere and rolled onto his back, again laughing uncontrollably. It was an unfortunate thing to witness.

"I doubt that I'll ever be able to un-see this," Grace commented.

Arlen and Grace helped the poor buffoon to his feet and held him up while he successfully negotiated the fabric, the button, and the zipper.

"Eliot Stern, reporter," said Eliot with a salute. "But, that's 'journalist' to you. Actually," he continued, raising a finger for emphasis, "that's 'former journalist' to you. To you..." he sang. "Happy birthday to you..."

A little more singing, then another outburst of laughter and another choking cough.

Arlen looked Eliot in the eye and asked, "Mr. Stern, how long have you been looking at that wall?" Arlen himself was careful not to look at the painted wall, gesturing toward it only with a nod of his head.

Eliot dramatically raised his arm and looked at his wristwatch. "Mmmm... Since about when-you-drove-away-thirty." He blinked, flashed a tightlipped grin and sat down on the floor.

Wren gasped. What had such prolonged exposure to her painting done to this man?

Eliot found his shirt just under the painting and crawled across the floor to it. He jammed his hands into the sleeves, then picked up a pair of sunglasses that was lying nearby. Wren quickly plucked them from his fingers.

"Polarized lenses," she said, shaking the glasses in front of Eliot's nose. "Did you wear these inside the barn?"

Eliot smiled and tipped his head to one side. "Oh, yes — these are my good pair! Do you like them?"

Eliot began to turn back to the painted wall, but Arlen pulled him around so that he was facing away from the painting.

"You know," Eliot sang the words rather than speaking them, "this has been even better than the time the woman with the black nails showed me the other painting."

Arlen, Grace, and Wren all turned their attention to Eliot.

Wren understood. "It must have been at the gallery," she said, "Jeanette Perdot has a painting. I never imagined she would show it to anyone — especially a journalist! I remember saying to her that she'd know what to do with it. I thought she understood that that meant storing it away and keeping it secret, not broadcasting it. What was she thinking?"

Maybe Homeland Security is right, Wren thought. *Maybe these paintings are just too dangerous. A glance might make you happy, but hours of uninterrupted viewing, with polarized enhancement, puts you permanently on the Magic Bus.* She felt like a criminal.

"Hey!" Eliot put a hand on Wren's foot. "That's *former* journalist. Do you have a flute? I hear some music that needs playing." Eliot squinted into the distance, held his arms in the air like a conductor and nodded his head in time with some melody that was available only to him.

Grace looked down at Eliot, shaking her head.

Eliot blinked. "Can we eat now?"

"I've always wanted a puppy," Grace growled.

They all helped the *former* journalist to his feet and steadied his walk to the house.

"Oh," Eliot cooed, "look at the little bunnies! Don't squish them."

In everyone else's perception of reality the cute little bunnies were simply stones along the edge of the gravel path.

Grace, a whirlwind in the kitchen, caused a spectacular salad to appear. Arlen sat at the table with the journalist — *former* journalist! — from another dimension, watching Eliot happily drifting on his new, untroubled waters.

Wren sat at Julia's bedside, wondering if they would really be able to care for her while she healed. Wren understood the casts, but the wired jaw was beyond her. She was resting her head on the edge of the bed when she felt her friend stir. Wren sat up straight, shocked to hear Julia moaning and chirping, trying to say something, trying to be understood through her immobilized jaw.

"Arlen," Wren called, "a little help here?"

Arlen pointed a finger at Eliot and gave him a hard look, hoping that would pin him to his chair, and strode into the living room, to Julia's bedside.

"I don't know what she's saying. Maybe she needs more pain medicine," Wren offered.

Arlen delicately took Julia's plaster-free fingers in his hands and looked into her eyes. "Julia, what do you need? Are you in pain?" he asked.

Julia looked at him and moved her eyes to look at the desk across the room. Blinking furiously, her eyelashes flapping like an angry bat's wings, Julia repeatedly turned her eyes toward the desk and back to him.

"iPad! She wants the iPad," Wren shouted. She dashed across the room, snatched up the electronic device, and powered it up. Holding the pad so Julia could easily see it and touch the letters with her somewhat useable fingertip, Wren asked, "Is this OK? Can you work it?"

Julia simply typed, "Y".

Arlen and Wren smacked their palms together, a resounding high-five, above Julia's chest.

Julia continued typing: "bring me paintingyouhave it"

She looked at Arlen.

He looked at the floor, studying the pattern in the rug, "Yeah. I've got it. It got pretty beat up, although Wren patched it as well as she could. I don't think you should see it...I mean, in your current condition, it might be too difficult."

Julia looked hard at Arlen, and he was surprised not to see pleading. Instead, he saw her eyes narrow into angry little slits.

"OK. I'll get it. Wren, please wait here with her so she doesn't try to follow me."

Wren snorted an uncertain little laugh when Julia winked at her.

"I'm coming with you," shouted Eliot Stern, his voice going squeaky with excitement.

Arlen walked to the old Winnebago, Eliot trailing along like his shadow. Opening the door, Arlen turned to Eliot and raised a hand. "You wait here," he stated firmly, and hopped into the RV. He found an extra blanket and wrapped the painting in it. Turning to leave, he bumped hard into Eliot's chest. "I thought I told you to wait outside."

"I just had to see inside this place," Eliot whispered. "Can I stay here?"

Arlen Divine looked around at his old home. He had slept in a small bedroom in Grace's house since his arrival, and suspected he might not need his RV any time soon. "Sure, pal. Sure." Holding Eliot's face between his two hands, he forced him to make prolonged eye contact and said, "Do not use the galley and do *not* use the head. Do you understand?"

Arlen was holding Eliot's face so firmly that Eliot was fish-lipped. "Yes. No. I mean, yes."

Arlen shook his head, doubting that the mentally-altered Eliot Stern could succeed at not blowing up the bus or overflowing the holding tanks. Pausing to take the key from the ignition, he went back to the house with the blanketed painting.

The aroma of tomatoes, peppers, and onions simmering together in a magical tangy blend tickled Arlen's nose and caused his stomach to rumble in anticipation. The whole day had passed without a meal, and now Grace was preparing a hefty spaghetti feast for the crew of kidnappers — and Eliot Stern, if he wasn't too lost in space to take food.

Wren remained at Julia's side and looked up at Arlen with a worried frown. "Arlen," she said softly, "I think she's having a lot of pain."

Arlen and his bulky armload came around the bed to where Julia could see him. She blinked and blinked.

"Wren," Arlen said as he pulled the sheet off the battered painting, "you may want to give Grace a hand in the kitchen."

Wren shook her head. "I'd like to take a quick look at the painting, just to see how the repairs have held up."

A soft, low-pitched bell rang from within the canvas, and Wren quickly averted her eyes.

"Julia, I'm going to hang the painting on that coat rack so you can see it, alright?" Arlen said, looking into her eyes. He could see that tears of pain had been streaming down her cheeks and his heart squeezed tightly against his ribs, making a lump in his throat. He removed a denim jacket and two baseball caps from the coat rack standing by the door and tossed them to the floor. Whisking the coat rack to a position beside Julia's bed, about even with her knees, he hung the damaged canvas from two of its hooks.

How does a painting leak sound and color? How does it happen that sounds emanate from the colors on the surface and from deep inside some hidden place in the canvas? Now colors seemed to be pooling on the floor beneath the painting. Arlen dared not look directly at it. Even holding it so close and hearing its peculiar bells was making him feel warm. Or was it cool? He thought about it a little and decided he simply felt receptive and open. "Hmm," he grunted as he noticed a splash of blue paint on his boot.

Julia was squirming a little. Arlen thought the pain had become too much for her and reached to touch her hand. He realized that she was using the hand to claw at the cast on her other arm.

"Julia! Whoa, girl, don't do that!"

She reached toward the iPad, and Arlen fumbled with it and got it in position for her to tap words.

"cutitoff"

Arlen looked at the screen in horror. "My God, Julia. Does it hurt that bad? Let me get Grace to give you some more painkillers."

"Nnnnno," Julia growled, then typed, "castoff".

Arlen stood and looked at Julia, studying the cast on her arm. He folded his arms across his chest and tugged at the corner of his mustache. He shook his head, made a little grunting noise, and strode out of the room.

Stepping calmly into the kitchen, Arlen asked Grace if she had a Dremel tool.

"Sure. It's in the breezeway in the cabinet. It's in the original box — I don't think I've ever used it," Grace said.

"Dremel tool? Isn't that some kind of tiny electric grinder?" Wren asked with a puzzled frown as she watched Arlen walk away.

Returning to Julia's bedside, Arlen placed the Dremel box on top of her blanket. Julia looked like she'd be smiling if her jaw hadn't been wired shut. Arlen poked around in the box until he found the disc blade he was seeking. He pushed the switch and the blade spun in a tiny fury, assaulting his hearing with a whining squeal like a dentist's drill. He turned off the saw, then glanced in passing at Julia's cast-free arm and saw something shocking.

Where before there had been a deep cut surrounded by a row of stitches, there was now just clear, healthy skin. Not even a scar.

Arlen could scarcely breathe. Julia was looking at the battered painting, and a blue aura glowed like neon all around her body. *Beatific*, thought Arlen. *Beautiful.*

He revved the Dremel tool and then guided it carefully as it sliced through the cast like a paring knife through an orange peel. Plaster dust devils rose toward the ceiling and settled back down onto the bed, the floor, and Arlen's hair. Finished, he set the tool under the bed, then carefully removed the cast.

Julia blinked and made a sound like a purring cat as she rubbed circulation back into her newly freed arm.

Unbelievable! Arlen thought.

They looked at each other in silence for a while. Then Arlen began to laugh. He took Julia's two good hands in his own. She blinked rapidly again and reached for the iPad, by herself this time.

Two handed, she typed, "This painting is extremely medicinal, don't you think? Legs feel OK... Let's take off the leg casts!"

Arlen stood up. "Let's wait until tomorrow. Maybe that cute little hamster cage you're wearing on your head can come off first."

As a retort, Julia typed a row of leering yellow smiley faces.

Wren was running the blender in the kitchen at the same time Arlen had started cutting Julia's cast, so she and Grace had been oblivious to the sawing in the living room. The blender ground away, crunching and screeching, for two minutes, then Grace handed Wren a straw for the protein smoothie she was taking to Julia.

"I'll come with you," Grace offered, "Sometimes manipulating the straw can be tricky when you're holding the glass as well. You don't want to choke her."

Wren and Grace came into the living room together — and Grace screamed, "What have you done?"

Wren nearly dropped the drink, but Arlen was across the room in a flash, wrapping his fingers around the glass. Without a word he took the drink and placed the straw, oh so tenderly, between Julia's lips. Grace and Wren leaned on each other, looking on in amazement at Julia's healed arms. She could have handled the drink and straw by herself now, of course, but she allowed him to tend to her anyway — and Arlen was surprised by the feelings that tumbled and danced in him from that simple act.

Arlen Divine, he thought, *you are still a living, breathing man.*

Julia finished the drink and Arlen insisted that she sleep.

She typed, "Just to make you happy."

And he was.

Wren scooped up the pieces of Julia's cast and carried them out to the side of the barn, in a paper bag with the rest of the household trash. She paused for a moment to listen to the quiet evening. It was so beautiful and so peaceful. She could almost believe that today, and all the recent days leading up to it, had been nothing but an extremely bizarre dream.

Pulled from her reverie, Wren's breath caught in her throat as she heard a rustling sound. It seemed to come from the blackberry bushes, about fifty yards away down by the pond. Sharpening her focus, she tried to peer through the darkness. Silence... She turned toward the house, but after only a step the rustling came again. She felt a chill prickle up the back of her neck. Moving cautiously toward the pond, she stepped on a twig and it snapped — *crack!* — like a gunshot. Looking up from the broken stick, she clamped a hand over her mouth to stifle a scream as a white-faced deer stepped delicately out of the brambles. The deer, a young buck, blinked at her and sprang out of sight with two powerful, graceful leaps. Wren leaned against the barn and waited for her heart to stop slamming against her ribs. Relieved, but still not at ease, she suspiciously scanned the bushes for a few minutes. Then, satisfied that the deer had been the only thing there, she walked back to the house.

Wren quietly joined Arlen and Grace at the kitchen table. Eliot, who had already eaten a vast quantity of spaghetti, stood and announced that he was going out to *his* Winnebago to sleep.

"Stay out of the barn," Grace implored.

Wren stared at Arlen as if she could pierce his skull with her eyes and look inside to find answers to her questions. "So," she asked mock-casually, "what's going on with Julia's injuries? Arlen, I just carried out the trash, and that trash included the cast that you cut off of Julia's arm — the arm that got broken only a week ago."

Seconds ticked by in silence.

"Come on," Wren nearly shouted, "you two must have *some* ideas about this insanely fast healing process."

"Wren," Arlen spoke cautiously, "I don't think you need to panic. The paintings simply appear to have something else to offer, and I think all we can do is accept it. It's not like it's anything bad."

Grace artfully slurped a strand of spaghetti as she hurried into the conversation. "Just what are you saying?" she asked, wiping bright red tomato sauce from her chin and forehead, eyes narrowed at Arlen.

After swallowing a big forkful of salad, Arlen placed his utensil on the table beside his plate, wiped his mustache carefully with his napkin, and leaned back in his chair. He rocked the front legs off the floor a few inches, then dropped heavily back down and splayed his hands on the table as he arrived at what he wanted to say. "It's simple. Wren's paintings make people feel good, but Eliot showed us what too much of a good thing can do — to some people, at least. But just look at me — the paintings healed my emotional wounds and got me clean, and I was alone with one even longer than Eliot was. We've seen the paintings take lots of people into intensely happy places. Now Julia is showing us that the paintings can also heal broken bodies." He shrugged. "There you go. Simple."

Grace looked skeptical. "But how is what happened to Eliot 'not anything bad'?"

"That's hard to answer — I never met the guy before he got into the barn, and I was mostly too sloshed to bother reading his articles in the paper. But if the painting was smart enough to give me what I needed, maybe what Eliot got is exactly what *he* needed. Maybe who he is now is who he really always wanted to be, who he's *meant* to be. He seems to think so."

Wren stopped eating, but held her fork in her hand like a dagger. "I don't understand my part in this. I don't know what I'm doing," she said quickly. She sped on, "I mean, I understand the paint, the color, the hues and tones, the layers, but I don't know why this is happening. I never willed it. Of course, I'm overjoyed that Julia seems to have been somehow healed by my painting. But it's the same damn painting that almost got her killed! And my studio is still burned, and Homeland Security is still hunting me like a rabbit."

Grace reached across the platter of spaghetti and placed a comforting hand on Wren's arm, "No one has said that *you* make this happen, Wren. It should be obvious that you're a channel, a conduit. You are the carrier of the energy, but you didn't *make* the energy." She paused for a moment, until she had Wren's full attention. "It's really amazing, if you think about it. What is the one thing a true artist hopes for?"

Silence.

Grace said, "Well?"

Wren studied Grace's eyes. "I think a true artist hopes that people will look at their work and see beyond the medium, past the paint or clay, the photo paper or steel, the poem or the music or the dance, and then feel that they have had a close encounter with eternity."

Arlen felt tears burning his eyes.

"Wren," said Grace, "how lucky you are, to be able to present this to the world. And how lucky we are, to be able to help you."

"Thank you... both of you. But I still feel more than a little weird," Wren said softly.

Grace sighed, got up, and poured Wren a glass of Pinot Noir. "I don't usually recommend self-medicating with alcohol, but this is a good vintage."

Wren smiled up at Grace and gladly took her medicine.

"Let's see what the painting does for Julia by tomorrow," Grace said. "Let's just let it happen, let it work. I agree that we should be accepting of this gift and not go trying to analyze it to death right now."

Wren set her wine glass on the table and said, "When she is up and walking around, Julia's going to want one of those nasty little cigars she loves. Unless my paintings don't approve of them…"

At last, laughter had a seat at the table.

"I was just thinking, though…" Grace said, pouring herself a glass of wine. "Isn't it funny how we keep wondering *why* Wren's paintings cause such interesting responses, we keep hammering at the question of *how* it is they do what they do. They are only causing good things to happen — assuming Arlen's right about our *former* journalist — so why is it that we can't just accept it, like we accept that the sun will come up in the East tomorrow morning? Like it's just a natural occurrence, nothing weird, nothing to freak out about? We don't have to dissect it to see if it has a spleen, we just have to see that the good is there. Yet when we talk about Billy Joe Bobb, who is the living, breathing embodiment of pure evil as far as I can see, we never ask one single question about where *that* comes from, even while his actions inflict pain on people. When he and his followers spew hate speech that breeds sorrow and suspicion and hurt, we never once ask what makes it work the way it does."

Wren looked at Arlen, then they both looked at Grace. Grace looked at the fresh tomato-sauce stains on her blouse. She took a sip from her wine glass and looked up at her new friends. "Anyway, I was just thinking about that. From now on we should try to accept beauty and goodness easily, with open arms." Leaning toward Arlen and Wren, she nearly growled, "And, instead, question the *shit* out of evil."

Arlen twirled his fork around his fingers like a tiny baton and said, "Speaking of evil, there is one other little thing we need to talk about. The Reverend Billy Joe Bobb…he's out there, somewhere — in this area — and he knows we're here. He really believes that Wren is some kind of satanic artist, and I believe he means to do her great harm. Or I guess Julia, because he's got them mixed up. We should probably make a plan."

"We've hatched some good plans so far…" Grace said.

Wren was now more than a little concerned about the rustling she'd heard in the shrubs. *Yes,* she thought, *a plan would be good.*

Arlen tipped his chair back again, tapped nervous fingers on the dining table and said, "So far, yeah. We should incubate this one soon...maybe even right now."

The table was cleared and dishes were washed.

Julia slept as the painting mysteriously moved atoms, causing her to continue to heal. A few drops of yellow paint lay on the floor below the painting.

Eliot slept in the Winnebago, awakening every hour or two to sit up and look out the window and laugh. He whistled a tune that made him sway like a snake charmer.

Wren and Grace sat side-by-side on the porch, hips touching lightly.

Arlen drank a whole pot of coffee, with plenty of sugar, while Wren and Grace drank the last traces of the medicinal Pinot Noir.

The Reverend Billy Joe Bobb hid in the blackberry brambles at the edge of Grace's farm, hunkered down under a camouflage tarp he'd picked up in Poulsbo. His thoughts rambled and roamed and leapt like the little frogs in Grace's pond. He watched the house from his thorny, distant vantage point. Hours passed and finally all the lights were turned off.

"This will be so easy," he quietly hissed, like a poisonous snake. Billy Joe Bobb loved the sound of his own voice, so he said it over and over and over.

Chapter 26

*H*omeland Security Agent Levi Bitters sat in his darkened motel room and stared a hole through his computer screen. He was watching a satellite image, zoomed in tight on Grace's farm. A tiny blue dot sat in the center of the picture. He was pleased that his intuition had led him to imbed a tiny tracking device in Julia Burlow's arm cast. It would've been nice if he could have just had the surgeon implant the "tick" directly under the patient's skin. But necessity is the mother of deniability. In the end, Bitters had relieved the guard for an hour and, with the aid of a simple pocket knife and a small tube of super glue, he'd created a traceable target. Now he would know exactly where the "weird-ass" artist's friend was being transferred to, "need-to-know" or no.

Yesterday, Bitters had sat at his desk and watched as the tiny blue dot went nowhere. Julia Burlow was severely injured, after all, and was confined to a hospital bed with her little beacon silently showing him her precise location. He was confident that she wouldn't be moving any time soon. He went out for lunch. When he returned, he'd looked at the computer screen, satisfied that the blue dot was still in its proper place. Pushing papers around on his desk, he had begun sorting his mail.

Then, out of the corner of his eye, a sudden blur of blue had brought his attention back to the computer screen. The patient was on the move! The blue dot was out on the street, and Agent Bitters' paperwork was now scattered all over the floor. He had watched her progress, his nose just inches from the screen. Bitters knew that Burlow was not scheduled to be moved for another five days. What the hell was going on? He phoned the agent on guard, but got no response. Protocol would be to phone his superior at this point, but he wanted to remain at the top of the food chain at this particular banquet.

"No need for panic, Levi," he said to himself.

He knew what to do. He was well trained. Levi Bitters closed his eyes and took several deep breaths. His composure regained, he looked again at the image and gave a short gasp of surprise. The blue dot was moving north on the freeway.

According to Agency protocol, now would be the time to call in a surveillance team to move in on whoever had absconded with the patient. But Bitters was feeling somewhat ambivalent about Agency protocol at the moment, especially as inconvenient questions would arise about how he had learned of the escape in the first place — questions that he much preferred not to address just now, or possibly ever. He would have to handle this on his own. He would watch, and then he would act.

The blue dot moved northward, then off the freeway, heading west. He watched his screen in fascination until the tracker indicated that the target was boarding a boat at the Edmonds ferry terminal.

Agent Bitters snapped his laptop shut, tucked it under his arm, and grabbed his car keys. He was out the door and down the road in seconds. He would find Julia Burlow, wherever she was being taken — and that, he was certain, would be where he would also find Wren Willow Hendrix.

Fair weather had brought out the tourists. Levi Bitters checked into what might have been the last motel room in the county, just five miles from the blue dot. It wasn't much of a room, but that didn't matter; he only needed a home base, a private place to keep watch on his target. Ignoring the odor of mildew and mold, Agent Bitters went right to work. The satellite image he watched was in real time, and was relayed from an array of satellites, so there were no lapses in imaging. He marveled at the resolution, but was dismayed that the blue dot actually obscured some details on the map. Nevertheless, Bitters had a fine view of what was proving to be an interesting scene. His target remained stationary inside an isolated farmhouse. He wished he could see inside the house, to see how many people were there with Julia Burlow.

What he *was* able to see, however, was an unexpected intruder at the far corner of the property. A man crept through the foliage and settled in, covering himself with a cheap hardware-store camouflage tarp. To someone who knew how to look, the thing reflected so much light that it might as well have been a beacon.

Dusk became darkness. Bitters stretched, yawned, and put the computer image into night-vision mode. He made adjustments to mitigate the glare of yard lights, house lights, and automobile headlights, and the image became brilliantly clear.

Camo-Tarp Man remained in the bushes. The blue dot was still in the farmhouse. A figure came lurching out of an old RV and went into the house. Bitters had the feeling he might have missed a few things while he was driving to the motel, but that was the price of working solo. Now nothing moved. Forty minutes passed, and then an hour. RV Man came out of the house — or at least it was some-one with the same erratic gait. What was he doing? Bitters chuckled as he watched the satellite image of the man spinning and twirling, flapping something that looked like a bedsheet. The man danced his way back to the RV.

A few more minutes went by before Bitters saw the blue dot move out of the house toward the barn. Tree limbs and rooflines obscured his view. How could this be happening? The woman was completely immobilized! But there it was — a Homeland Security blue dot cannot tell a lie. Agent Bitters watched the screen for an hour more before he dozed off. He jerked awake when his chin dropped to his chest.

"Asleep at the wheel," he whispered as he tried to refocus. The blue dot was now just outside the barn. Nothing was moving. The lights were off in the house, the RV was dark, and the camouflage tarp was glowing from the same location as before.

Bitters closed the laptop and lay down on the bed. *Just a ten-minute nap,* he thought.

Six hours later he had not moved, deeply asleep with his shoes still on his feet.

Chapter 27

Arlen threw off his blanket and sprang up from the recliner he had slept in. Julia was moaning loudly. He was at her bedside in two long strides.

"What is it? What do you need? Water? Bedpan? Painkiller?"

Julia held the iPad in her solidly healed left hand and typed with the index finger of her right hand.

"get these casts and wires off me now pls"

Arlen stood, grinning under his grand mustache. The sun wasn't up yet and the rest of the household was still asleep, but he obediently took up the tiny power-saw and patiently cut through Julia's leg casts. Plumes of plaster-impregnated gauze dispersed and formed a dust storm around Arlen and Julia. The stiff plaster molds fell away and Arlen stepped back in disbelief as Julia bent her knees to her chest.

There was no sign of injury. Not a bruise. Not a scratch. Not a bump. The injuries were completely healed. Arlen felt oddly afraid, as if a little fetal alien might spring forth from Julia's abdomen. He told himself that this was reality and not a science fiction movie. That did absolutely nothing to assuage the fear now chewing at his gut.

For the first time in many days, Julia sat up. "Gnt. Gnnnt," she pointed aggressively at the wire contraption on her head. If her eyes had been needles, Arlen's skin would have looked like a pincushion.

"OK, OK... I've got to study this a minute. I think I'm going to need some tools."

Grace had just come into the living room and quickly assessed the situation. "Specifically, you will need a needle-nose pliers and a wire cutter," she stated.

Arlen started to speak, but Grace interrupted. "Arlen, why don't you go to the kitchen and make some coffee? I've got this," she said softly, nudging him toward the kitchen.

Julia reached out and took Grace by the hand.

"I've seen this done before, my friend, and it could get rough," Grace nodded toward the painting, "You might want to take a good long look at that painting while I get the tools."

Grace retrieved the needed tools from a drawer in the kitchen.

"...OK, Julia, you do know that there have been times over the years of our friendship that I may have actually wanted to do you bodily harm. I hope you understand that this is not one of those times."

Julia blinked and then gripped the blankets in a white-knuckled defense against anticipated pain.

Grace held the wire nippers firmly as they bit crisply through the metal strands that held Julia's halo in place. She then gripped the needle-nose pliers and gently, steadily pulled out the first wire that was piercing Julia's flesh. She swallowed hard, and pulled just as steadily on the next. A lone drop of sweat dripped off the end of her nose.

Julia looked at Grace, wondering when the pain was supposed to start.

Grace examined the wire. Not a trace of tissue, or even a drop of blood. She pulled out another, and then another. Soon, the whole cage was gone. Julia was free.

Julia worked her jaw back and forth, up and down. "Well, that was just fucking odd," she finally said, raising one eyebrow.

Grace sat on the bed and frowned at Julia.

Julia swung her feet to the floor and stood, stretching so completely that several vertebrae popped loudly with relief. "I need potato chips. You got any, Grace?"

Wren was just easing down the stairs from her bedroom when she saw Julia sprinting for the kitchen. She opened her mouth and sat down hard on the stairs. Grace walked over and put her arm around Wren's shoulders.

Wren took in the wire cutters in Grace's hand, the bits of wire cage scattered around Julia's bed. "This is just too much," she said, breathlessly. "How can all of this happen from a damn painting?"

Wren was floundering in deep uncharted waters. She wanted to run after Julia, to tell her how amazing it was that she had miraculously recovered so fast, but she was afraid. She needed to grab onto something that was far away from the shocking power of her paintings. She turned to Grace.

"Grace, how did you know what to do for Julia, just now, with the wire cutters?" Wren was probing cautiously. "And I was thinking about the hospital...how did you know so much about how it worked? And even the disguises..."

Grace studied Wren and said, "I don't know if this is the right time for that story. There's a lot of pain in it."

Wren's face was a mask of resolve. "Are you sure? There may never be another time."

Grace sighed deeply, "OK, here's the thing. When I was younger, in my 20s, I fell in love. We were together for nineteen years. We did everything together, our work and our home, but mostly, we sailed."

"That sounds wonderful. What was his name?"

"*Her* name, Wren. Jane. Her name was Jane." Grace sat quietly for a moment, looking back at a lifetime. Arlen and Julia were laughing in the kitchen. "So, anyway, one day we were out on the water and a halyard jammed at the top of the mast. Jane went up the mast in a bosun's chair, something she had done loads of times. It was a defective metal ring. Damn thing snapped like an icicle and the line raced through the blocks and Jane dropped like a rock. Broke her neck, but she survived. Survived... Well, Jane was in a coma for two months before she died."

Grace stoically told Wren about that two months: the ventilator breathing for Jane, the feeding tubes, and how Grace had secretly wished long before the end that the machines could just be turned off.

"Wren, you know that people in those years were a little dim about relationships that were *different*. Honestly, more than dim — most people were hateful. Jane's family forbade me to see her, to even show my face at the hospital. I was probably a little insane with grief and fear. I just had to be with her. At first I was sure she'd get better, maybe need a wheelchair in the worst scenario. I started planning how we'd remodel the house to accommodate her new requirements. I needed to be with her, to give her energy, so I invented different disguises to let me be there to encourage her. I was a phlebotomist, an intern, a janitor. I was even a chaplain for a whole day. It wasn't much, but I got to be near her, to at least look at her face and stand in the room with her. When I was disguised as a nurse or a doctor I got to take her pulse. Her skin felt like paper, and her heartbeat was a shallow whisper. It didn't take long before it was clear, to me at least, that Jane was going to die."

A single tear streaked a path down her cheek, and Grace paused to dab at her eyes with a shirt cuff.

"It was pretty funny, though. Her parents and even her twin brother were often in the room when I was there in one of my "official" roles, and they never recognized me. This was all back east...

The real stink was after Jane's death. Her lawyer said there was an insurance policy, and I was the beneficiary of $1.5 million. Guess what? Jane's parents went berserk, claimed that nineteen years as a couple didn't count for shit because we weren't a *normal* couple."

Grace brightened as she recalled, "Jane was tough, though, and extremely intelligent. The policy was iron-clad; her family didn't have a case. God, they were nasty, though… So I sold our house, I sold that damn boat, and I moved as far from that place as I could get. I went off the map. Off of *their* fucking map, anyway. I came here and bought this farm. After a while I even bought another boat."

Grace studied Wren seriously for a moment, and then said, "There is one other little detail. Only two people know it; one is Julia, and the other is Jane's brother. Now you will know it, too." Running her hands through her hair, Grace gathered her courage and calmly finished her story. "One afternoon Jane's family was away from the hospital, or so I thought. I was playing the part of a volunteer that day, bringing magazines and good cheer to patients. I came to Jane's room, opened the door, and started to walk through when I saw her brother standing beside her bed. He was talking to her, something I had never seen him do. He said he was sorry, and he hoped that it wouldn't hurt. He told her he loved her and he promised her that he would keep their parents from harming me."

Grace sighed heavily, and then continued, "I never saw it coming. He had found a way to shut off the ventilator's alarm. He was so much braver than I was! With the alarm off, he switched off the ventilator, calm as anything. I didn't stop him. I just watched from the doorway. At first, Jane seemed to breathe, but after a few seconds it wasn't really breathing at all, just some shaky rattling sounds. It only took a few minutes. Then she was gone. The heart monitor alarm went off, so he quickly turned the ventilator back on, but it was too late — or just late enough, depending upon your feelings about torture and prolonged, pointless suffering. I stood aside as a herd of nurses and doctors poured through the doorway. Jane's brother was

shoved to the wall. I will never forget the way he looked. Drained...
No, he looked hollow. He never said a word, and no one ever questioned him. I managed to stay in the room unnoticed. The doctor made a time-of-death pronouncement, and the medical entourage left the room. I was shaking and really no longer in control of myself. I went to the bed and adjusted Jane's blanket. The whole scene was fairly blurry through the tears and all, but I looked up and saw Jane's brother, and I knew that he knew that it was me in that disguise. He knew that I'd seen what he had done. I turned and ran. I ran for years, really. He kept his promise to come to my aid, though, and he eventually got Jane's parents to give up their fight against me. It wasn't like blackmail — he knew that I held his secret, but he'd looked into my eyes in that moment, and he knew that I would always *keep* his secret."

Drawing a deep breath, Grace sat up straight and nodded her head, "That was a long time ago, Wren. But...you asked."

Wren looked at Grace a moment, and then, her heart sliding open just a little wider; she wrapped her arms around Grace and held her tightly.

A loud commotion in the kitchen interrupted the moment, and Wren and Grace ran in to see what new catastrophe awaited them.

Arlen held a piece of burned black toast, water dripping from his face and soaking his shirt.

Julia was laughing so hard that she had to lean on the kitchen counter for support. She held an empty water glass in her hand. "Your toast was in flames," she said, still laughing and gasping for air. "I should have used the fire extinguisher." She gestured toward the red tank hanging on the kitchen wall near the stove.

"I'm lucky you just used the faucet, then," Arlen said. Laughing himself, he grabbed Julia in a bear hug.

"Hey, you're getting my hospital gown wet," Julia protested, giving Arlen a shove. Then, remembering that a hospital gown offers no posterior privacy, she quickly turned her back to the wall.

"Julia, I just don't even know what to say to you," Wren began. "…I feel so responsible for the accident."

Forgetting about the unfortunate hospital gown, Julia stepped forward and embraced Wren. "You made some special paintings, I showed one of them around, I got in a fight, and I fell down in the wrong spot. That's all that happened. It looks like I'm OK, though, doesn't it?" Julia said, still clinging to her. "Wren, you are my friend, and the only thing you are to blame for is making my life very interesting."

Grace and Arlen began to applaud and shout, "Beautiful! Well said!"

Everyone fell silent, however, as a disturbance of goats, bleating and crashing around in the garden, drew them to the window.

"Oh, crap," shouted Grace, "they've gotten loose again. Julia, you and your bare ass stay right here. You two, come with me. We have to round up those rambunctious marauders before they devour all of my profits."

Julia leaned on the counter, laughing at the comical scene outside the kitchen window. A goat head-butted Arlen and he fell over backward. Wren chased a big brown goat into a fence corner, but then was too intimidated by the goat to wrap her arms around it, and it shot past her. Grace was creeping up on a white goat that had ten inches of fresh organic chard sticking out either side of its mouth.

Julia laughed out loud, enjoying her friends' antics and reveling at being alive.

She was leaning over the sink to get a better view when she heard a clicking sound from the hallway. She sensed a sudden change in the room. An aroma — something out of place for this room — was beginning to overpower the smell of burnt toast. There was a subtle movement of air, and she thought she saw a blur of motion reflected in the window. She turned quickly, but no one was there. She waited, not moving, but she was alone in the kitchen.

Outside, there was a loud crash as Arlen fell over a bucket, and Julia returned her attention to the action. As she watched Arlen, she saw something in the window, and instead of focusing outside the window Julia concentrated on the reflection. In that reflection she saw a man behind her, and a chill of fear slid through her. She whirled around in slow motion, time crawling as in a dream. For a long moment she was paralyzed with shock as she looked at Billy Joe Bobb, standing before her with a blazing tiki torch that he had plucked from the garden. The pungent odor of citronella made her cough. Citronella, and something else that she couldn't identify.

Reverend Bobb's eyes were hidden behind dark glasses, but Julia could see him gazing at her with suspicion — suspicion mixed with what looked like real fear.

"So, there you are — the Devil's own painter. How is it you're on your feet? Your body was broken. Is this not proof that you've been dancing to Satan's song?" Billy Joe Bobb hissed.

Julia's mind reeled as she realized that Billy Joe Bobb thought she was the painter of the otherworldly paintings. Not that it mattered much.

He thrust the torch theatrically toward her like a dull-witted villager in an old Frankenstein movie. The movement frightened her out of her stupor. She edged steadily along the counter, moving away from the sink and past the stove, to the wall where the fire extinguisher hung. Never taking her eyes off Billy Joe Bobb's smoldering torch, Julia hoped that she accurately remembered the location of the red tank. She moved another step, easing toward the canister.

"I'm going to burn you. God told me that it would come to this! I'm going to send you back to Hell, wrapped in the purifying flames of my torch." Billy Joe Bobb's voice rose, both in volume and in pitch, and he jumped toward her — faster, Julia thought, than humanly possible.

She felt the searing heat from the torch's flame. Diving away from Reverend Bobb, Julia grabbed the red tank and pulled the safety pin in one glorious pirouette. With the torch just inches from her face she squeezed the lever.

The fire extinguisher sputtered, then shot out a thick jet of fire-suppressant foam. The torch went out, and Billy Joe Bobb's trajectory sent him directly into the path of the foamy cloud. He screamed and choked as chemicals covered his face, falling to the floor and clawing maniacally at his eyes.

Julia raised the heavy tank to bring it down on Billy Joe Bobb's head ... when a dark shadow loomed up behind her. Her heart lurched as she felt someone grab her arm in a vise-like grip.

As she turned to face this new threat, the man holding her arm stepped back, but didn't let go. "Agent Bitters, Homeland Security!" he shouted. "I've got him. Step away — I've got him!"

Julia sighed with relief and leaned against the wall, lowering the fire extinguisher to the floor with a metallic clang.

At that moment, the goat wranglers rushed into the kitchen, piling into one another, slapstick style, just in time to hear the handcuffs snap closed on Reverend Billy Joe Bobb's wrists.

"Let go of me, nigger!" Billy Joe Bobb shouted, as Agent Bitters lifted the foam-covered man to his feet. The preacher was literally foaming at the mouth, and Julia fought an urge to giggle at the metaphor made real.

"Not terribly creative, as insults go." Bitters growled. Turning to Julia, the tall Black man smoothed his rumpled suit and said, "Let's start over, shall we? I'm Agent Levi Bitters of Homeland Security. I'd like to say that I'm arresting this man for being an obscene excuse for a human being, but unfortunately that law isn't on the books yet. For now, we will have to make do with inciting hate crimes and murdering his nephew."

"What?" Billy Joe Bobb screamed. "How did you know I killed him?"

"Actually, sir, the evidence we already had is proof positive, but I do enjoy hearing it from your own mouth in front of multiple witnesses. Your nephew's body was dumped into the Columbia River. It seems there was an eyewitness to that, Reverend, a hiker who saw it and went to the police. And more recently, Delbert Florian Bobb's body floated to the surface. It scared the hell out of three guys just out for a quiet day of fishing. Seems they hooked your nephew instead of a salmon. And you know the best part, Reverend? When the local cops found the fellow that dumped your nephew — your other dear nephew, Buddy Sol Hargis — he told the officers that he was just following the orders of young Delbert's Reverend uncle."

Julia and her friends stared at Agent Bitters, speechless.

Bitters pushed Billy Joe Bobb ahead of him through the kitchen door; then, holding him by the collar, he turned to the shocked group and said, "I'm going to lock this fellow in my car, but I'll be back in a minute to talk with you. All of you." Shaking his head and pushing Billy Joe Bobb ahead of him, Agent Levi Bitters stepped outside.

Julia turned to say something to Arlen, but suddenly everything seemed to happen at once. She heard a shout and a loud thump, and Arlen went still. Julia turned to see Reverend Billy Joe Bobb struggling with Agent Bitters. As she watched, Bobb grabbed a heavy metal object near the door. *Gas can*, thought Julia incongruously. *That was what I smelled earlier.*

Her thoughts were interrupted as Billy Joe Bobb brought the can down on Agent Bitter's wrist, hard. Bitters lost his grip on the chain of the handcuffs, and Billy Joe Bobb managed to get one skinny, slippery hand out of its cuff. He sprang up with all his rage-fueled strength and rammed the top of his head into Bitters' jaw. Agent Bitters dropped in slow motion to his knees, then fell forward. As Bitters lay sprawled in the grass, Billy Joe Bobb grabbed the gas can and dashed around the side of the house.

"Stop him!" Wren yelled.

"The barn!" Julia shouted. "He's going to burn down the barn!" She jumped out of the way instinctively as Arlen rushed past her in hot pursuit. As she turned to follow — hospital gown forgotten for the moment — her foot crunched on something on the ground. Looking down, she saw a pair of sunglasses, and she recognized them as the ones that Billy Joe Bobb had been wearing when he threatened her with the torch.

Agent Bitters, meanwhile, had risen to his feet and dashed after Arlen toward the barn, grumbling something about goddamn one-size-fits-all handcuffs.

A few seconds later everyone else was running behind him. Julia wasn't sure whether they were more concerned with apprehending Billy Joe Bobb or keeping Agent Bitters from seeing the painting.

Eliot Stern, sitting on the floor in front of Wren's barn-wall painting, was rocking and humming, wearing only his underwear and a garland of berry vines from the garden. He turned around upon hearing a loud thud. Reverend Billy Joe Bobb was staring slack-jawed, his arms dangling like ropes, a metal gas can at his feet. Billy Joe Bobb did not even look at Eliot, but only at the painting looming over him. Suddenly, he fell to his knees, his lank hair flying around his head although there was no wind, his eyes seeming about to leap from his skull.

Eliot jumped up and sang out, "It's an alien! It's an angel! It's my old friend the preacher-man!"

Not wishing to disturb this alien angel's communion with the painting, Eliot backed slowly away toward the barn door. He bumped into the doorjamb, his eyes never leaving Billy Joe Bob, who was now developing a light blue aura. Smiling a knowing smile, Eliot turned and ran toward the house to share his news, leaving Billy Joe Bobb in front of the painting, glowing and swaying like a top spinning its last revolution.

The Reverend Billy Joe Bobb finally stopped swaying, and struggled to stand. His body straightened and his eyes squinted with resolve. He was a man with a clear vision — clearer than ever before. Turning abruptly from the painting, he stumbled then ran out into the yard. Nearly colliding with Agent Bitters, who had been poised to burst through the barn door, Billy Joe Bobb cut left and ran toward the house and the cliff beyond.

Rubbing his jaw, Bitters ran after him, and Eliot scampered after Bitters. They could hear Billy Joe Bobb shouting, "I didn't know. I just didn't know!"

Wren, Julia, Arlen, and Grace streamed around the house from the other side, following closely behind Eliot Stern. Everyone stopped abruptly as they saw Reverend Billy Joe Bobb standing at the cliff's edge, just one step away from eternity.

"Reverend Bobb," Bitters shouted above the wind, "it doesn't have to be like this. Come back and stand with me."

Gulls were spinning overhead, squabbling and calling. Far offshore, a pod of orcas breached all at once, as if in expectation. Somewhere in the distance, an otter yipped.

Billy Joe Bobb turned to Bitters and said, face placid, "It's OK now. I just didn't know." Without turning, he calmly stepped backward and disappeared over the lip of the cliff, down to the rocky beach eighty feet below.

Eliot fainted, and Wren sank to the ground because her own legs had deserted their posts. Arlen and Julia stood hand in hand beside

Grace and Agent Bitters, and watched as the high tide pulled Billy Joe Bobb's broken, lifeless body from the beach to be swallowed by the sea.

In the yard at the edge of the cliff, Grace revived Eliot, and the small group gathered themselves and slowly made their way to the house. They collapsed into chairs around Grace's kitchen table, sitting in shocked silence, until Wren finally spoke.

"What happens now?" she said in a whisper.

Grace had brought Bitters a bag of ice and he was now pressing it to his rapidly swelling jaw. Arlen had found Julia a house robe.

"Well," Bitters said, barely moving his mandible, "you should probably all stay off the scene a while. Take a vacation." He smiled, then winced. Turning to Julia, he said. "That was some quick thinking on your part, using the fire extinguisher. Brave, too."

"Toast," she said vaguely. "I owe it all to burnt toast."

"Well," he went on, "it was quick, and very sharp, considering your extensive injuries." He paused, straightened his tie, and regarded Julia with some disbelief. "…Injuries that you seem to have completely recovered from in an unusually short time."

"I'm a fast healer. Everyone in my family is," Julia said with utter sincerity.

Arlen spoke up to deflect attention from Julia's unusually fast recovery. "How did you find her? I know it was Julia you were tracking, but how?"

"You know I can't tell you that. Can you tell me how it is that Ms. Burlow is up and walking around, strong enough to attempt to bash in the head of a lunatic, days after being run over by a loaded Duck?" When no one answered. Bitters smiled thinly. "Exactly. So we'll just agree to leave it at that."

Agent Bitters drew himself up into his official posture and set his voice on Maximum Sincerity. "Ms. Burlow," he continued carefully, "I'm sorry that you were harassed and pursued in what is now an obvious case of mistaken identity. It is clear that you were abducted from the hospital by an antisocial madman and suspected murderer. You were really quite lucky to have succeeded in overpowering him and escaping; it's only unfortunate that he committed suicide before he could be brought to justice."

He looked straight at Wren and winked. "And, that — as my boss likes to say — wraps up this case."

The heaviness was lifting, and while no one was ready for food, they agreed that coffee was a good idea. They were, after all, in the Pacific Northwest, where coffee consumption is a legal requirement for residency. Eliot Stern was still excited about his angel sighting and swooped around the room in an impersonation of the creature, humming something that sounded a bit like "Son of a Preacher Man".

Handing the ice pack to Grace, Agent Bitters thanked her and, muttering something about the inescapability of paperwork, stood to leave. Turning to Wren, he paused and leaned close.

"Keep it under the radar, Ms. Hendrix. I'm on your side."

"I can't stop painting," Wren said, lifting her chin.

Levi Bitters looked deeply into Wren's eyes. "I didn't say 'stop'," he said. Pausing at the door, he turned for a long look at everyone seated at the table. "I'm never going to forget any of this," he said quietly, "or any of you. But I promise you that my memories will remain strictly off the record." He looked down at the floor a moment, then turned and left the house.

As Agent Bitters walked to his car, Wren caught up and walked with him. "Thank you," she said.

Opening his car door he paused, looked intently at her, and said, "What do you think made the Reverend Billy Joe Bobb go suicidal like that? He was always crazy, but he wasn't that kind of crazy."

Wren looked up at the impossibly blue sky, at the tall fir trees, and the barn. She almost put her hand to her mouth as she noticed the barn door was open and the giant painting was partly visible. She quickly stepped around the car, closer to Bitters, positioned so that when he faced her he faced away from the barn, safe from the painting's influence.

"I just can't imagine," she said, smiling slightly.

Bitters smiled a knowing smile and nodded slowly. He shook Wren's hand and got behind the wheel. Glancing back at the house, he raised his hand in a wave, and drove away.

Chapter 28

*S*ummer days seem to pass more quickly than rain-laden winter days. Too soon, the days become weeks and summer slides into autumn. In the maritime Pacific Northwest it is one particular day. You won't find it noted on any calendar, but it is real: It's the day the earth shifts its tilt just that little bit and, in an instant, summer is over. The spiders become weavers of diamond-studded webs; the hummingbirds start asking for handouts; and people start hanging raincoats on the pegs by the back door, and maybe keeping an extra one in the car.

It was late in September. It may have been September nineteenth, still summer by a whisker. Grace was standing at her back door, coffee cup in hand, watching Arlen, Julia and Eliot harvesting carrots for the farmers' market. She was wondering how she had suddenly managed to acquire a family. Mostly, she was amazed at how much she was enjoying this new life. Wren came up behind her, taking her hand.

"He's kind of like a pet. Eliot, I mean," Wren said.

"Yeah. Sometimes I think it's a little bit like having another goat," Grace said. "Gordon told me he's going to start driving Eliot to town. I'm a bit worried about what will come of that."

What came of that was this: Gordon gave Eliot a bamboo flute, and Eliot soon became a local star, making beautiful, enchanting, ethereal music with it. On any given day now, you can hear him playing outside the food co-op or on the street corner by the galleries. Offer him money and he will take it, grinning, and tell you, "OK, it's for Grace." If you are fortunate you will encounter him at his favorite place on the beach. Tourists and locals alike stop and listen as Eliot the Flute Guy hops across the rocks and driftwood, digs his toes into the sand at the edge of the Salish Sea, and breathes the sound of Wren's paintings through his flute, onto the breeze.

On this day in September, maybe the nineteenth, Grace set her coffee cup on a fencepost and walked through the damp gardens to where Arlen was working. "I have a proposition, Mr. Arlen Divine," she announced.

Arlen stood straight, removed his muddy gloves, and wiped his sleeve across his forehead. Sweat removed, mud applied. "What's on your mind, Grace?"

"The farm has always been good, but it could be better. I need more hands. And you need a home." Grace paused and held her eyes steady on Arlen's. A breeze unraveled her hair and brought with it the primal scent of warm earth and of seawater. She drew a long breath and asked Arlen, "How'd you like to be partners? Own this farm together, run it as a solid little business?"

The air was still, and a lone seagull sang out as it glided overhead. Wren watched from the garden gate. Julia came over and stood beside Arlen, surrounded by a sea of plants. Eliot sat between the rows, eating a bright red carrot, his crunching adding percussion to the seagull's song.

"Grace," said Arlen, "I would be honored. Partners... It's...I don't know what to say, other than yes." As Grace and Arlen embraced, a tear could be seen escaping Arlen's eye.

"OK, that was easy," Grace said, stepping back. "Now we need an official name, and I have the perfect one." She made a grand, sweeping gesture with her arm and made her pronouncement: "From now on, this place shall be known to all as the Divine Grace Farm."

Everyone whooped and applauded, even Eliot, who might or might not have been really clear on what was being celebrated.

"Now, Mr. Divine, Julia, Eliot, please carry on. I am taking Wren sailing today," said Grace.

And off they went, Grace and Wren, down to the sweet salt sea.

Julia was standing with her arm around Arlen's waist as Gordon pulled into the driveway in a new, tall, windowless silver Mercedes cargo van.

"How do you like your new wheels, Gordon?" Julia asked. She had bought the van for him when he became her delivery man, taking the occasional canvas to wherever it needed to go. Julia's paintings had become the second-hottest thing in the art world when the news broke of her miraculous escape from the clutches of the late, unlamented Reverend Billy Joe Bobb, and his subsequent fortunate demise. Her agent knew a good craze when he saw it, and was happy to help the dollars roll in.

"I'm getting used to her," Gordon grinned his spacious smile as his two black Labradors bounded out of the van.

"Good!" Julia said, "I'm enjoying all this success myself. I just wish it was based solely on the merits of my work." She chuckled. "But I guess it seldom is..." She thought for a moment, gave a single "Hah!", then turned and walked toward the barn.

The large building, with its mounting collection of paintings by Julia — and by Wren — seemed to vibrate, barely able to contain the energy of it all.

"I'm going to help Gordon load a canvas," Julia called to Arlen. Seeing him standing there in the sun, she was overwhelmed with pure joy. "I love you, Arlen Divine!" she shouted.

Arlen took one step toward her, and Julia came running back to him. Arlen swept her up into his arms and they spun around and around and around. He threw back his head and yipped like a coyote, looking like... like what? Looking like the happiest man on the planet.

Chapter 29

The boat basin was a cornucopia of sights and sounds and smells. The edgy fragrance of salt water and sea creatures merged with the pungent tang of diesel fuel and creosoted pilings. Halyards snapped and rang against masts, and the masts danced and swayed with the inhale and exhale of the sea. Grace and Wren finished loading the day's supplies aboard *Evermore*. Although she had long lived beside the water, Wren was not a sailor, and was now more than a little anxious. Grace's sailboat was thirty-two feet long — not really a big boat — but appeared much larger to Wren's inexperienced eye.

"I know what you're thinking," said Grace. "She's got some rust stains and a few scrapes. *Evermore* is a little ragged looking, but she really comes into the wind like a champ."

Wren swallowed hard. "What I was thinking, Grace, is that I don't actually know the first thing about sailing. I don't know a halyard from a jib. I *do* know that the water out there is awfully deep and cold and unpredictable."

She was thinking that sailing might be a little like life itself, so much danger and so much joy, and that it was difficult to own the joy without buying the danger along with it. That was when Grace leaned toward Wren, pulled her close in a precarious embrace, and kissed her. Wren was surprised, but even more surprised at how natural it felt to kiss Grace back. They looked far and wide into each other's eyes, *Evermore* rocking gently beneath them.

"Oh, my. Well, I guess that was my first sailing lesson," Wren said. They both laughed. What could possibly be next?

Wren was surprised to find herself trembling, certain it had little to do with her lack of sailing knowledge. She held Grace's hands and, looking into her brilliant green eyes, said, "I don't exactly know what to do."

Grace gave Wren a quick hug, and then stretched out her arms in an expansive gesture toward the sky and the boat and the whole of their new world. Then, reaching deeply into wisdom that she knew to be true, Grace said confidently, "Listen — there are really only two things you need to understand. First, know which way the wind is blowing. Second, have the courage to cast off the lines and go where that wind takes you."

Wren nodded a smile at Grace and, with the confidence of a woman who knew how to grasp a good metaphor, slipped the lines and released *Evermore* to the wind.

Epilogue

The Huxley-Lavelle Gallery, under the astute "temporary" direction of Ms. Jeanette Perdot, has a vault containing some 200 paintings, 173 assorted drawings and prints, and 26 sculptural pieces. In this collection you will find two sketches by Salvador Dali, four signed Chagall prints, two small guitar sculptures by Pablo Picasso, and 85 new paintings by Wren Willow Hendrix.

In the climate-controlled cool dimness of the vault, Wren's paintings appear to pulse slightly as though they are breathing in and out, in and out — as if they are attuned to the waves kissing the shore near their birthplace.

Occasionally, special clients will call and express their need for a certain kind of painting. The client list for these works by Wren Willow Hendrix includes scientists, leaders from every major religion, teachers, politicians, and physicians — all of whom will quietly admit the limitations of their chosen professions.

On this particular evening, the world stands at the edge of a gaping abyss. The climate is changing, economies are shriveling, populations are growing where sufficient food and housing are not, and nuclear exchange seems entirely too possible. It is hard to say who is doing a bigger business — religious institutions, extremist politicians, or the taverns. Desperate people seek their own particular salves and healing balms.

In Washington, DC, the President has called his generals to the war room — a scene being replicated across the globe by prime ministers, presidents (for life and otherwise), and kings.

In rainy Seattle, the phone on Ms. Perdot's desk rings.

"Huxley-Lavelle, this is Jeanette Perdot," she lilts. "Ah, yes, Madame Prime Minister, thank you. One moment while I link you to the conference call."

Jeanette thumbs a couple of buttons on her phone, and then sets the device on her desk. Several images of grim faces appear on a computer screen that had been glowing blue in the darkened gallery space.

Jeanette smiles into her computer's camera, draws a calming breath, and speaks. "Honored ladies and gentlemen, I am so pleased that you are all here this evening. I am happy to tell you that I have *exactly* the paintings you've been looking for."

The End

About The Author

Sam Weis is an accomplished painter with works in private collections across the US, the UK, Europe, and Israel. She is also an award-winning 12-string guitarist/recording artist and songwriter. Sam has toured with two hard-rock bands based in Chicago, and in Seattle, and enjoys a successful solo music career. Abstraction is her first novel.

Sam is a vagabond living in Iowa, Florida and Washington State's Puget Sound region.

Acknowledgements

There are so many people I wish to acknowledge for their contributions to this book through their friendship and encouragement. I could probably write another book just about everyone who said or did some small thing that pushed me forward.

But for now, thank you to my dear friend Cheryl Rife for encouraging me to write the book after I presented her with a bare outline and asking if she thought I should pursue the novel or if I'd lost my mind.

Thank you to Holly Gwinn Graham for her sharp eye, keen wit, and perseverance.

Truly, this book would not exist without the boundless energy and encouragement of my beloved friend, Chanale Hidegkuti. She has been my biggest fan for four decades, and I am so grateful.

I am especially happy to acknowledge Chuck Gumpert, Christopher Mathie, Jim Napoleon, Rich Holliday, and Renee Salant for being my test audience and listening to me read the entire book aloud to them over the course of three dinners and dessert.

Certainly, this book would be less readable if not for the extraordinary editing skills of Don Radlauer and Yael Shahar. They saved me from many blunders and made this book shine.

And I acknowledge you, dear reader, for taking a chance and reading my first novel.